THE SURROGATE

IAIN MAITLAND

INKUBATOR
BOOKS

Published by Inkubator Books
www.inkubatorbooks.com

Copyright © 2025 by Iain Maitland

ISBN (eBook) 978-1-83756-496-5
ISBN (Paperback) 978-1-83756-497-2
ISBN (Hardback) 978-1-83756-498-9

Iain Maitland has asserted his right to be identified as the author of this work.

THE SURROGATE is a work of fiction. People, places, events, and situations are the product of the author's imagination. Any resemblance to actual persons, living or dead is entirely coincidental.

No part of this book may be reproduced, stored in any retrieval system, or transmitted by any means without the prior written permission of the publisher.

For Tony, Ann & Julie

PROLOGUE

My name is Sophie. I am thirty-five years old. I should be the happiest woman in the whole wide world. I am married to Matt, my sweetheart, the love of my life. We have been together for ten years now. He is my big teddy bear.

We both have jobs that are steady and secure. I work in shipping administration at the docks here in Felixstowe in Suffolk, England. Matt is a self-employed plumber and always has plenty of jobs. We normally work Monday to Friday and have the weekends off.

We have a nice home that we scrimped and saved for. It is our pride and joy. We love everything about it. We live by the sea, and it's a nice place to be. I enjoy running down the promenade to the pier and back.

I have everything that I could ever have wished for in my life.

Almost. There is one thing I don't have and never will.

I don't have what I've always wanted more than anything else.

I don't have a baby. There is a great, big, jagged hole in

the middle of my life where a baby should be. I see women of my age, and younger, pushing buggies and walking hand-in-hand with toddlers. I want to snatch one and run away with them. Madness, I know.

We tried for so, so long. Naturally at first, holding off and making love two or three times a day at my most fertile times. It never worked. Nothing. Not at all. It broke us, or me at least. Not being able to be a mother is the worst thing in the world.

We've been through the NHS, done all the tests, and had our rounds of IVF. We'll have to pay if we want more. But we're exhausted and heartbroken, and it's just ridiculously expensive for us. As Matt says, we're already maxed out on our borrowings with our mortgage and his van and my car. Our mortgage is currently more than the value of our house. I wish we hadn't bothered with any of it.

Deep down, I'm so unhappy. I can't talk to Matt about my feelings. I don't want to upset him. And I've no close friends, no friends at all, really. Haven't had for years. I'm a bit of a loner. I have a mother and brother. I don't really see them anymore.

Matt says, in his most cheerful (and irritating) voice, that we can foster or adopt, but I want our own child. He's also suggested getting a kitten or a puppy. He means well, but he's such an idiot at times.

I've no idea what to do or which way to go. I know I can't go on like this, though. I am at breaking point. Something good – overwhelmingly joyous – has to happen soon. Otherwise, I'm just going to snap.

PART 1
BEST FRIENDS FOREVER

CHAPTER ONE

SATURDAY, 24 AUGUST, LATE MORNING

Lucy sits opposite me at the table at the back of the coffee shop, her face all shiny, flushed with excitement. She is thrilled to see me after all these years. I'm happy enough to catch up. We were once best friends forever – our two families went on holiday together to Florida when we were fifteen, and we wore matching tee-shirts emblazoned with "BFF" on the front.

I have not seen her for about eighteen years. Since her family moved away when she was sixteen. They had to, really. They'd have been chased out of town. But now she is back – just her – in Felixstowe, where I have stayed all my life: GCSEs, A levels, working in a shipping office at the docks, getting engaged and then married. To Matt, my handsome plumber. The love of my life.

She emailed me at the start of the summer, to say hello and to tell me her news – she had got a job working in a care home in town starting at the end of August, just a couple of days away now. Had since found a place to live on a caravan park within easy walking distance. Been in on various induction days and made friends already. I did not ask how she got my email address. I don't really do social media, as I don't want everyone to know my business. But Felixstowe is a small town where everyone seems to be related, or at least knows each other. She'd have got it from a mutual old friend, I assumed.

"*Coffee tomorrow morning?*" she emailed last night. I agreed. She's been pressing for a get-together at least every week since that first email. I can't keep making excuses. I don't particularly want to offend her. And today is a Saturday, and I've nothing much else to do except go to the gym. Matt is off to the football at lunchtime with his mates in the North Stand at Portman Road in Ipswich, the nearest big town to us – about twelve miles away.

So here we are, and it's not been as awkward a meeting as I'd imagined. When I arrived, she was sitting at the table, two lattes and two muffins in front of her. Just like we used to have when we came into town together on the bus so many years ago. I've not eaten a muffin since whenever. But no matter. I smiled at what I saw.

She was up and across to hug me, without hesitation, as I came towards her, and much longer and harder than I'd have expected. I hugged her back well enough. I bear her no malice. We were, after all, both victims in a way.

She looks smart in her white blouse, black skirt and heels. She says she's going to the care home afterwards to sign some forms.

She adds I look good, and I reply that she does too. I've kept fit and have lost the puppy fat I had when we last saw each other. I run regularly, once or even twice a day if the weather's nice. Swimming occasionally at the leisure centre near the pier. She's still beautiful. Blonde hair. Blue eyes. Shapely. The boys always loved her. Much more than me.

We chit-chat for such a while, about how Felixstowe has changed, and how such-and-such happened at school, and what became of old friends and teachers. And, I have to say, we fall so easily into each other's company again.

By the time I go and order two more lattes, the years we have been apart seem no more than a few days. We then chat more personally, in between sips of coffee, about our lives.

She says she is married, but is getting divorced. She does not mention his name nor any children. I do not press her. She sounds bitter, but is putting on a brave face. I'll wait for her to tell me more when she's ready. Coming home to Felixstowe, she says, is a new beginning. "Meeting you again ..." She stops speaking, choking slightly. Then she excuses herself, going to the cloakroom.

When she returns, having reapplied her make-up, I talk more about myself, but in a matter-of-fact manner. I don't want to say how happy my life has been, well, in almost every way. I'm not going to rub it in when things haven't gone so well for her.

There is a silence, slightly uncomfortable, as we drink our coffees. We both know what we are going to move on to next. She asks me how my family is, and I just say my mother and brother are well and working in Ipswich. I don't say we're kind of estranged these days other than birthday and Christmas cards. I don't want to bring that up. I hesitate and add that my father passed away the year before last. I say he had a bad heart. I don't tell her how he died, though. She nods sympathetically.

I ask her how her family is, and she tells me her mother and her sister are "fine" and still living in Milton Keynes where they moved, which is more than a hundred miles away. She does not say much about them, and I do not wish to pry. It's obviously a sore point. We look at each other, and she adds, "My ... father's out of prison now, but we don't see him." I nod, unable to think of anything to add.

We've both finished our second lattes, and ate our muffins a while ago, and our conversation – our meeting – seems to be coming to a natural, ever-so-slightly awkward end. Unexpectedly, I feel a sudden sense of sadness. I've never had a best friend like Lucy since she went. No true friends at all, really. If it hadn't been for her father, Lucy and her family would never have moved away, and we'd still have been best friends to this day.

We sit, waiting for the other to get up, saying, "Well, it was nice seeing you ..." I cannot bring myself to do it first. And neither can she. We look around the coffee shop, full of customers, noise and hubbub, searching for something to talk about to keep things going. As teenagers, we'd have done impressions of the people around us and then run out, laughing hysterically. I look at Lucy. She looks at me. We smile. We both realise this is the end.

She shakes her head, then blurts out, "You didn't have children, then? I always thought you'd have had three or four by now!" She says it brightly, almost desperately, something to say to keep us here together a little longer. And we gaze at each other again, and I am sure she can see the pain etched across my face.

I tell her, in as steady a voice as I can, that we, Matt and I, tried for years without success. That despite all our efforts, nothing ever worked.

I then add that, lately, we have had IVF on the NHS. That it just hasn't happened. We are now thinking of going private, but, you know, it's way too expensive for us and, anyway, we are so shattered by the endless heartache. I gulp and think that now, really, is the time for me to get up and leave.

Lucy flushes and swallows. She then leans forward, puts her hand on mine, looks into my eyes and says, quite simply, "I'll have a baby for you."

MY MIND REELS. I cannot believe what Lucy has just said to me. Her instinctive reaction to my obvious pain. I'm speechless.

"I'll have a baby for you." Her exact words. Said so casually. As if it's little more than offering to take in an Amazon parcel off the doorstep for me.

I laugh, a stunned reaction to what she's said. I can't take it in. But then Lucy always was impulsive.

"Wow!" I say eventually in a high-pitched voice. And then again, "Wow!" my voice cracking this time. I go on after a moment or two, "I don't know what to say."

I look at Lucy, and she seems as shocked as I am. I think she said it without any thought. Perhaps she's regretting it now, and we're both feeling as embarrassed as each other.

"You don't mean it," I say and then add, "Surely?" My voice sounds far more hopeful – desperate – than I'd have expected.

There is a long, long pause as though she's realising the enormity of what she's just said and is going to back away.

"Yes," she replies quietly, almost a whisper. She picks up her long coffee spoon, using it to scrape the froth from the rim of her glass mug and into her mouth. "I do."

We look at each other. For a few moments, we are those two sixteen-year-olds again. Sipping our lattes like proper grown-ups. Joking how, when we were in our eighties, we'd still be meeting here every week for coffees and muffins. I am moved by the thought.

"Why," I ask, "would you do that for me?" I know the answer – pretty much what she is going to say before she speaks. Heartfelt words we both said to each other when we were teenagers.

She sighs, searching for the sentences and how to say them. "Because you were ... you still are ... the best friend I've ever had. I thought we'd grow up and our husbands would be best friends ... our children would be playmates ... be at school together ... we'd all go on holidays to Disneyland." She stops for an instant, seeming emotional, and I reach out and put my hand on hers.

She goes on, "I mean, if it weren't for what Da ... my father did ... that's what would have happened, I'm sure of it. We'd still be like sisters."

I nod, thinking that would probably have been the case, but even so, it's been a long time, and we've led different lives – we are adults now – and it's such a big thing to do. Overwhelmingly massive, really.

"Let's not talk about ... I don't want to ... your father ..." I stumble over speaking about Uncle Daniel, as I once called him. "It's such a kind offer. Thank you."

She leans forward, gripping my right hand tightly with both of hers, sensing, I think, that I am backing off. I'm not. I'm just blown away, really. I need time to consider it fully, from all sides. And I have to discuss it with Matt. See what he thinks. (He'll be beside himself with joy.)

Lucy always seemed to know what I was thinking before

I said anything. It was uncanny. It's the same now. "I promise you I'll have your baby for you. One hundred per cent. But think it over, talk to hubby, see what he says. He might hate the idea. A baby with my big nose!" (Her nose is perfect, by the by.)

I smile and nod and do not say that, after the last round of IVF failed, Matt had gently broached the idea of surrogacy. And I had said – I shouted – "No-oo!" because I could not bear the thought of someone else carrying our baby. But it seems somehow different with Lucy. Maybe. I'm not sure. I'm so bewildered. I can't think straight right now. It's too much to take in.

"I will," I reply, suddenly feeling emotional again. "Whatever we do, we can be friends ... like we used to be ..." I stop, not wanting to say "best friends forever" in case my voice betrays my feelings.

Then Lucy is up and coming round to my side of the table, hugging me again, and it feels so good to have her back in my life. I've no idea how things will go from here. A rollercoaster ride, I expect. Our friendship always was, one way or another.

I THOUGHT our hug would be the end of our meet-up. We'd put our numbers into each other's phones and agree to meet again, perhaps same time, same place, next week. Lucy would head off to the care home. I'd go and get some shopping.

But then Lucy says, "Lunch somewhere?" and it seems rude to say no to someone who's just offered to have a baby for me. So I answer yes and suggest we go down to the Spa

Pavilion theatre on the seafront. It has a nice restaurant looking out over the North Sea.

Lucy agrees, checking her phone and saying, "I've got until half past one, well, let's say one forty-five. I've said I'll be there at two." At that, we leave the coffee shop, walking out on to the high street and down towards the sea.

We talk as we go, just this and that, mostly pointing out to each other the places we used to go, and reminiscing about them. The Wimpy Bar for our tea. Woolworth's for pick 'n' mix sweets. Greggs the baker's, where we'd buy hot chocolate to drink on cold days.

Lucy loops her arm through mine, and we keep walking, like we used to do on the way to the beach all those summers ago. And she says, "Ah, do you remember those huge lads at the pier? The creepy twins? Ugh."

I laugh and say, "Ugh," too and tell her that they both work somewhere at the docks and look the same ... and that neither of them married, and they still live at home with their mother. We both mock shudder at the same time.

We get to the bottom of the high street, where the road slopes down to the seafront, left to the theatre, and right towards the pier and the leisure centre and, further on, the amusements around the bay. "Do you remember when you won that Scooby-Doo toy on the claw machine?" Lucy asks. "That boy grabbed it from you, and you punched him to get it back?"

I laugh. I've always had a quick temper. We then talk about our various teenage escapades up and down the seafront.

As we walk down the twisty-turny path towards the theatre, Lucy gestures to a wooden bench, indicating we should sit for a few minutes. We've sat on this bench many times, talking about different things, but boys mainly.

It's a sunny day, and the promenade and beach below are packed with holidaymakers. It's quieter up here. It will be nice to sit in the sun for a while and remember the shows we saw at the theatre when we were young, the Chuckle Brothers and the interminable amateur pantomimes every Christmas.

But I sense, as Lucy unhooks her arm from mine and sits back without saying anything, that we are going to talk of other matters. Her father. And what happened.

"I ... I ..." She hesitates, and I think, and want to say, that we don't need to talk about this; we don't have to go over everything, scratching at scabs, tearing open old wounds. What's the point now? None at all. But she goes on; she has to do so. To get it out of her system. I can tell she's prepared what she's going to say.

"I just wanted to tell you, to stress, that it's just me here. Coming back. Not my mum. Nor my sister. And certainly not my father. You haven't got to deal with any of that. It's just me. I've come back to ... begin again."

It strikes me that it's odd coming back to the town where everything went so horribly wrong. Her father, accused and convicted of sex offences against young teenage boys. Including my brother. The family left before he was sent to prison for six years. A wickedly low sentence, really. Out, I'd guess, in three, as most prisoners seem to serve only half their sentences inside, from what I've read. It's disgusting. But I hold my temper and my tongue.

Lucy goes on. "You were brave to speak out about Joel. I remember your mum coming round and speaking to mine. Them shouting at each other. And we weren't allowed to see you anymore. God, I hated it when we moved to Milton Keyes. I cried for months. Missing you. None of it would have come out if it weren't for you."

She makes it sound like all of it – her perverted father, moving away, prison, her family imploding and mine – is all my fault. But I'm sure it would have all come out anyway. Joel spoke to me about it when I saw him crying and punching his bedroom wall. And there were others, of course. Someone, sometime, would have gone to the police.

I put my arm around her and pull her close, our heads touching, and I say, "It's okay, it's okay." And she asks, in a tearful voice, how my mother and brother will react when they know she is back. And I hug her and reply, "They'll be fine ... they always liked you ... they know it wasn't your fault." I go to add that they'll be pleased to see her, but I think that's pushing it too far. Fact is, they probably won't ever know. I'm not going to tell them.

"Come on," I say suddenly, getting to my feet, "race you to the Spa!" It's what we used to do as teenagers after sitting on this bench. One of us would leap up and shout, "Let's go!" and start running towards the theatre, the other chasing to catch up.

And I am away, racing at full pelt, as there is nobody in front of me on the pathway. I hear Lucy shouting, "That's not fair!" and laughing as she runs after me.

I get to the doors of the theatre restaurant, then stop and turn and shout, "Beat you!" Lucy's bending forward with her hands on her knees, saying she hasn't run like this in years. We then high-five as we used to do and go into the restaurant arm in arm. And you know what? I think that, maybe, things are going to be just fine.

CHAPTER TWO

SATURDAY, 24 AUGUST, LUNCHTIME

The restaurant is busy, and all my favourite tables by the windows facing out to sea are taken. It's so peaceful and relaxing there. "Never mind," I say to Lucy. Maybe next time.

There is a table with two chairs towards the back by the bar, and we make our way to it, picking up menus as we go.

"On me," Lucy says and asks what I want. We agree on a Pepsi Max each and a bowl of cheesy nachos to share. As Lucy goes up to order, I have a proper look around.

There is a mix of people here, mainly white-haired old folk and harassed young mums with babies in their arms and toddlers jiggling about. I cannot take my eyes off one little boy with long blond hair who's running up and down. He is so sweet. A gang of four teenagers come running by, laughing, heading from the toilets to the front doors.

There is a commotion behind me. I glance around, and a woman with carrier bags in both hands is struggling to come out through the door of the women's toilets. My heart sinks when I recognise who it is. Emily. She went to school with

Lucy and me, and she bullied Lucy at every opportunity. Probably because Lucy was so pretty and she wasn't. Lucy called her, cruelly but accurately, the Blob back then. I've lost count of the number of physical fights I had with her, defending Lucy and other girls whom she bullied too.

Worse than that, she now lives next door to Matt and me. The day we moved in, she came round with twelve dry-looking cupcakes with childish stickers on top, shouting, "Surprise!" I never knew – we definitely wouldn't have bought the place if I did. She doesn't work, never has done, and lives with her widowed mother, Big Blob as was, who has mobility issues. Emily's something of a stalker: she's always watching me from a window.

Emily sees me and comes across. She thinks we are best friends. We're not. I cannot stand her. I loathe her, actually. She's going to be trouble now that Lucy is back.

"Mum's asleep," Emily says, sitting down in the chair opposite me without being invited. "I've been for a walk and just came in to use the lavvy. Bloody kids kept banging on the door when I was in there." I try not to pull a face at the image I now have in my head. Not that she'd notice. She's too wrapped up in herself and her inward-looking life.

"I've been into town," she goes on, gesturing to her bags. "I had to get Mum's ointments and a new cushion for her commode." I turn my grimace into a good-natured smile as she looks at me through her thick-lensed glasses.

I know I need to avoid getting into a conversation, as it will just go on, and I will have to walk back to town and home with her. And go in and say "hello" to her mum, who'll start talking about her ailments, and that's the afternoon gone. Emily has an expectant look on her face, assuming I'll offer her a cup of tea. She doesn't seem to realise I'm not here for her, let alone that I might be with someone else.

Then Lucy is coming back with two pint glasses of Pepsi Max, and she stops as she sees Emily sitting in the seat across from me.

Emily half turns to see who I am watching coming up behind her. I see the look of recognition in their faces at the same instant. Emily flushes as she gulps and doesn't know what to do. "Hello, Lucy," she says eventually, in her monotone voice.

Emily makes no effort to move, even though it must be obvious that Lucy is with me, has gone to get two drinks, and has now returned, ready to sit down.

"Hello ..." Lucy says. I think for one awful moment that she is going to add, "Blobby." She does not. Instead, she says, "Hello, you're looking good." That's more cutting. Even by the wildest stretch of imagination, Emily does not "look good".

She has mousy brown hair, cut in a pudding-basin style. She wears a matching lime green top and skirt, polyester I think, presumably from a local charity shop. And sensible shoes. And for reasons best known to herself, a hi-vis yellow jacket. It still feels like summer outside.

Emily blinks, one, two, three times as she gazes at Lucy, thinking of a comeback comment. At school, she would have just barged Lucy over and sat on her if the teachers weren't looking. I'd have dragged her off. She gets up out of her seat, and for a second, I think that's what she's going to do now.

But Lucy is stepping back out of her way, the Pepsi Max in both glasses spilling over the top onto her hands.

"So nice to see you again," Emily mutters, an insincere

smile on her face. She gathers up her bags and, without a backwards glance at me, is about to walk away.

Lucy smiles and then laughs. So, Emily bumps into her, accidentally or not – not – and spills more of our drinks. Lucy does not react. And then Emily is gone. I'm thinking that, somehow, there will surely be trouble ahead with Emily.

LUCY PUTS our now two-thirds full glasses of Pepsi Max on the table between us and then shakes her wet hands. I pass her a wipe from my bag as she sits down, and she cleans her hands with it.

"Emily is still here, then ..." Lucy says, smiling, and I laugh and tell her that Emily lives next door to me. Doesn't work. Cares for her mum. Wants to be my best friend. Aargh.

For good measure, I add, there's an odd man downstairs – we have the top two floors of a three-storey, terraced Victorian house – and he's really strange. He doesn't seem to work either and often sits there by the window, watching me come and go. "It's like being in a goldfish bowl," I explain.

"Apart from that ..." Lucy says, echoing our childhood conversations.

"Apart from that ..." I reply, knowing where we are going with this.

"Life is perfect," we both say at the same time, laughing joyfully. We clink our glasses.

"She's your best friend now, then!" Lucy makes a joke of it, sipping her drink and gazing out towards the windows and the sea beyond. It seems to be of no importance to her. I think it is.

It would be good to have a friend again, a proper best friend forever, like we were as teenagers. Like I say, Lucy is the only friend I've ever had like that. I've had none since. I'm not drawn to girly women. And I tend to speak my mind. There are always lots of people around me, but I still feel alone. Other than Matt, of course. My lovely man.

"No," I reply in the same jokey manner. "It's always been you." I find myself reaching out to take her hand. Lucy lets me hold it for a second, then pulls her hand away, turns it into a fist and hits me on the back of my hand. It's a thing we used to do. We smile at each other.

"Tell me about Matt?" she says, taking another mouthful of her drink. "The love of your life. How did you meet?"

"At the Bandbox, you know, on the seafront by the Alex? I'd had a few drinks and fell down some steps and landed by his feet. He helped me up, and it went from there." I smile. "He told me, later, that he knew I was the one for him that first night. I didn't remember much of it, to be honest. He held me up when I was being sick at some point; that's about it. But I gave him my phone number, I think, and he started texting me for a date. I couldn't remember him properly, but I said yes, and here I am now ... Mrs Curtis."

"Matt Curtis?" Lucy says in surprise. "The same Matt Curtis who was two years ahead of us at school. That Matt Curtis?"

One and the same, I think, although I don't say it. When we were at school, he was the boy – one of several, to be honest – all the girls liked most.

"Yes," I say. "That Matt Curtis. He's every bit as handsome as he was and just the nicest man in the world. When he asked me to marry him, he promised that he'd spend the rest of his life loving and adoring me. I said I'd be happy if he got me cheesy chips whenever I wanted them ... and then gave him his answer: yes."

"I remember Matt. He once ... doesn't matter," Lucy says abruptly as I look up, wondering what she was going to say. That they liked each other probably. Maybe more. Kissed at the prom or something. Lucy was never shy with boys.

She looks down into her glass, not wanting to say anything else. I could pick up on this, but decide to let it go for now.

I'll come back to it later at the right moment. I change my next comments, though, so I don't sound all lovey-dovey naïve about Matt.

"He had partners before me, and I did too." I shrug, as if it's no big deal. "But once we were together, that was it for both of us. We've never, you know, with anyone else. And now," I go on, "we live in Ranelagh Road, just up from that church where they had that fete that time – when Emily wore that bright yellow dress?"

We both smile at another memory.

"Anyway, it's all been ... just great really. We're both equals. I'm not some little doormat." Just so she knows I'm not like my mother.

"Yes," Lucy replies, finishing her drink. She checks her phone, for the time rather than messages, I think. She's about to say, "Got to go."

But I have something to ask her. I need to know. I just do.

"Do you have children, Lucy?" I put it simply and in as friendly a voice as I can.

She looks at me with a pained expression. It's not something she wants to talk about. But I must know. I add another comment.

"And tell me about your husband; what's he like?" I think for a fleeting instant that she's going to get up and walk off, she looks so distressed. But, finally, she speaks.

"My name now is ... Lucy Yilmaz ... no one pronounces it properly, nor can they spell it ... Yilmaz that is, not Lucy," she adds, in an attempt at a humorous afterthought.

"Go on," I say, intrigued.

"I met Ahmed on holiday in Turkey five years ago ... we had a ... fling." She looks into the distance, her eyes shining and a smile on her lips, recalling happier times. She always loved her "flings", as she put it. More innocent back in the day, of course.

"He followed me home to England. I thought he was infatuated with me ... but he ..." She stops, shaking her head, exasperated; she is not explaining things properly.

"So you have children, then?" I ask, cutting in as nicely as I can. It seems to help her clear her thoughts.

"Two, a boy of four, Emen, and a girl of three, Ceren. He ... wanted Turkish names ... I wanted English ones ... so, anyway ..."

It's not like Lucy to give in like that, I think, but I don't respond.

"We were good for a while." Her voice becomes melancholy. "He worked in a car wash with his brothers who'd been here a while, and I made stuff and sold it on Etsy, online. Money was always so tight. And then ..." She stops and is close to tears this time.

"Go on," I say again, reaching out and holding her hands. She looks at me tearfully as I add, "What happened?"

"His father died ... they're very big on family in Turkey

... and he wanted us to go back there for the funeral and stay. I ... I couldn't ... it's quite a ... male-dominated society."

She stops and ponders a while, and I wait.

"Ahmed's gone off with the children, and I don't know what to do, who to turn to, how to get them back. I have no money to do anything."

I stand up, walk around the table, and as Lucy gets up, we hug each other for what seems like minutes.

And then I speak, saying, "Best friends forever ... forever," I repeat for emphasis and can feel her body move as if she is sobbing.

Eventually, we pull apart, and we are both obviously emotional.

"Thank you. Thank you," she says.

We stay like this, so close, for a while.

Finally, we step back, both of us then checking the time on our phones. We're back to grown-up platitudes before we go. "You'd better hurry ... can I give you a lift?" ... "No, my car is parked by the pier ... yours?" ... "I walked into town."

We hug and then kiss each other's cheeks, first one, then the other – as we did as teenagers, pretending to be adults – and we part on the steps outside the theatre. Lucy waves her phone at me – "I'll call you" – and I wave mine back.

I don't know what to think as I start walking up the hill to home. Lucy. Matt. A baby. It's all almost overwhelming. Part of me is excited. Matt will be so thrilled. He's always longed to be a dad. But I feel sick as well. Something nags at the back of my mind. I'm not sure what it is. But it worries me.

AFTER I'VE PARTED company with Lucy, I walk through the town, picking up a bagful of shopping from the Tesco Express on the corner, close to where Matt and I live. Our road runs parallel with the high street, Hamilton Road, as it's called here.

As I come up the pathway to the house, I glance at the windows on the ground floor. There are dusty net curtains, unchanged since we've been living here. They twitch, and I can see a shadowy figure sitting behind them.

I stick the middle finger of my free hand up towards the window. If the man who lives downstairs is watching, it reminds him I won't be intimidated by his constant gaze. If he's not, it's no matter.

I open the main door and stand for a moment in the hallway, listening. The house has been partitioned. We have an inner door to the left, which opens on to a staircase leading upstairs to the two floors where we live. The man downstairs has an inner door to the right to his apartment. I don't hear anything, and I hurry on up.

After unpacking the shopping, I sit on the ledge in the bay window of the living room at the front, looking down into the road. I like watching the comings and goings, and I cannot be seen easily, as I've pulled the curtains close to each other.

I don't know all that much about surrogacy – I think it will be different in countries around the world – and I realise I need to know how it works here in the UK. I open Google on my phone, finding a page on a government website and reading the key points from it.

> *Surrogacy is legal in the UK, but if you make a surrogacy agreement, it cannot be enforced by the law ... If*

you use a surrogate, they will be the child's legal parent at birth. If the surrogate is married or in a civil partnership, their spouse or civil partner will be the child's second parent at birth unless they did not give their permission.

That worries me slightly, but I go on.

Legal parenthood can be transferred by parental order or adoption after the child is born ... If there is disagreement about who the child's legal parents should be, the courts will make a decision based on the best interests of the child.

That's better.

You cannot pay a surrogate in the UK except for their reasonable expenses ... You must apply for a parental order or adoption if you want to become the legal parent of the child ... One of you must be genetically related to the child – in other words, be the egg or sperm donor.

I sit back happily enough.

The man downstairs is at it again. When he's not sitting at the window, watching me coming and going to and from work, he's banging about or drilling or making odd, haphazard noises that make no sense.

There is a drilling noise today. Not the short *zzz* of placing a clock on the wall or the *zzz, zzz, zzz, zzzz* of putting up shelves.

It is a whirring noise; he is sawing something up – an

unwanted chair or a table, perhaps. Sometimes, I think he is taking all the furniture in his flat and cutting it up into little pieces. But I never see him taking anything to the dump. He does not have a car.

I try to ignore it, even though it sets me on edge. I think instead about Lucy and Matt and surrogacy and how I will raise the subject tonight with Matt.

I imagine his face, his jaw dropping. He will be beyond words. So happy and enthusiastic. I suspect that this – Lucy having our baby – will not be as simple as it first sounds. But if we both want it to happen – if the three of us really, really want it – I am sure it will.

CHAPTER THREE

SATURDAY, 24 AUGUST, THE EVENING

Matt and I usually take turns to make dinner – whoever's there first. In the week, I finish work at my shipping company at five o'clock and head home, but then I like to go for a run and have a shower before anything else. Matt rarely works late, but he has been going further afield lately, on a big restoration project, out towards Bury St Edmunds, which is a forty-five-minute drive.

Weekdays, we only have quick and easy meals – spaghetti Bolognese or chilli con carne. Weekends, Matt likes to have a go at fancier dishes inspired by the cookery shows he watches on the television. Today, being a Saturday when his football team, Ipswich Town, is playing at home, he won't be back until mid-evening. He goes for a beer or two with his mates after the match. We have soup and sandwiches when he gets in, sitting and watching something on Netflix.

I tidy and clean the house, as it's my turn. Then I sit back on the window ledge in the living room, looking out to the Victorian terraced houses to either side and the road and pavements full of cars. I'll have a run along the promenade later, then shower and get everything ready for Matt's return. He usually texts as he leaves the pub.

Matt and I have been living as a couple for nine years now, married for three, and we moved into this narrow, three-storey mid-terraced house in Ranelagh Road soon after our wedding. We went without so much to get our deposit and our mortgage together. Even the wonderful wedding I'd dreamed of all my life. We just had a simple registry office ceremony with a few friends of Matt's – neither of us really get on with our families – and a nice meal afterwards. We then had a week's break in the Lake District.

It means the world to us, our little nest. The first floor, front to back, comprises a living room, a bedroom, a second bedroom, a bathroom and a kitchen, with an iron staircase down to the garden. I sunbathed there the first summer but felt uncomfortable that the man downstairs might be watching. We have a loft floor – two small bedrooms up a narrow staircase. They are both full of boxes and suitcases and junk at the moment; one, the bigger at the front, was earmarked to be our baby's nursery.

Matt and I are soulmates. Our lives together are perfect, or at least they were not so long ago. We've always seemed to have the same thoughts and opinions about things. We both always loved the idea of having children, a boy and a girl, or so we imagined when we were younger and our heads were still in the clouds.

It was horrible, what we went through, tests on my eggs and on Matt's sperm. I know he felt humiliated but didn't say anything so as not to upset me further. There was such a long wait for IVF on the NHS – and we were so full of hope during that time. Two goes, both failures. And we were back where we started, but now demoralised and broken. To try again, we'd have to go private, and we just don't have the money. But now, here comes Lucy and her life-changing offer.

My phone tings; a text message is coming in. I click through and see it is from Matt.

On way home. Anything from Sainsbury's? Back at 7. Exciting news!

I'm taken aback – Matt never comes home that soon after football. I wonder what the *exciting news* is. The last time he had news for me was when he was offered a share in a greyhound by Baz, one of his football mates; it took me ages to talk him out of that so-called investment.

I text back.

Ok! I've been to Tesco. See you soon.

Then I go into the kitchen and make sandwiches, putting them on plates and covering them with foil, ready for later. I've time for a run, up Ranelagh Road and round and down to the promenade to the Sea You café at the far end of the bay and back again. Home in time for a shower and to put crisps and cans of drinks on trays with our sandwiches.

I wonder again, as I leave the house, what the exciting news is. I'm hoping he's not met someone new at football who wants to sell him a top-of-the-range car at a suspiciously low price. We have my seven-year-old Ford Fiesta and his five-year-old small white van, I forget the make, for work. I know Matt would love a head-turning car, but we just cannot afford it. More importantly, I wonder how I will broach the subject of surrogacy and, of course, Lucy.

MATT and I are sitting on the sofa in the living room, watching a programme about alien disclosure on Netflix. Matt's more interested in it than me, as he claims he once saw something in the sky when he was a child. Probably a kite with a little green man on it. I'm happy enough to watch. Later, when he nods off, I'll switch over to one of my *Time Team* programmes on YouTube. We'll go to bed around midnight and maybe make love. He often rallies surprisingly well after a sleep.

We had our sandwiches and soup and cans of fizzy drink after we'd both showered. I could tell he was buzzing with excitement – tickling my waist at either side as I carried the tray through into the living room. We eat and drink before we watch television. It's a chance to catch up on what we've been doing. Matt can be reluctant to chat at times, but tonight he was more than happy to. He was fit to burst, actually.

"Go on then!" I said eventually. "What's your exciting news? You've won a million pounds on a scratch card?"

He said that Lee, one of his mates at football, is breaking up with his girlfriend, and they are looking for a home for their Jack Russell dog, Stanley. "I thought, you know, if we're not ... um ... having a baby ..." He looked at me with his big, wide eyes. He means well, but he can be such a fool at times.

Still, at least he didn't suggest getting a pair of hamsters, as he did when I was struggling to conceive in the early days. I say, firmly, so he doesn't go on about the dog, showing me photos, "We both work all day ... can't keep him locked up ... we're both really busy." I reeled off a few other reasons, and that seemed to satisfy him.

We took our dirty bowls and plates into the kitchen, and I loaded the dishwasher. Matt came up behind me and put his hands around my tummy, saying, "I'm sorry, Soph, I'm such a ..."

But I turned round and kissed him before he could say the final word. We then cuddled for a little while, and he gave me one of his *bed?* looks.

I said, "Later," as I wanted to talk first about Lucy and the surrogacy idea. If we went and made love and he fell asleep, we'd not discuss it until tomorrow. And I cannot wait.

Matt watches his Netflix programme while I simply feel distracted. I've never told Matt much about Lucy and her family. At least, not in any detail. I've mentioned her in passing a few times, how our two families were once as close as they could be, and that we holidayed together in Florida.

I've also said how upset I was when they moved to Milton Keynes. He knows about Lucy's father but doesn't like to talk about it. It's almost as though if it's never mentioned, it never happened. And he was more interested in his PlayStation back then rather than talking about feelings and emotions.

I think it was just one of those things where, because I didn't say anything significant to Matt at the start of our relationship, it became harder to talk about as time went by. And we've not had much to do with my family, my mother and my brother, for a while. I believe my parents felt a terrible sense of shame, that they never noticed what was going on, and, later, they too wanted to pretend it never happened. There was some contact, but once my father died, that pretty much ended. It's all been something of a taboo.

Anyway, I need to raise the idea of surrogacy and see how Matt responds. He mentioned it once before, so I suspect he will be in favour. We can discuss it in general terms. I will talk about Lucy too. The idea of Lucy carrying our baby is a lot to take in, and I want to get to know Lucy again, as adults now, before I discuss it with Matt and we commit fully to that path.

"I HAD LUNCH WITH LUCY TODAY," I say suddenly as the credits roll.

"Lucy?" he replies, waiting patiently for the next alien documentary to begin. "Donoghue?" I notice that there is surprise in his voice. Lucy Donoghue used to work in my office. She left to join the police. I never really knew her, as she was on a different team.

"Lucy Kingham. As was," I reply.

He nods in recognition, then reaches for the remote control to fast-forward to the next programme.

I look at him, pretending to be busy. He's always so bloody transparent.

"You did, didn't you?" I ask, my voice sounding angrier than I expected. "Had sex with her."

He shakes his head and laughs slightly nervously. "No, we just, you know, kissed once, that's all. At a fete. Just mucking about."

"Yeah?" I respond.

The potential argument's over already. Although it – the fact that they kissed – is interesting to know.

"Yeah. God, it was years ago. When we were kids. Honestly, it was nothing much. I'd forgotten about it." (Obviously, he hasn't.)

I summarise what happened – our email exchanges, then coffee and something to eat and drink on the seafront. He glances at me once or twice, pretending to be interested, but I can see he is itching to watch the next aliens documentary.

I don't talk about her family moving away or the father. I don't want to rake it all up again in my own mind, let alone share it. I sense he's losing interest in the conversation anyway.

I say she's married, has two children, has broken up with her husband and has moved back here to start anew. He pulls a "that's interesting" face as the programme starts, and that really, really annoys me. So I just come straight out with it.

"Lucy's offered to have our baby. To be a surrogate for us." I say it quite harshly, the annoyance clear in my voice.

That's got him. I can see the shock in his face. He nods normally, as if we're simply discussing what we'll have for breakfast in the morning. Croissants for a change? But he swallows so loudly that I can hear it. His eyes flicker, his brain going through everything, before he eventually replies.

"Is it ... would it be better if we ... I don't know ... I thought the surrogate would be anonymous ... to start, anyway ..." The longest pause. "Um, it's a lot to take in ... what do you think ... what do you want to do?"

"Well, it's not happened for us, has it?" I respond, my voice still harsh. "And it never will. We can't afford more IVF, can we? And we both know Lucy, don't we? In our different ways. And she's not going to want money for doing it. I don't think so, anyway."

He looks at me and nods. Agreeing with what I've said but still looking uncertain. He's in shock, really. I'm not sure he's going to reply or add anything further, so I go on.

"I suppose, at the end of the day, the question is: do we want a baby or not?"

"Yes," he says, faster and much more emphatically than I expected. "I'd love a ..." I think he's going to say son, but he stops and corrects himself and says instead, "I'd love to be a daddy."

"I'd love to be a mummy," I reply. Matt then uses the remote control to turn off the television, and he turns to face me, all emotional and weepy. I am too, and we both lean forward, hugging each other tight.

This way certainly isn't perfect. I'm sure there will be issues ahead. But we will deal with them as we have to, and one day, not so very far away, we'll be a perfect little family.

CHAPTER FOUR

SUNDAY, 25 AUGUST, JUST BEFORE MIDDAY

Matt and I went to bed and made love and then chatted about Lucy and surrogacy and made love again. I finally watched him fall asleep next to me, spent and contented. I got up and used the bathroom, changed into my pyjamas and came back to bed, thinking about where Matt and I should meet Lucy. I wanted it to be somewhere relaxed and informal where we'd feel at ease and could just chat quietly. It had to be special too – for such a momentous occasion.

I thought about inviting Lucy to our home – I'd ask Matt to make one of his fancy meals – but something about that didn't feel quite right. I don't know why. And I didn't want to go for a more formal meal at a smart restaurant, waiters hovering about, overhearing and interrupting us. Then I decided, texting Lucy and suggesting a time and a place. She replied almost immediately: *Yep!*

Sea You is a nice café on the beachfront down towards the docks. It's the place I sometimes run to in the mornings or evenings, turning round there before heading home. It's usually busy, but it's really spacious, and there is plenty of seating outside where we can tuck ourselves away. The food's always good. That's where Matt and I are now, late Sunday morning, with three full English breakfasts and three pots of tea on the table in front of us. Waiting for Lucy.

She texted fifteen minutes ago, stating she was running late, *See you in 10!* but that we should order, and she'd have a *fry-up & a cuppa, please!*

Now we sit here, like two statues, looking out at the promenade and sea in front of us. Neither of us are speaking. We're so nervous. I've no idea what we're going to ask or say to Lucy. I should have written down some questions.

Matt sees her first, pointing to get my attention. I look to my left, watching her approach. She's sauntering along the promenade, collecting admiring glances as she comes towards us.

She walks quickly to me as I stand to greet her. She's wearing a straw hat and a thin blue summer dress and flat sandals, and she looks naturally gorgeous, and it's all so effortless. I feel a swell of jealousy, which I ignore. We embrace, both of us emotional.

She steps back and smiles warmly at Matt. Like they're old friends. I guess they are. Sort of. My great bear of a husband looks overwhelmed, but then he too gets to his feet and comes round to hug her.

For a moment, Lucy and I are both wrapped up in his arms as he pulls us towards him. He makes a gaspy, breathy noise, fighting back tears. I am too as I go to sit back down at the table. They then follow my lead.

The first few minutes of our meeting are taken up with grown-up comments on the weather, what a lovely place this is, and how stunning the view is with lots of different boats going by. It is a glorious, sunny day. Then we are pouring tea and passing serviettes and sachets of ketchup and mustard to each other, and checking we're all happy and have got everything and are ready to eat and drink.

And so, we start our breakfasts and eat quietly for a few minutes, as though this is something ordinary rather than, potentially, the biggest moment of our lives. I don't know what to say, nor how to begin a meaningful conversation.

Halfway through, Matt leans forward to Lucy, ready to speak. I think he's going to ask about herself and her life and her children.

She'll answer and then ask him about our life. Round and round we'll go. Never getting to the point – which is, of course, Lucy having a baby for us.

He takes a mouthful of tea, swallows it, wipes his mouth with the back of his hand, and then he says what he's decided to say. A planned speech of sorts. I never knew.

"We've always wanted a baby so much, haven't we, Soph?" I nod as he reaches out a hand to mine. We hold hands. "And we've been trying for years, and we've had IVF and ... Soph's probably told you all of this ... but, anyway, nothing's worked."

He looks at Lucy and reaches out his other hand to her, the one he's just wiped his mouth with. She takes it without hesitation and looks at him as he speaks.

"It's, you know, the eggs ... um ..."

He glances at me as I sit there, mortified that he's said it like that, just so ... I don't have the words.

"Thank you, Lucy, for doing this, thank you so much." This time, he sobs and pulls us towards him again, across the table full of plates and breakfasts and teapots and cups of tea. It's rather embarrassing, and I notice that people all round us are looking this way.

I'm the first to pull back, politely enough, and I continue eating my all-day breakfast. Matt and Lucy do too. I sit there, waiting for Matt to come out with a series of, I don't know, "what, when, where and how?" questions. But instead he's just chomping away and smiling and making those silly small grunting noises he does whenever he's really happy. Like he's chuckling inside to himself.

I glance at Lucy, and she looks back at me, laughing. So I do, too, in a friendly way. Matt looks up, and I see him thinking, *What are you two finding so funny?* Lucy grunts, "Uuh, uuh," a rough impersonation of him. Like they've been best friends, more than that, all their lives. Matt laughs. I smile.

We carry on, eating and drinking and not saying anything about everything we need to discuss, for another fifteen minutes or more. Matt reminisces about school days and teachers and what happened to various people we knew. Like I don't know any of this! As if I've not gone through it all already with Lucy! She keeps smiling and laughing indulgently at all the things he says.

Eventually, when I'm feeling frustrated and expecting us to get up and go in a minute, Matt goes, "Aaaaahhhh." He always does this when he's full of food he's enjoyed. I wait a moment. He doesn't burp (or worse) as I half expect. That's something, I suppose. Instead, he says, far too enthusiastically, "Let's have another brew for two ... I'll get three fresh cups; we can split it between us somehow!"

We watch him go. "Shouldn't we," I ask, "be asking each other lots of questions about surrogacy, you know, like, which clinic and, I don't know, the practicalities of it ... legal stuff, signing forms and things?" I look at Lucy, and she smiles back, seeming completely at ease with the situation. She shrugs cheerfully enough.

"He wants to be friends first, get to know each other, hang out, before we get to all of that." She says it in such a matter-of-fact way. Like it's obvious. And she knows Matt really, really well. That annoys me. Then she goes on, "He's like all men, really, a great big boy." She laughs delightedly. I don't laugh at all. Matt comes back, following a waitress carrying teapots and cups on a tray. He smiles at Lucy and then at me. I don't smile back.

THE REST of the day went well enough. After we'd finished our cups of tea, the three of us walked along the promenade to the pier, just chatting generally, like old friends. No mention at all of Lucy having our baby! They seemed cool with that. I just kept quiet, feeling irritated.

I thought we'd go on the pier and put some two-pence pieces into the machines and that we'd struggle to know what to do after, with Lucy hanging round forever. But she suddenly checked her phone and said, quite brightly, that she was off to see someone she'd hit it off with during her induction at the care home. I looked at her, thinking, *A man ... already?* She replied before I could say it, "Jo. J-O. Not Joe. J-O-E." We all laughed.

Matt and I went to the cinema, had a drink and a bite to eat, did some shopping in Ipswich and came home. We spent our usual evening, eating one of Matt's meals, getting our things ready for work the next day, then falling asleep in front of the television. It felt like it had been a long day. Matt seemed happy. I felt frustrated, wanting to have sorted everything out more than we had with Lucy.

We now lay in bed, chatting – at last – about having a

baby. It's the first time in ages that we've really gone into it in detail. We haven't dared for so long. Boy or girl, we don't mind. I'm sure Matt would prefer a boy so he could one day put something like *Curtis & Son – Plumbers Extraordinaire* on the side of his little white van, but I know he'll never admit it.

Names? We didn't like to talk about names before; it somehow seemed unlucky. Now we can dream. Even so, we have no idea of names yet, only all the ones we don't like. Max, Oscar, Fiona and so on. They're awful. And I've said we're not having Matt Jnr, no way. Still, it's such a big decision.

Then we talk about where the baby will sleep. In the smaller bedroom on this floor, I suggest, not upstairs as we first planned. We need to hear the baby, and I don't want to risk carrying him or her down the stairs and tripping.

To be honest, it's mainly me talking while Matt fiddles with his phone. I'm about to say something about it – I've noticed he's almost always on his phone when we're talking about anything important. But he turns suddenly and shows me the screen. I can't read it clearly. No matter, he tells me what I need to know.

"Oh, Soph, we can't do it." I hear him swallow hard. "This surrogacy thing is really expensive, way more than IVF." He sighs, reaches out and holds my hand, then goes on, telling me much of what I already know.

"We'd have to do it through an agency, and they'd take my sperm and either your eggs or Lucy's … Lucy's, I guess." He looks at me, but I don't react, just sit there staring into space. "And it's like IVF but twice the price … and we'd have to pay Lucy reasonable expenses. We can't afford it, any of it."

I know all this – that we cannot realistically do it formally – because I've read everything online about surrogacy in the UK over and again. It's a long and complicated, official process with doctors, nurses, solicitors and all sorts of professionals getting involved and taking their cut. It's more about making money – at our expense – than giving us a baby. I'm sorry if that seems hard, but it's how I feel.

So I already know we need to do it informally, and that's what I wanted to talk about when we had our brunch at Sea You this morning. For me, there are three issues. One, how Lucy will conceive. I know I am going to have to be grown-up about that. Two, whether Lucy will want to be paid. My fingers are crossed. Three, how we can draw up a legal agreement that the baby will be ours, mine and Matt's. I'm sure that's possible. Even if we have to use a London solicitor and pay their expensive fees.

"It's okay," I say, turning towards him. I can see how upset he is. "Don't worry. We can do it another way, just the three of us. You and Lucy will have to, you know …" I don't want to say it, *have sex*, out loud, so bluntly. There are other ways, of course, such as home insemination, but the success rate seems to be far lower. He looks surprised, thinks about it, taking it in, and then nods in agreement.

I go on. "It will be alright – and we'll have the baby we always wanted." He looks at me for reassurance. "Will it?" he murmurs, and I add, "One hundred per cent." He seems happy with it. I'm not happy about them having sex, of course I'm not, but I tell myself I'll have to be grown-up about it if I want a baby of my own. And I do, so, so much. More than anything.

CHAPTER FIVE

MONDAY, 26 AUGUST, EARLY AFTERNOON

Even though I knew today, a bank holiday Monday, would be Lucy's first proper day at work, I texted her after Matt and I had talked, asking her if we could meet at lunchtime. I sometimes work overtime on bank holidays, as the pay is good, and we always need money. Matt works too, doing fiddly one-off jobs. Anyway, it turned out both Lucy and I have breaks at the same time. We agreed to meet on a bench by the Ferris wheel on the seafront. She didn't ask why, assuming, I guess, that we'd now meet regularly just for the fun of it.

Lucy was there when I arrived. She was swigging from a Coca-Cola can and eating cheesy chips from a cardboard cone. She's still a teenager at heart. She offered me a chip. I took the cheesiest one. I declined the can, holding up the bottle of water I was carrying.

We sat next to each other in the sunshine for a while, exchanging pleasantries about each other's work that morning. I'd been dealing with the usual import forms one after the other. She'd been talking to an old lady with dementia sitting on a commode. I had the better time.

I have to tell Lucy that Matt and I cannot afford to go down the formal surrogacy path. That we cannot even afford to pay her reasonable expenses. I have to hope that, somehow, Lucy will go ahead with the surrogacy anyway.

It's our last chance – our only hope – of having a child. I have to persuade her. But my pride won't let me beg.

After we've had our drinks and eaten the chips and laughed at things we've seen around us, including a dog chasing an empty crisp packet caught by the wind, I get to the point of our meeting.

"I've been talking to Matt; he's been going through all the NHS pages about surrogacy – so much to take in!" I hesitate and then go on. "Clinics and lawyers and legal documents to sort out ... let alone actually having a baby." I try to laugh, to sound cheerful, but it does not come out quite right.

Lucy reaches out and holds my hand as I continue. She seems to sense what I'm going to say; perhaps she's been reading up on it all as well.

"And money, so much money." I stifle a sob, pause and then add, "It's ... the formal route ... twice the price of IVF ... and we can't afford that, nowhere near. We're stretched so tight right now."

Lucy squeezes my hand. I can't look at her.

"And expenses, reasonable expenses, it says on the website ... can double the cost of it all. We don't have that sort of money ... were you relying on expenses to live on ... to pay for a lawyer to get your children back? I'm sorry, I'm so, so sorry."

Lucy shuffles on her bottom along the bench towards me,

putting an arm around my shoulder and pulling me close to her.

"It's okay," she says. "It's okay, it doesn't matter. I've somewhere to live, and I'm earning now. I don't need your money."

I wait, hoping she will say the words I want to hear: that, somehow, she will still have a baby for me, for us.

"When we were young." Lucy sighs. "I imagined we'd be best friends forever, that our husbands would be best friends, and our children too. That we'd be like sisters. We were like sisters, weren't we? For so long. And I've always wanted to be back with you again."

I nod, agreeing with her.

"I'll have your baby ... I don't know how ... rubber gloves and a syringe most likely ... to start with ... if not ... we'll have to do the deed." She laughs her dirty laugh. "And I've no idea how I'll manage when I can't work for a bit ... but I guess we can sort something ... you can bring me sausage rolls from Greggs."

We used to love those.

I turn and embrace Lucy clumsily. I want to say thank you, but I can't say it without choking on the words. So I just squeeze her tight – three times – squeezing all the air out of her. It's what we did when we were young and were too embarrassed to express affection and share words of love.

"Shall I come round to yours later to talk about it?" Lucy asks as, eventually, we pull gently apart from each other. "Eight o'clock after we've eaten?"

I wipe my eyes with the backs of my hands and nod once and then twice: "Yes, yes."

"I'll text Matt," I say, reaching for my phone and clicking on messages. Lucy crunches her can in her hand and then throws it towards a bin. She misses – she was always a poor shot – and goes and gets it and drops it in with her screwed-up chips cone. She waits patiently in the sunshine. "All done," I tell her eventually, having messaged Matt, ending it, *Yeah! Yeah! Yeah!*

We hug for what seems like forever, and then we go to leave our sunny spot on the bench. Lucy is wandering along in that aimless way of hers towards the care home. I offer her a lift, but she says she prefers the walk, as it's not that far. So I go to my car and wave at her as I pass by.

I'm thrilled by what she's said – even so, the thought of how she's going to conceive with Matt still troubles me. It will be more than rubber gloves and a syringe. That was just Lucy's silly joke. We both know it will have to be proper sex to give it the best chance of happening. I try not to think about it. Just the baby I will one day hold in my arms.

I GET in from working overtime at five fifteen and sit down for ten minutes, texting Matt, *Don't be late!*

He replies a few minutes later, *Leaving now!*, so I've probably got forty-five minutes if he's working Bury-way.

I go for a quick run to the pier, picking up some ready-made salad bowls and cream cakes from the Tesco Express in town on the way back.

After a hasty shower, I put everything out on plates, with a jug of water and beakers, on the kitchen table. And then I sit waiting for Matt and thinking about things, making sense of everything and how I feel, in my head. I go over it all repeatedly until I am at ease with my thoughts.

So – I want a baby more than anything else in the world.

My heart aches for a baby. The only way we might do it by using the official surrogacy route is five years down the line, when the cost-of-living crisis may have eased and our house will hopefully have risen in price from where it stands now, which is below what we paid for it. We could maybe then remortgage to raise funds. But I'd be gone forty, and I think I'd feel too old to be a new mum.

So this plan – Lucy having a baby for us – is the only option left other than fostering or adopting. I know I could not bear to foster a child in case I fell in love with them and they were then returned to the birth parents. With adoption, and I know it sounds awful, but however much I try to reason my fears away, we'd not know what we were getting, what the parents were like; I always worry, what if the father was like that character in *Bates Motel*, Norman Bates. I shouldn't think like that, but I do.

Then Matt is back, hurrying up the stairs and into the kitchen, giving me a brief kiss, then dipping his head under the tap for a drink of water. Typical man. My brother used to do the same.

"I'll have a shower, change, and we can then eat before she arrives," he says. "Okay?"

I nod my agreement, and then he is gone.

I listen to him moving back and forwards, and then the sound of the shower. There were times, not so long ago, when we'd shower together. We've not done that for a while. So many sweet things drifted away when we were trying so hard to conceive and everything became so practical. I resist the fresh urge to follow him into the bathroom, as I'm still thinking about Lucy and the baby.

I wonder, deep in my heart, why she would do such a massive thing for us, for me, really. We were always so close, like sisters, it's true. She was a loner, the girls hating her because of her looks and her manner, and the boys always wanting to be with her, even from an early age. And I was a loner too, still am, really, never finding it easy to make friends. We just bonded.

There was a time, years back, when we would have done absolutely anything for each other. We were both in the Brownies, although we never went on to the Girl Guides, as it just felt too prissy for us. One night, on an overnight trip to a campsite, we both cut our hands picking up broken glass that had been left near the toilet block. We put our hands together, our blood mixing, and we swore we'd always be best friends until the day we died.

I've never, since then, met anybody who came anywhere close to being like Lucy. Women don't seem to like me – maybe because I speak my mind. If someone asks, "Does this top suit me?" I tell them the truth. That no, it shows too much of your tummy, which is, er, you know. And I've been told I frighten men. They've never bothered me, with their insecurities and desires, put it that way. I think perhaps Lucy feels the same about me, and she wants to be like sisters again.

I hear the shower still going – Matt always spends longer in there than anyone I've ever known. When we started living together, the first time he had a shower, he was in there for such an age that I thought he'd had an accident. I went in, and there he was, out of the shower and by the bathroom mirror, carefully putting cream around his eyes. I believe he spends longer in front of the mirror than he does in the shower.

Then he's getting out at last. I hear the cascade of water go off. He whistles tunelessly, as if he can't think of a song.

He'll still be a while yet before he comes out of the bathroom. If I asked, he'd say he's "grooming". I think he just likes looking at himself.

A few minutes later, Matt is moving about again, into the bedroom to get changed. He sometimes gets into his PJs at this time, but I hope he'll wear everyday clothes for when Lucy arrives.

I'm torn, thinking about Matt and Lucy making a baby together. Yes, we've both had plenty of other partners. I've had just into double figures. Matt's had a similar number, I think. Body count some call it – like we're murderers. But I've not been with anyone else since we met, and I'm pretty sure it's the same for Matt. No, not "pretty sure" – I'm certain.

I don't like the idea of Matt sleeping with Lucy; in fact, I hate it so, so much. But I think it can probably be limited to when she is at her most fertile. And it does not need to be done in anything other than a practical manner. It will be a short act rather than a long lovemaking session as it is with Matt and me.

It's not so much the act, if it can be limited to that, I realise, but also the fact that they will, I don't know, have some sort of bond between them – and it will last forever. They will have created a child, something Matt and I can never do. Now that I've forced myself to explore the thought, it's that bond rather than the act of sex itself that troubles me most. I will have to live with that realisation bottled up inside me, forever.

Then – at long last – Matt appears, stinking of body spray and aftershave as per usual. He's always OTT with them, like he's covering up a bad smell. (He isn't. I love the natural scent of his body.)

Finally, he sits down opposite me at the table. He looks at the salads but knows better than to pull an *ugh* face. I notice he is dressed smart-casual instead of his usual black tee-shirt and jogging bottoms. For Lucy's benefit.

"So," I say as he jabs at a vine tomato with his fork and lifts it to his mouth. "I've talked to Lucy about having a baby, and we've agreed ... You're definitely going to have to have sex with her."

Then I laugh as he sits there with his mouth open.

LUCY TURNED up just before eight o'clock, clutching an opened and half-empty bottle of Pernod; it was our favourite grown-up tipple when we were teenagers. Stolen from Lucy's mother's cabinet. We'd get into trouble and be grounded for weeks, but we didn't really care. Lucy obviously still drinks it. I've not for years.

The three of us sat down in the living room for a while, and Matt got out various bottles and mixers and glasses. And peanuts and cashew nuts. Like it was some ghastly dinner party our parents might have had. Funnily enough, we all seemed to be at ease with each other from the start, though.

I had a glass, or two, maybe more, of Pernod – just to be polite. Matt had wine. I'm not sure what Lucy drank, but I don't think she joined me in the Pernod. I remember, when Matt had put on some music – he still has a record player for his vinyl collection from when he was younger – that we talked about them having sex and Lucy saying, in a silly Suffolk accent, that she was as "fertile as a big moo cow today, actually". We laughed and carried on; I remember thinking she was just being daft. The comment didn't really make much sense.

I'm woozy now, kind of drunk, but it somehow feels different. I don't seem to be able to think straight. And my body is uncoordinated. I try to get comfortable in my armchair, but all I manage to do is slide off onto the carpet. I've not felt drunk like this for so long.

Matt is on the sofa opposite. He is laughing at me, his head thrown back, roaring. I can see Lucy sitting next to him, and she's looking at me too. She seems to be smiling. But I can't quite make it out.

Then Lucy comes across, bending over, her face so close to mine. She crosses her eyes as if that's what I'm doing, and then laughs. I try to sit up and focus, but it is all too much, and I slip back down, bumping my head on the carpet.

I turn my head to the side as Lucy goes back to the sofa, and I watch the two of them looking at me. And there is something I want to say, to shout, very much. But I cannot think what it is, let alone form the words. All I know is that it's not a nice thing.

I lift my head, feeling that I might be sick any moment and not wanting it to fill my mouth, choking me. I don't want to die here.

I look at Matt and Lucy, wanting them to do something for me. I'm not sure what. I have the word *help* in my head but do not want to say it. I don't think I could even whisper it.

I can hear Matt saying something, his voice sounding so far away. It's as though he is singing. I can't make out the words, just the tone of his voice. Oh, so cheerful.

Lucy just sits there, her hand on his thigh now, smiling at

me. And I want to tell her to stop. Don't do that! And I try to get the words out. But I cannot.

Then, later, she rests her head on his shoulder. He just sits there, smiling gormlessly. He doesn't move away or do anything to stop her. I want him to stand up and come over to me.

Then I am nodding off. I can't help myself. I fight it, struggling to stay awake. I have to.

I need to do something. Watch them. That's it. I need to shout no if I can, when they get up and go.

I do not want them to do whatever it is they are going to do. My mind can't ... it's something really bad. Awful. Shameful. But I can't think. I am losing my thoughts. My stream of ... whatever it is.

CHAPTER SIX

TUESDAY, 27 AUGUST, AFTER MIDNIGHT

I am awake again now, and it is dark, moonlight streaming through the living-room window. My mind seems to be working again. Sort of. I have a shocking headache, but my thoughts are becoming clearer. My body aches, though, and I don't know why.

I feel around, and I find a cushion beneath my head that was not there before. I don't think it was, anyway. Someone – Matt or Lucy – must have placed it in position. But they did not cover me with anything; they didn't put the throw on the sofa over me to keep me warm. And they've turned the main light off.

I sit up slowly, gasping in pain, or at least discomfort, and I peer towards the big clock we have on the wall opposite the fireplace. There is just enough moonlight for me to see that it is coming up to one o'clock.

Matt and Lucy are not here, although the debris of the night – bottles, cans, glasses, packets of nuts and so on – is on the coffee table. An empty bottle lies on its side on the carpet in front of me. A broken wine glass, bowl and stem, is next to it.

It hits me, suddenly, that they are not sitting in front of me, waiting for me to come round. They have gone off together somewhere. And then I remember what we were talking about. Joking. Laughing. Matt getting Lucy pregnant. Her being as fertile as a moo cow.

I struggle to my feet, slipping back down once onto my knees before I can rise and stand steady. My head hurts. My body too. My mouth is bone dry. I stand there, knowing I have to find them. I realise where they will be. In our bed.

I walk, aching, to the living-room door. Open it and stand, listening. Nothing. Our bedroom is the next room along the hallway. Just beyond the fire extinguisher we keep on the landing by the top of the stairs. I move to the bedroom, the door slightly ajar. I listen again, for sounds of lovemaking or post-coital murmurings.

I want a baby so much. But not like this, I think. It's somehow so wrong. And dirty. I don't want them to make love – even if it's, as Matt might put it, "having sex, just once". They didn't ask my permission, I think angrily.

I lean my head on the door in despair, and it's enough to push it open. I stumble in, losing my balance, tipping unsteadily onto the carpet. Then I stand up, expecting to see Matt and Lucy there, both naked, in each other's arms. Or worse, still making love.

MATT LIES THERE ALONE, the duvet thrown back, the lamp on his bedside cabinet still on. He sometimes has nightmares and can't bear to sleep in the dark. A childhood legacy.

His father wasn't a nice man when he was young. That's one of the reasons he keeps away from the whole lot of them these days.

He's wearing his pyjama bottoms, but no top. That's how he usually sleeps in warmer weather. I'd normally just slip in beside him, pulling the duvet over us and snuggling up close. But I need to wash my face and hands first and clean my teeth. And there's something else I need to do. To know. Was Lucy in this bed with him, or did she simply go after another glass or two on the sofa?

I move forward, checking my side of the bed, seeing if there are any signs that Lucy has been here. A strand of her blonde hair. A mark on the sheet from Matt. There is nothing. I look at my bedside cabinet and carpet. For something. An earring, maybe. I don't know. Again, there is nothing unexpected there.

I don't know what to think. I assumed they came into our bedroom. I was sure they'd have sex. I'd come in and find them. We'd have a blazing row, and Lucy would gather her clothes and be gone. I've no idea what we'd do from there if she were pregnant. Unlikely, though. Unless it was a case of first time lucky.

I think, most likely, they got up while I was asleep – passed out – on the living-room carpet. They were polite but embarrassed, feeling awkward. Maybe Matt kissed her on the cheek to indicate a polite goodbye, and then she was gone, and he went to bed as normal.

Something bothers me though; that scenario doesn't feel right. The whole thing just seems off and really odd. If Lucy had gone like that, Matt would have come back after seeing her to the door, and then he would have lifted me up from the living-room carpet, saying, "Come on, Soph, time for bed." He didn't. He left me there. He just wouldn't do that.

I go into the living room, searching for something. I'm not sure what, but I'll know it when I see it. There are no signs that Lucy was ever here. I turn on the living-room light and study what's on the carpet. That's it. I know what I'm looking for. The half-empty bottle of Pernod that Lucy brought with her and gave to me. It is not there.

Pernod is what Lucy and I used to drink down by the pier and along the amusements. I thought she'd brought it along tonight for old times' sake, a little in-joke between us. But it was not a new bottle, but a half-full one. I think my subconscious registered that was strange, but I didn't say anything, maybe assuming she couldn't afford a fresh new bottle.

I'm sure I was the only one who drank any. And although I haven't drunk properly, drunk-drunk, for so long, I know that it's what knocked me senseless. It never used to do that. A horrifying thought strikes me hard.

Did Lucy put something in the bottle to drug me so she'd feel easier having sex with Matt? She must have access to stuff at the care home.

I go to the bathroom, washing my hands and face and brushing my teeth. I stand there looking at myself in the mirror. I'm not sure if I am staring at the face of a victim or a, not a bully exactly, but someone who is not a very nice person. Someone full of suspicions. Matt has always been a wonderful husband. He'd not behave like this. I tell myself I'm being unfair.

As I walk back into the bedroom, watching Matt breathing gently, I think I may be creating a monstrous wrong against Lucy. She was always my best friend. She had no choice but to go away. She has shown nothing but kindness and generosity towards me since she came back. She is, still, my best friend.

Lying down and pulling the duvet over me, I can feel the heat of Matt's body. He has always been lovely and warm, my hot water bottle in winter.

But as I lie there, I work out what might have happened. And now I'm sure that it's what did. Quite simply, they came in here, had sex, and Lucy left before I came round.

As I stare at the ceiling, I can't shake off the thought. I don't wish to lie here in turmoil, nor do I want to start an argument by sleeping on the sofa in the living room. I'm torn and troubled, and at this moment, I'm full of a seething anger. I can't make sense of things in my head, which is throbbing like my brain's about to burst. I'm not sure if I hate Lucy, Matt or maybe simply myself.

MOST WEEKDAY MORNINGS start the same, both of us in in a hurry. Matt usually gets up first and showers while I go into the kitchen and put together a basic breakfast: cereals, maybe some toast, orange juice and mugs of tea. We eat and drink quickly, and then Matt heads off to work – he's helping to convert a country house into apartments at present – and I go for a run before showering, changing and setting off to work.

Today it's different. I'm woken by Matt getting up early and heading for a shower as usual. As he goes, he pokes his head back round the bedroom door and says, "I'll do a fry-up … give me ten minutes in the shower?" He is moving down the hallway before I can reply. I sense he feels as awkward as I do.

I lie here for ten minutes or so, listening to Matt showering and then moving about the kitchen. I get up, feeling dirty somehow, pulling off the sheet and pillowcases and the duvet cover, taking them into the kitchen and putting them into the washing machine. I'm then into the living room, with a bin bag, clearing up.

Matt calls, "Ready!" and I make my way back to the kitchen, throwing the half-full bin bag into the corner by the door to the outside staircase down to the back garden. The bottles clink together, and Matt says, "I'll sort the recyclable stuff from the rubbish later." He gestures to me to sit down.

It's a nice breakfast – a fry-up but not too much of anything. I'm not keen on slabs of meat. This has two slices of crispy bacon, two chipolatas, scrambled eggs, button mushrooms and vine tomatoes. Even so, I can't face any of it. I'll sip at the mug of hot, sweet tea in a minute or two.

Matt is jolly, unnaturally so. He's usually a real Steady Eddie, but now he is talking away, about the breakfast ingredients, in a faster- and higher-pitched voice than normal. As I drop my knife and fork back down to the sides of my plate, he hesitates, looks at me, then glances away.

I know the answer to my question just from that glancing look. Still, I ask it, "You did, didn't you? With Lucy?"

He leans back in his chair, looks at me again, then away, and back again. He is embarrassed, and I suddenly feel sorry for him. Almost. But not quite.

"Yes," he says suddenly, meeting my eye and then dropping his head down, in something close to shame. He fiddles with his knife and fork, then sits there with them pointing upwards, like he's waiting for permission to start eating.

I expect him to add something defensive, accusatory, as most men would do. "I thought it was what you wanted," they'd say, almost implying, "You made me do it!" But Matt's not like that, he just sits there, waiting for my response.

And I don't know what to say. In my head, I have an image of the two of them together, naked, in our bed. Both of them moving towards ecstasy. It is that thought – the sense that Matt enjoyed it, relished it, was having the best sex ever – that tears at my heart.

I want to hear him say that it was just an act, to impregnate her, without feeling or enjoyment. That it was just to make a baby for us. But I hate the thought of that, too, our baby being created in such a cold and unloving way. But then, of course, Matt must have been aroused enough to have begun and ended the act. And I am back to that image again.

Matt sighs, stirring his mug of tea with a spoon. Then he looks at me, holding my gaze. I think he is going to say, "I love you." He sometimes says it at unexpected moments, but I'm sure he knows better than to say it now.

"I want to be a dad so much." He stops, his voice cracking as he repeats the last words, "So much." He thumps his heart with a clenched fist. I have never seen him do anything like that before. It moves me. Then he adds, "I want a baby with you ... my soulmate." He hesitates for such a long while, and then he says, "How else can we have our baby ... but like this?"

He sounds almost despairing as he goes on, "It wasn't like you think ... we didn't ... it was just ... we didn't even get undressed properly. And ..."

I put my hand up, a gesture: stop! I don't want to know any more. He is going to say it was quick and he had me in his thoughts when he was doing it. I really don't want to hear anything like that.

Matt reaches his left hand across the table and puts it on mine. I don't pull away, nor do I wrap our hands together as I might normally do. I wait to see what he says.

"We've always wanted a baby, more than anything. And we can't ... so this, after, you know, last night, is the only way ... she said it was the right time ... we had to take our only chance ... it will be perfect. We'll have our baby at last!" He grabs both my hands, going to pull me forward. I resist.

"If she's pregnant!" I say, my voice louder than I expected. "What are the chances of that ... first time!" He looks startled, and I realise he's been assuming she would be pregnant instantly. "It doesn't happen like that ... it might take three or four goes every month for months." I see the expression on his face, faking eager anticipation, and I laugh. "You're not doing it again ... ever!"

And at that, he is around the table and taking me in his arms. He goes to kiss me, but I turn my head slightly and just hug him. I have a sudden image in my head of him kissing Lucy last night. Oh, so passionately, I don't want him to kiss me now. Not properly. Nor do I want him doing what he sometimes does, lifting me up and carrying me to the bed, expecting to make love.

"Not now," I say decisively, reaching for my mug of tea. He sits and starts eating his breakfast. "You'll be late for work if you don't get a move on."

He hurries before putting bacon and chipolatas between two slices of bread to take with him as a sandwich. Then he's up and away, clattering his mug and plate and cutlery into the sink and going off with his sandwich. I sit there at the table, picking at my breakfast.

He comes back in to say goodbye before he goes, and I angle my head so he can kiss my cheek. "Cinema this evening?" he says, even though we've just been. He loves his cinema visits and popcorn and pick 'n' mix. My big kid. I nod and ask him what he wants to see. He tells me to check online and find something "funny ... cheerful". And I reply that I will see what I can do. And then he is gone. And still I sit here, pushing my breakfast around my plate.

I think I should be pleased, thrilled, that Lucy may be pregnant, already carrying our baby for us. It is, or should be, the greatest moment of my life. But my head is so full of negative thoughts. Lucy and that half-empty bottle. Matt leaving me on the living-room carpet all night. And I do not believe I will ever shake off that image of Matt and Lucy in bed, the two of them reaching climax together. Is the thought of us having a baby enough to blot that out? I'm far from sure.

CHAPTER SEVEN

FRIDAY, 6 SEPTEMBER, MID-MORNING

The next week or so Matt and I just carry on as we always have done, getting up, going to work, coming home, eating, going to bed. Repeating the cycle.

We don't talk about Lucy. Matt seems awkward and embarrassed. I don't want to dwell on what happened. So there's a kind of mutually agreed silence on the matter.

I've not heard anything from Lucy. I thought I would. I decided I'd text her on Saturday morning to ask her how the new job is going. Matt is off helping his friend Baz clear out his garage. I might ask Lucy if she wants to have lunch.

But now, today, Friday, mid-morning, I receive a text from Lucy.

Meet? McD. One?

The message does not surprise me. I'd half expected it. I know what it means.

Sure! See you then! I reply, adding an exclamation mark to sound cheery. I'm feeling rather sick, to tell the truth.

I'm not sure McDonald's down by the docks is where I want to learn Lucy is pregnant. But still.

It would have been better – nicer – if she had come round and told Matt and me together.

That way, it would have been a shared experience and felt more like our baby.

I get to the McDonald's just after one o'clock. It's always busy at this time of day, and I can't find a car parking space, so I go and park by the supermarket behind McDonald's and walk back.

I see Lucy sitting by a window. She's pulling a goofy face and waving at me with a little red McDonald's flag. Like she used to do when we were children. Like she's still ten years old. I smile and wave at her as I approach the entrance.

As I go across to the table, she says she ordered two wraps of the day, fries and two Coke Zeros, and she hopes that's okay? There's a plastic thing, I don't know what it's called, with a number on it, 634, on the table between us. I nod, pleased at least that she hasn't bought us Happy Meals with chicken McNuggets. As I sit, I look over, and her beaming face confirms what I've been expecting.

She opens her handbag, then her purse, fiddling to the side of it before pulling out a little white stick.

She glances around to make sure we're not being watched. The place is packed, every table taken and queues at the counter, with staff collecting trays and cleaning floors. But nobody is taking any notice of us.

Lucy holds the white stick out in a cupped hand and points to the blue line on it with her other. "Congratulations," she says, then adds, "You're going to be a mummy." She smiles. "And don't worry, I gave it a good wipe before I put it in my bag."

I take the stick from her, checking it is real, that the blue line is there. It is. For sure.

Despite everything – being in this crowded McDonald's, Matt so far away, my mixed feelings about Lucy as a surrogate – I am close to tears. I dip my head down as a young McDonald's employee plonks a tray of food and drink between us and wanders off.

"Thank you," I say at last. It's all I can think of. We look at each other. Her face is triumphant. I must look emotional. I rally by fiddling with wrappings and straws and serviettes. Despite all the loud and lively teenagers around us, it feels like we are alone. We eat and drink quietly for a few minutes, lost in our own thoughts.

I notice, behind Lucy, two teenage girls from the local school. They are getting up, putting their leftovers on a tray, taking it over to a bin. One's lively, the other quiet.

They could have been us, Lucy and me, so many years ago. The "Lucy", pretty and slender. The "Sophie", less so, plainer and more solid. I don't know why, but the sight of them makes me feel unbearably sad.

As four teenage boys, all spikey haircuts, rucksacks and honking noises, bundle in where the girls were sitting, I grab my wrap and drink and say to Lucy, "Come on, let's go to my car." Lucy does the same and follows me.

As we sit in my car in the supermarket behind McDonald's, finishing our food and drink, Lucy says, "You seem ... are you okay? It's a lot to take in, I know."

I nod and smile and reply, "I'm thrilled ... really ... so thrilled." I make my voice sound as excited as I can. In truth, I have such mixed feelings. Massive negative ones. Too late now, though. "It's just ... Matt." It's all I can think of to say.

There's a long pause. Then Lucy responds, a catch in her voice. "I ... ah, I'm so sorry. I was excited to tell you ...

McDonald's wasn't the right place … how stupid of me … it's just that it's so convenient for both of us. And we used to go there all the time, didn't we? I have such happy memories."

I nod, thinking, really, that I am so churlish, so unreasonable – wanting everything my way and just so, so perfect. It's mean-spirited of me. I say, "It's okay, no, it's fine … it's great!"

"Tell you what, Soph. Let's do it again. I'll come round this evening after you've had your tea. Pretend we've not met today. I'll tell you both at the same time. Okay? Half past eight?"

I nod: yes, please!

We finish our food and drink in a happier silence, thinking our own thoughts. Lucy is delighted, I'm sure of that. Matt will be fighting back tears of joy. And I will do my best to put on my happy-every-after face. I'm not sure it will fit me perfectly. An image of them together in my mind's eye still troubles me.

MATT, of course, is beyond chuffed. He is thrilled-to-bits speechless. He stands there with his mouth flapping open like a fish out of water. Not knowing what to say or do.

Lucy arrived, as she said, at eight thirty, a bottle of wine in one hand – "Non-alcoholic!" – and a small bouquet of flowers for me. Freesias. They are so sweet, and I know Lucy does not have much money, so it was a kind thought.

I led her upstairs to the living room, and she stood in the doorway, looking at Matt and me standing up and gazing back at her. *Ta-da!* She raised her arms in the air, triumphant, bouquet in one hand, bottle in the other.

"Mummy and Daddy!" she shouted, and Matt, big, tough Matt, burst into tears.

He doesn't know what to do, how to react, which means that whatever he does will be instinctive. And telling, it suddenly strikes me.

I think he will turn to me, holding me tight, saying something loving, with "mummy" at the end of it.

Instead, he rushes to Lucy, hugging her, and she makes a silly "ooh-ooh" noise, pretending he's touched her bottom and she quite liked it. She puts her arms around him as best she can, what with the bouquet and bottle.

I think, for one appalling moment, that they're going to dance – actually dance, like lovers, a slow dance, the last one at the school prom – and I rush forward, taking the bouquet and bottle from her.

She steps back, and he moves forward, embracing the two of us, and we stand there awkwardly in something like a group hug, the bouquet crumpled against my tummy and the bottle between my thighs.

I pull away, gesturing Matt towards the kitchen to put the flowers in water and to uncork the bottle and come back with glasses.

"I'll not stop," Lucy says as the two of us sit down opposite each other in the two armchairs, with Matt busying about in the kitchen. "Just a celebratory glass and I'll leave the two of you to it."

Something in her voice and the way she glances at me, almost hopefully, perhaps wistfully, suggests she'd like to stay longer, maybe for the rest of the evening. I smile back and say, "Yes." As in, don't stop.

Her face twitches ever so slightly, and I feel I am being

mean again, but it's really for Matt and me to be together now on our own, absorbing the news, talking things over, making our plans. Not Matt, me and Lucy!

Then Matt is back, with wine glasses and the bottle, mumbling nonsense about leaving the flowers in the kitchen ... some stems have broken ... I'll have to do something with them. And so on. Like only a woman can arrange flowers.

I shake my head, the flowers can wait, some instinct warning me not to leave Matt and Lucy together at this moment. I have a sense they may kiss.

Stupid, of course. They have already been together, so to speak. But that was a, what's the word, practical matter. Of sorts, anyway. What I don't want them to do, I realise, is to actually fall in love, which seems horribly possible at this moment.

Matt puts the three wine glasses he has been carrying onto the coffee table, and then pours wine from the bottle in the other hand into each of them in turn. "Low alcohol!" he states.

He stays standing, about to raise his glass. Lucy and I get to our feet. She already has her hands around her tummy, like she is cradling an about-to-be-born, nine-month-old bump. This infuriates me, but I say nothing.

I think for an awful moment that he is going to say, "To us!" but he stumbles over his words and then raises his glass: "To the baby!"

Both Lucy and I echo his words. "To the baby!" Lucy takes a step forward and puts one arm behind Matt's back and the other, holding the glass, around mine, and we're all pulled into another embrace.

I see Lucy looking up at Matt, all simpering eyes and

fluttering eyelashes, and Matt looking back at her almost adoringly. Because she can have a baby and I can't. And just at this moment in time, I feel a surge of negativity rising up and almost overwhelming me. Something down deep inside tells me this isn't going to go well. Really, it isn't. It's not going to be happy ever after.

PART 2

TWO'S COMPANY ...

CHAPTER EIGHT

SATURDAY, 7 SEPTEMBER, THE EARLY HOURS

I am lying in bed now, three hours on, and I cannot sleep. My mind is full of troubling thoughts. About Lucy. Matt. Me. And the baby.

Matt is sleeping next to me, breathing gently. No matter what, he is asleep within minutes of putting his head on the pillow. He would stay sleeping through an earthquake.

He wanted to make love when we came to bed. I did not. We only make love when we're both really keen. It didn't feel right tonight somehow.

Lucy went to leave just after we'd toasted the baby. "I really must be going," she said once she'd downed the first glass. I know Lucy of old, of course. The way she said it sounded plaintive, almost sad. Some men fall for the "poor little me" routine.

"No, stay!" Matt answered, reaching out his hand and holding one of hers. "At least let's finish the bottle. Another glass!"

She agreed, surprise, surprise, and we had one more glass each. I'm not sure she should be drinking even low-alcohol wine if she's pregnant. I didn't say anything. The word *if* sticks in my mind.

I didn't mind that she had a second glass. What bothered me – angered me – was the way he reached out and held her hand. And she held his. Quite naturally. It's as though it doesn't matter if I am standing in sight of them or not.

I lie here, getting ever edgier. Lucy came round this evening in full make-up and dressed to kill. She is prettier than me. And shapelier. And more outgoing, easier to talk to.

Matt is smitten with her; I can see that. He is what I'd call a simple man. Straightforward, that is, not stupid. Lucy can be sweet and charming. She always has been. Only I, her best friend of old, know she can also be cunning and manipulative. But never with me. At least not then. Now? I'm not so sure.

Then there is the baby. The fact that Lucy is pregnant, and so easily, makes her so much more attractive than me. I've not been able to get pregnant even after years of trying every month. I feel such a failure.

Lucy left after we had finished the bottle. She said, this time, she'd really better be going. Matt replied, "You don't have to." I wanted to shout, "Yes, go, go on, go."

Matt showed her out, leading her downstairs to the main door, where they stood talking. I moved to the top of the stairs but couldn't hear them clearly. I imagined him kissing her goodbye. I didn't want to think about that.

Then Matt was back upstairs, in leaps and bounds, following me into the bathroom, where I was cleaning my teeth. He put his arms around me and hugged me tight. I was as cheerful as I could be. Then we went to bed, and he put his hand on my shoulder, and I said I was very tired. He asked if I was happy. I replied, "Yes, really, really happy," as positively as I could. It seemed to satisfy him.

As I lie here, still unable to sleep, my mind working things through, I realise what it is that's keeping me awake. It's not that I am jealous of Lucy or that I feel a failure or that I am worried about how Matt looks at Lucy. Well, there's all of that, of course, but more. Something that's somehow much worse.

I am angry that Lucy has got pregnant immediately. That's the crux of the matter. She has done something I've never been able to do. And so easily. Effortlessly. Just once. And Matt is able to be a dad, a real dad. And he could be a dad again, if he wanted. But not with me, not properly anyway. I can never be a real mother.

My mind goes on, click, click, clicking its way through everything. I always think too much. Overanalysing. Weighing things up. Making sense of them. I'm doing it now.

Lucy is the same age as me. Thirty-five. Past her prime fertility-wise. What are the chances of a thirty-five-year-old woman getting pregnant first time round?

I then work through the dates – from when she'd have got pregnant to, today, when she announced her pregnancy. Eleven days, maybe a day or two before her period is due? There are tests that reveal you're pregnant six days before your period. Even so, it's tight. I think she takes us for fools.

My mind crystallises into a single thought around that word that's been nagging away at the back of my mind. "If".

You know what? I don't believe Lucy is pregnant.

AS MY THOUGHTS CRYSTALLISED, I knew, in my heart, I had to act quickly on my suspicion – no, my certainty – that Lucy is not pregnant with Matt's baby.

Otherwise, it would all escalate out of control oh so fast. Decorating the spare bedroom. Shopping for baby clothes and stuff. That's what Matt is like. A big, overenthusiastic kid at heart.

Lucy would be with us at all of these moments. Right in the middle of our lives. Helping to choose a cot and a buggy and picking the colour scheme for the baby's room. Just being there. All. The. Time. I can't have that.

So we're sitting here now, Lucy and I, at lunchtime, having a makeshift picnic, just the two of us, on a blanket on a grassy plain by the Grove woods on the outskirts of Felixstowe.

I don't usually do picnics, either making or eating them. I can't be bothered with fiddly bits of things. Hard and soft cheeses. Different types of silly chutney. Lettuce. So many types. And I hate wasps and flies buzzing about and ants crawling up my legs.

But I need to deal with this, so I made a makeshift picnic, texted her first thing as Matt headed out to clear Baz's garage. *Lunch? 1? I pick you up?* and she replied with *Working overtime today!* and then an enthusiastic *YES!*

So here we are.

"What's the matter?" Lucy asks, almost straight after we've set everything out and taken a can of Coke Zero and a sandwich each. She says it before either of us have taken a bite. She knows me so well.

She goes on before I can answer, making assumptions about what I think, how I feel, who I am. Like we're still sixteen-year-old schoolgirls.

"I'm not going to hang around all day, every day. Once the baby's born, you're mum; I'll just be auntie." She reaches out and puts her hand on my arm, and I feel, for a moment, ever so churlish with my doubts and suspicions. "Honestly, I know what you're thinking. You've nothing to worry about. It will be you, the baby and Matt." Then she says, "When the baby's born, if you want, I can leave town and never come back again. Not a word. Not even birthday and Christmas cards ... well, WhatsApp gifs. Is that what you want, Soph? You only have to say so."

I shake my head and reply, "No, no, of course not. I'm just being ..." I shake my head again. What else can I do? She leans forward and hugs me. I hug her back. We start eating and drinking.

"That's where we saw that muntjac deer that time," Lucy says unexpectedly, pointing towards a line of trees.

"No one believed us," I answer. "Might as well have said we saw a three-foot grey alien." Lucy laughs, spluttering on her sandwich.

"God, you're terrible at sandwiches," she says, pulling the sandwich apart. "Cheese slabs, still."

I laugh too.

"What was the name of that horrid teacher who had the allotment – where I pulled up all his vegetables?" Lucy asks. "I remember him screaming when he saw what I'd done."

"Mr Watson ..." I answer. "God, he was creepy." We both chuckle, lost in our own thoughts. We eat and drink on in a more relaxed mood.

But it scratches away at me, the thought – the dreadful, instinctive feeling – that Lucy is not pregnant, and just as significant, why would she say she is? Maybe this is a desperate ruse to get close to me. Perhaps to us. Or only to Matt. Yes, to Matt.

I can't work out how she'd think that would work, though. Would she pretend to lose the baby in a month or so's time? When she'd wheedled her way into our lives – and Matt's affections?

And where did the stick with that faint blue line come from? It's not something she could get easily unless she did it herself. Possibly, it's something she kept from when she got pregnant with one of her children. Some mothers are sentimental like that. Yes, that seems most likely. Possible, anyway.

I can't stop myself. I open my handbag, take out a pregnancy testing kit I had left in a drawer, with three tests still in it, open it and hand her a white stick. She looks at it, her sandwich halfway to her lips, her mouth open in surprise, and then at me. I see sudden anger flare in her face.

"You're kidding," she says, throwing it back at me. "You're fucking kidding me." She never used to swear much, and hasn't done since she came back, but I can tell she's so angry, not just by the words but the way she spits them out.

I go to say some nonsense about Lucy not leaving the blue-lined stick with us ... Matt really wanted to have it, to keep it as a memento, he's so thrilled ... that's all. But I don't get the chance. Lucy is already getting to her feet. She sees straight through me. The picnic's over.

She checks her phone, then says, "I've got to go. I'm supposed to be back at one forty-five. Will you take me? It's miles to walk from here."

I nod, feeling awkward but also cheated, and then we both start packing away the picnic into the two big carrier bags I used.

"How could you?" Lucy says as I drive out of the car park, heading for the bypass that's the quickest way to the care home. "What, you think I'd say I'm pregnant because ...?" She leaves the question hanging in the air, expecting an answer.

I'm driving the car at seventy miles an hour down the bypass to the docks, close to where she works. I just want this over. "I'm sorry," I reply. "I ..." I shake my head, unsure what to say. "I don't know what I was thinking." We drive on in silence. I'm feeling humiliated. Lucy's still stiff-backed and fuming.

We arrive at the care home. She is up and out as the car comes to a halt. Then she turns, and I expect her to give me a mouthful of abuse. Instead, she simply says, "Fuck you, Chunky." And then she is gone, and I wonder, because she used my childhood nickname, if despite this, all will be well between us.

I drive back by where I work, a big soulless office block at the docks, with my thoughts and feelings all over the place.

Is she pregnant? Is she fooling me and Matt? Why? Why? Either way, I'm not happy.

I just know this is all going to end badly. I wish none of this ever happened. If only I could turn back time. All I want is Matt and me to be together again. Exactly as we were. Happy.

MATT and I get on with things, having a meal at the pub round the corner on Saturday evening and going over to Framlingham on Sunday afternoon for a pub lunch and a walk round the castle grounds. Matt huffs and puffs his way up and down the path. He can't be bothered with it.

He keeps asking about Lucy and when we'll see her again and "go shopping for things". Like there's now three of us in this marriage. Lucy isn't replying to my text messages – she's playing silly beggars – and so I fib to Matt, telling him she's gone to see her family for a few days.

By now, Sunday evening, he's eased off with the questions although I keep seeing him on his mobile, looking at cots and pushchairs and things. He's a softie at heart.

After we've eaten and before we go to bed, Matt and I are watching a Channel 5 thriller about a man caught up in a murder. He's meek and mild. The murderer is obviously his butter-wouldn't-melt, but deeply repressed wife.

It's a four-parter, and Matt loves these sorts of things. He'd binge-watch the whole lot. I have to persuade him to watch one episode each evening.

We're on part three now, and Matt is second-guessing what will happen next. He's almost always wrong, as I'm sure he is tonight. If anyone looks even a bit shifty, he accuses them. I usually get it right – nine times out of ten – but keep quiet so I don't spoil things for him.

"It's definitely him," Matt says, engrossed. "You watch. They'll do a flashback and show him losing his temper." He reaches for the bowl of popcorn I've made and pushes a handful of pieces into his mouth.

"Why do you think that?" I say innocently, knowing his mouth is full.

Matt tries to speak, chokes, then turns towards me and laughs, spraying bits of popcorn over me. Accident or not (not), I laugh too, going "uurgh" and brushing them onto the carpet. He can pick them up later when we tidy round before going to bed.

As I go "uurgh", there is a noise from the buzzer on the landing. Someone is downstairs, on the front doorstep, pushing our bell on the main door.

"Ignore it," Matt says, swallowing his popcorn and taking a mouthful of Coke Zero. He then turns and looks at the clock. "It's gone eleven. Some drunk teenagers playing knock and run."

I wait, not so sure. We've never had anyone ring our bell at this time of night before. And we've had plenty of drunks and teenagers going by over the years. And why our front door? It's tucked well back from the pavement.

It goes again. Buzz.

Buzz. Buzz. Buzz.

Buzz. It's something urgent.

"Freeze it," I say to Matt, gesturing towards the television and then the remote control on the sofa between us. "I'll go see. It's probably the man downstairs gone out without his keys."

It isn't. As I open the main door, Lucy is standing there. Cowed and tearful. It looks like she's been in a fight; her clothes are all awry. She is barefoot, holding her shoes in her right hand, one with a broken-off heel.

Before I can speak, she steps unsteadily over the threshold and falls into my arms. "I've been … there's this man at the caravan park … I can't go back … please don't make me go back." I hug her tight, and pulling our door to behind us, I help her into our home and up the stairs. She stumbles over the fire extinguisher on the landing, banging her knee, and I help her up. She's in a bad way.

Matt is turning the television off as I help Lucy to sit in

an armchair by the fireplace. She hugs herself tight; she seems in pain all over. Or perhaps she is just really upset. It's hard to tell. Matt glances at me, unsure what to say or do. Then he takes a fleecy throw from the back of the sofa and wraps it around her shoulders. She smiles waveringly up at him.

"What happened?" I ask. She tells us that there's a man at the caravan park where she lives, a kind of handyman, and he's been coming on to her. She's just been polite and friendly with him. But tonight, she had a problem with the gas cylinder under her caravan, and he came and replaced it and said he needed to come into the caravan to do something or other. He then tried to force himself on her. She managed to shake him off, get out and run away, leaving her belongings and her car behind.

"Don't make me go back. Please," she says, close to pleading.

I go to answer, to say she should call the police, report it and then return with them to the caravan park. They'll have a word with the handyman. But Matt, big-hearted Matt, is saying she can stay here, not just the night, as I would have done at most, but for as long as she wants. I go to pull a *No!* face at him, but he's already saying he'll get the front bedroom of the loft tidied and hurries out of the living room.

"I'll not be any trouble to you, Soph, I promise." Lucy struggles painfully to her feet, dropping the throw on the armchair. "May I use your bathroom, please?"

I nod, feeling somehow angry that she's now here – violating our marriage – and also pangs of guilt that I'm being so unreasonable. I watch her leave the living room.

Thing is, I know Lucy too well. She won't sit in her room, or maybe go out every other evening to give Matt and me time together. She'll be here each breakfast and all through every evening, and at weekends, she'll come shopping with us, want to go round the shops with me and to the cinema all together – the three of us trying to squeeze into one of the two-seater comfy sofas on the back row.

A few minutes later, Lucy and I meet at the bottom of the staircase to the loft, just as Matt comes down and says, almost like he's expecting a round of applause, "All done." And I look at her, and she is wearing a pair of my pyjamas and a headband of mine to hold her hair back. She must have gone into our bedroom and rummaged through drawers like everything were hers. She seems better now, uninjured and cheerful, and smiles at me. Then she turns and smiles at Matt too, and he smiles – no, beams – back at her. And I feel another flash of anger as she heads upstairs.

I look at Matt as he watches her go. There is something about this that troubles me more than just Lucy being here. It's Matt, of course. Most men, even happily married men, automatically look women up and down, often without realising it. But this is more than that – he is looking at her a little too intently.

I suggest we go back into the living room to finish the episode we've been watching on the television, and we do, although we are both ill at ease. Towards the end of the episode, with a close-up of the meek and mild husband, Matt turns to me with a smug, "told you so" expression. I can't be bothered to explain what the final twist will be. It's so obvious. The ending of thrillers always are.

My mind is full of thoughts about Lucy. Her angry reaction at our picnic – her overreaction! – followed by the childish silence. Planning, I think, her next move. Her arrival here tonight, supposedly beaten and bruised and then miraculously cured.

As we go to bed, Matt puts his hands on my hips and moves close. I say, "Not tonight." He sighs and backs off. I think he is excited by Lucy's presence in the house. Her lying upstairs in my nightclothes. That's the reason I don't want to do anything, not with her listening to us. That and, of course, my growing certainty that Lucy is not pregnant. It's all part of a plot. The ending of this story, the killer twist, inevitably being Matt and her together.

I LIE HERE into the night, with Matt snoring softly next to me. He snores sometimes, mostly when he's been drinking, but it's never loud enough to keep me awake. Even if he was as quiet as a mouse tonight, it would make no difference. I'd still be unable to sleep. Thinking about Lucy.

I hear her getting up, the floorboards and the steps creaking as she makes her way downstairs and to the bathroom. I sit, checking Matt is still asleep, as he is no longer snoring. I wait a few minutes – she's taking an age – eventually listening to her making her way back upstairs. Then I follow, two steps at a time.

I knock lightly on the door, pushing it open before she can answer. The room is half lit by moonlight coming through the skylight. She sits up in bed, now wearing a baggy white tee-shirt of Matt's. I suppress a sudden flash of anger. How dare she. I want to take two, three strides across the room and rip it off her. I calm myself, taking deep breaths. Before I can say anything, Lucy speaks.

"I'm not pregnant anymore, Soph. I'm so sorry." She

looks at me from the bed, pulling the duvet up to her chin. All I can see are her big, tearful eyes. Somehow, that news does not surprise me. I resist the urge to shout back, "You never were!"

"I felt ... something ... I don't know ... during the attack ... I just grabbed my bag and ran ... I had one of the sticks left in the side pocket, so I ..." She stops, seeming emotional and pointing to her bag on the carpet.

I rummage in the bag and find the white stick, angling it in a shaft of moonlight. There is nothing there, no blue line. I feel an overwhelming sense of relief.

She sits up. I sit down next to her. We hug. Lucy does not say anything. I cannot think of any words.

She pushes her face into my shoulder. I can feel her body shaking.

I pull back gently, but she holds on tight, and we sit like that for several minutes, in silence, other than the sound of Matt getting up, coming out of our room, blundering his way, half asleep, to the bathroom. He never moves about quietly.

"Will you tell Matt?" she asks, moving back and dipping her head down. She wipes her nose and eyes on the duvet. "Will he be upset? I know he was longing for ..."

I get up. "I'll talk to him ... explain ... He'll be alright ... Is there anything else you need?" I turn to leave.

She shakes her head. "We can try again ... I'm sure ... if you want to?" I can sense her looking at me with her plaintive little face. I nod briskly. I can't really say no at this moment, just in case. But I don't want it now.

"Love you," she says suddenly as I head for the door.

I hesitate. Thing is, I don't think I do.

"Love you too," I reply, trying to sound enthusiastic as I pull the door to behind me.

Matt is standing by the bathroom door, waiting for me. I imagine he woke and rolled over, saw I was not there, and then got up to find me. Went to the bathroom first. Checked the kitchen too. Listened and heard Lucy and me talking, so just stood there. "She okay?" he asks quietly.

"She's lost the baby," I say, my voice blunter than expected. "So she says." I can't quite manage to keep the sourness out of my voice. Matt doesn't seem to notice, standing there with his mouth half open.

Then he's moving by me, the word *No!* on my lips but not spoken out loud, as he's hurrying off to see her, to say kind words, to comfort her. I go to bed. When he comes down some ten minutes later, I am not asleep but simply lie there with my back to him.

I think he's going to say something stupid like, "Don't worry, we can try again," in his jolly voice. "No, we bloody won't," I'll snap. But he doesn't. Instead, he sighs and gulps, expecting me to comfort him. I don't. Eventually, he falls asleep.

I just lie there, next to him. I imagine my so-called best friend forever sleeping above us, curled up in my husband's tee-shirt.

CHAPTER NINE

MONDAY, 9 SEPTEMBER, BREAKFAST TIME

Breakfast, such as it is on a rushed Monday morning, is a tense affair. I'm dashing about, busy, busy, busy. Eventually, I sit down for a few minutes at the table opposite Lucy. I need to leave for work but want to know what Lucy's going to do today. If she's here alone, she'll snoop through every little thing.

Matt is over-the-top solicitous, fawning over her, making sure she has everything, a glass of water, more toast. She nibbles at a slice. I sense he wants to ask her if we can try again for a baby next month – no chance – and I keep pulling angry "go away" faces at him, but he doesn't seem to notice.

Lucy sits there all hunched in, the classic victim's pose. She doesn't fool me – and she knows it; she won't meet my eye. Matt falls for it, hook, line and sinker. He's hanging around, hoping I'll go to work first so he can give her some sort of sympathetic pep talk. I imagine he'll put his arm around her shoulders. She'd like that, leaning her head in towards him.

"If you're ready in the next ten minutes," I say through a mouthful of cereal, "I can drop you at work."

"I'm not going in today," she replies after pulling a pained face and pushing her plate of toast away. "I've got the day off."

"Oh yes?" I respond, wondering how she arranged that given that her mobile phone has supposedly been stolen. I don't respond. She'd just come back with a clever answer.

I look at her as I finish my cereal and pull across my plate of toast. She doesn't meet my eye. Instead, she watches Matt move to boil a kettle for a mug of tea.

He turns, and she smiles at him. Quite honestly, I could slap her face. She's so transparent. "Cuppa?" he asks her in his brightest voice. She nods demurely.

We sit there quietly until he comes over with two mugs of tea, one for her, the other for me, babbling about how it might be too strong for her. She looks at it, saying, "It's perfect," (obviously), and he puts his hand on her shoulder. For Christ's sake.

He stands there looking down at us, and I can see he's going to make some sort of clumsy speech. I shake my head, but he takes no notice. "Lucy," he exclaims, waiting for her to look up at him. She does, adoringly again. Seriously, this is too much.

"We just wanted to say you're welcome to stay here for as long as you want … until you're back on your feet. And while you sort out your clothes and cards and money and phone, we can help you with some cash … and Sophie's clothes … you're about the same size." He smiles. It's meant to be comforting, but it just annoys me even more.

That's bad enough if he stops there, but he goes on, and I am screaming inside for him to stop, to just shut up. He then says, this elephant in a china shop, "And, you know, at some point, when you're ready, we could maybe try again." He lunges forward, hugs her, then me, utterly oblivious of his insensitivity, and ends by saying he must be going. Yes, please do.

So Lucy and I are now left sitting here with our mugs of tea, half ignoring each other, waiting for the other to speak. I glance at her. She is looking away. She gazes at me. I'm looking down at my mug.

She puts out her hand, reaching for my soft grey cardigan, picking at a strand to see if she can unravel it. She used to do it when we were young whenever I was angry with her about something or other – so many things, actually, so many times – and I'd laugh and swear at her and slap her hand, and things would be okay.

Not this time. I pull my arm away and just say, "Don't." We look at each other, my angry face, her pulling an exaggerated "woebegone" face, as my mother used to call it. Still trying to make me laugh. "Just don't," I say again. "I'm so fed up of ... whatever." I stare at her.

"I'm so sorry, Sophie, honestly I am. About the baby. I was hardly ... he punched me." She goes on, her thoughts going here and there confusingly. "I don't mind ... sometime ... trying again." Like having a baby is no big deal either way. I don't say anything about that. My mind is in turmoil.

I look at her as so many questions race through my mind. Why did she come back to Felixstowe and hook up with me again? Why did she offer to have a baby for us just like that? Is it the most wonderful thing ever? Or, somehow, the most monstrous? I just don't know. And all this – being pregnant, not pregnant, being beaten up. Is it terrible misfortune or some appalling scam. If so, why?

Lucy must see the agonies of uncertainty on my face as she ups and rounds the table, hugging me. She smells nice, as always. I think, hand on heart, that I am being unreasonable in my suspicions. Maybe I am. Then I realise Lucy smells so nice because she's wearing my favourite perfume. And I slowly pull out of the embrace and start clearing away the breakfast things.

"I'll do that," Lucy says brightly. "You head off to work."

I feel suddenly emotional, close to tears, as I turn to leave the room. I'm not sure why. I've got myself into a mess with all of this.

"I'm going to go to the bank today, sort my cards and stuff out, get a phone," she calls after me. I suppose I should offer her some cash, but she adds, "I've got some cash in my back pocket."

"I'll have tea on the table for you at six o'clock," she shouts as I'm going down the stairs. "Your favourite!" Whatever that might be. It used to be fish fingers and Alphabetti spaghetti. I don't know whether to be happy or angry. I'm so confused.

THE DAY PASSES SLOWLY. It's pretty dull being a clerk at a shipping company at the docks in Felixstowe. Still, it's the biggest container port in the United Kingdom, which means there's always plenty of paperwork.

I sit at my computer, checking forms, sending them where they need to go. I'm completely fed up with it, but am not sure what else I can do. I've been doing this all my working life.

There are times when I am simply waiting for forms to

come in. I can't do any work without them. They are the work. I usually sit and listen to music on my phone while I am on standby. Late morning today, I am thinking about Lucy, working things through.

I understand Lucy coming back to Felixstowe; things had gone badly wrong for her in Milton Keynes. A nasty husband. Children taken away from her. Heartbreaking stuff.

Where else could she go to lie low and lick her wounds? Felixstowe is her childhood home. It's a place where she'd feel safe. Other than that beating at the caravan park, of course, which ... well, I'm not so sure about that. There's something not quite right about it.

Anyhow, she has a job and had a place to live in that caravan. It's a chance to draw breath and then rebuild her life, to save some money to try to get her children back. I get all that.

I text Lucy before I begin processing forms again. *How you doing?*

Sorted cards at bank. Got cash. Blocked phone. Bought old phone. Spag Bol tea?

Another from me. *OK. You getting car and clothes from caravan park?*

One more reply: *Not now. Bastard waiting. Day or two.*

I acknowledge that with a thumbs-up and go back to my computer screen.

Even when working, I cannot block out my thoughts about Lucy. Getting in touch with me was a natural thing to do; we'd been so, so close. I doubt she could imagine being back in town without me by her side. Like old times.

Truth is, we were more than sisters. Lucy was closer to me than she was to her own sister. We shared all our thoughts and feelings, our hopes and dreams. It was love and hate at times, though. Lucy could be cutting with her words. I lashed out in anger. But we always made it up.

Offering to have a baby was pure Lucy. Looking back, she was always instinctive in everything she did: act first, think later. I think that's what happened here.

At lunch, I sit in the car park over the road from the office, eating a banana and an apple and sipping from a bottle of water. It's good to sit quietly without noise. The office is full of young lads; they're all nice, but boisterous. One of them keeps bursting into song – some Ipswich Town football chant – for no apparent reason. He's loud and tuneless.

Matt texts, as he sometimes does at this time of day. He'll tell me something funny that's happened or relay a joke someone's told him. It's usually garbled nonsense. Today, he just puts, *You OK?* I send a heart emoji. I know what's coming.

Then he unleashes what's been on his mind. Hours of his thoughts in a few sentences. *Good that Lucy's here! She can help round the house. Cooking! Ha! After the baby's born, she could be our nanny?*

You. Have. To. Be. Kidding. Me. That's what I think. I want to put that. But much stronger. F. Off. I place my bottle and banana skin and apple core by the passenger seat, then think how I will respond as I walk back into work. *Talk later*, I reply. I should have added, *Dumbo*.

Lucy is still on my mind as I work into the afternoon. It all started off well enough. But then it came to having the baby. All that early nonsense about using a syringe. It could only happen one way, and it had to be done naturally. I had to be grown-up about it. But I struggled with it. Who wouldn't?

Sitting here now, staring into space, I can see how I was consumed with jealousy. Was I drugged that night, or was I woozy because I hadn't drunk much for years? More likely that.

Have I been eaten up with jealousy ever since? In the cold light of day, I suspect so. Matt has always been polite and friendly. My big bear. Lucy has always been Lucy. Am I seeing more into it than there is? Is all of this angst purely down to me?

What are you doing? I text Lucy late into the afternoon. Just trying to be polite. I add, *Anything from supermarket?*

Going through your things, she replies. *Your knickers are so old.* Then adds, *And so BIG!!!* I chuckle, getting the joke. Same old Lucy. Then she adds, *Where's that top you wore first time we met again?*

I laugh out loud, ignoring the young lad opposite me giving me a strange look. Like I'm a mad old woman, at thirty-five. Old to him maybe, at twenty. I reply to Lucy, *LOL!* She's joking. I think.

I eventually turn off my computer, at the end of another dreary day, say goodbye to those around me and head to the car. I text Matt one last time, *Be home for 6. Spag Bol special from L.* I wait for a reply, but nothing comes. He must be on his way home.

As I drive towards town, my thoughts are stuck with Lucy – and myself. I know I was so envious that Lucy got pregnant straight away. But was she? First time out, it seems so unlikely. I guess it happens. I've known a couple of women at work who always seemed to be bragging about it. They seem to be Most Fertile Egg of the Year winners. Why would Lucy lie about such a thing, though? What could her plan possibly be?

Matt fell in love with her – that's the first time it's struck me hard – when she announced her pregnancy, and he has been all over her, so attentive, so caring, ever since. Or is that just me and my almost overwhelming jealousy? I know they had sex, and I will never forget that, but is there really anything there beyond smiles and looks of happiness and contentment?

And now, supposedly beaten-up and the baby gone, Lucy is in our home, living with us. Is this a master plan to snare Matt for herself? If so, what happens to me? Or am I just being an idiot who's going stark, staring mad?

You know what? I'm going to act nice and friendly, all sweetness and light, for the next week or so. I will curb my emotions and my temper and try hard to not be so jealous of Lucy.

But I will keep a close watch. I will monitor Lucy and Matt and how they look at each other. I will listen to what they say. I will stand at doorways when they think I am in another room, and I will take it all in.

If it is me – and I have been consumed by my own foolish, negative feelings – then I will try to change and be a better person. Even so, I do not want Lucy in my home, and I certainly don't want her to have a baby for us. I'll come to that in due course. And if all of this isn't me? If it is Lucy? At that idea, thoughts of revenge fill my mind.

WE SIT around the kitchen table just before half past six, Lucy, Matt and I, ready to eat. I am determined to be cheerful no matter what. I will lull Lucy into thinking I am happy with everything. I will set a trap, and she will fall into it if – *if* – she is up to no good.

We – Matt and I – had our showers. Lucy fussed around the kitchen like Queen Bee, even though spaghetti Bolognese is little more than basic student fare.

And now we sit here, with Lucy gesturing towards our piled-up plates, a jug of water, and our tumblers. I didn't go to university, but I imagine this would how it would be most nights. Slop on a plate. I bite my tongue. It's a mean thought.

I start eating, cutting my spaghetti into pieces with my knife and fork, and then mixing it with the Bolognese before putting it into my mouth.

Lucy, who is normally a shoveller when it comes to eating anything, is twiddling spaghetti round a fork, using a spoon, and then trying to eat it. For Matt's attention, I believe. I notice she is made up perfectly; I imagine she has raided my side of the bedroom again. She has a pair of my pyjamas on. And no bra.

Matt eats normally, but makes various appreciative, over-the-top grunts and groans as though he has never had spaghetti Bolognese before and it is the best thing he has eaten in his life. It's not; the meat doesn't taste great to me. I try to catch his eye – *shut up* – but he does not notice me.

Once we've got the "how are you?" and "nice weather" and the "how was work?" comments out of the way, the conversation moves on to more important topics.

"You got everything sorted, Luce?" Matt asks. So I'm "Soph" not "Sophie", and she's now "Luce" not "Lucy".

She smiles and goes through her cards-cash-phones story, and before he can respond, she says, "I'll go back to the caravan park at the weekend for my clothes and the car. Let the dust settle."

He nods and replies that he'll go with her ... make sure she's safe.

I stay quiet, already edgy. I can't think of any reason why she'd not want to go back tonight, with Matt, to get her things now instead of borrowing mine. And she needs a car for work! Now she's here, her job is further away. It's not around the corner anymore. I'm not driving her in and picking her up every day.

Matt repeats, like an old, cracked vinyl, the same tedious comments about she's very welcome for as long as she wants, we'll do whatever to help, blah, blah, blah, blah, blah, all of that. She beams at him. He's virtually purring. He turns to me to back him up.

Before I can speak, she reaches out and touches him lightly on the arm, looks at me and says, "I'll be no trouble, Sophie, I promise. I got enough cash out to buy some clothes so I won't need to keep borrowing stuff." (Even though she sits there in my pyjamas with an extra front button undone.)

She goes on, between mouthfuls of spaghetti, seeming to read my thoughts. "And I've a friend at work, we're pretty much doing the same shifts most days, so she'll pick me up and drop me home." It's not your home, I think, but I don't say it. I just smile at her.

She stands up suddenly, reaching for the almost empty jug of water. Then she turns to go to the kitchen, to fill it up.

It's so obvious, from the silky fabric of the pyjamas, that she's not wearing a bra. I glance at Matt, and he flushes slightly. He's noticed too. I stare at him; he looks down, continuing to eat.

She's back, putting the jug on the table and almost bouncing onto her seat. Matt looks up. He's so obvious.

As we continue eating and drinking, I want to ask what plans Lucy has to get her own place. I know, though, that if I do, Matt will jump in and say there's no hurry, that she can stay as long as she wants – forever, basically. The idea that she can be our nanny, of all things, in the back of his mind.

I keep my thought to myself while Matt and Lucy chat away; she asks him where he's working at the moment, what he's doing, and, after that, he asks if she enjoys working in a care home. She nods. "They're so sweet, the old men especially. They're like children again, really. There's one old fellow called Ronnie. I'm his favourite." And she proceeds to chat about him for a while.

I could lean across now and slap Matt, half jokingly, under his chin. He sits there, mouth open, taking in everything, her words, her little looks, the way she shifts in her seat towards him. She has him eating out of the palm of her hand.

As we finish the meal, Lucy makes a statement, out of the blue, that takes me by surprise. "Jo and me ... that's my friend at work ... we're going to try to get a place together ... we're about to start searching." She looks at me. "I'll be out of your hair soon." Trying to make me feel guilty.

"No," he says. It comes out as "No-oo-oo", all shocked and desperate. It's so OTT that I wonder if he's joking. But Matt doesn't really do humour, not like this anyway. Not ad libs. He goes on, "Stay with us, Luce, have, you know, when you're feeling better ... sometime." He means have a baby, and frankly, she's better already – it's all a big con.

She smirks and nods in agreement. Then she stands up, leans forward – Matt instinctively eying her cleavage – and reaches for our plates to take them to the kitchen. "I've got a cheesecake for afters," she states. Matt makes a childish "yum-yum" comment as I follow Lucy along the landing.

"You're welcome to stay a while," I tell her, biting my tongue and controlling my feelings. "For a while, but not forever."

She glances at me – a neutral expression – as she puts the supermarket cheesecake onto a plate and gathers up smaller plates and forks from cupboards and drawers.

She nods as she passes the cheesecake on its plate to me, then leans forward, sticking out her tongue, urging me to push it into her face like a custard pie.

"Honestly," I reply, anger in my voice, "you're too much." She laughs, and she thinks she's got me on her side again. But she's misread me this time.

"Honestly," she replies, mocking my words and tone, "if you don't want a baby, don't have one. It's your choice, Sophie. I know what I'd do if I were you. I know what Matt wants." With that, she twirls round and waltzes off with plates and forks.

I stand in the kitchen, alone, counting to ten – many more than ten – as I hear Matt and Lucy saying something to each other in the living room and then laughing together. A hot stream of anger comes up inside me. I go through, holding the cheesecake on its plate in the flat of my left hand. Matt's head is thrown back as he laughs uproariously at something Lucy's said.

How I resist the urge to push it in his face, I do not know. But I place it on the table and smile at them both.

"I'll be mother." Lucy giggles as she cuts it into four pieces with, of all things, the fancy paper knife from our honeymoon that we keep on the sideboard for opening letters and parcels. I suppose it saves her going back to the kitchen for a proper knife. We eat. They chatter away. I smile. Matt takes the last piece.

The rest of the evening, as we all sit around watching some Disney+ film about The Beatles, passes in a daze. I nod off in my armchair, waking up as the film ends to see Matt and Lucy – a bit too close on the sofa – watching me. They laugh, but I don't. We go to bed. Matt wants to make love again. I don't. I'm sure he has Lucy in his head. The thought sickens me.

CHAPTER TEN

MONDAY, 16 SEPTEMBER, EARLY MORNING

Lucy's been here for more than a week now. She hasn't been to collect her stuff. Nor has she mentioned moving out.

But she is bright and cheerful and bubbly at all times. As though this is now her forever home.

Matt, of course, loves it. The attention from two women. I wouldn't mind, but he treats us both the same when we're all together. Like Lucy and I are twin sisters.

Actually, she is driving me mad. And I really, really want her to go.

At breakfast, she sits there to the side of us, eating and drinking daintily (for Matt's benefit), and she's always starting inane conversations even though we usually prefer to sit quietly with our own thoughts.

Matt stays later than he used to, but still gets up to go to work first, chastely kissing me goodbye. By the end of the week, he has advanced to patting her on the shoulder. He'll be kissing her goodbye soon.

I'm not running while she's here. I don't like leaving the two of them alone together. I just don't. I want to trust Matt, of course I do. I don't trust her, though. If she plans to get her claws into him, she will do. He is so trusting; he won't see through her.

I wait here, fiddling about, until her friend picks her up in her funny little car, parking in the street, toot-toot-tooting. Then I go. She texts me on and off through the day, five, six, seven times. Someone at work said this. *Lol!* Someone at work did that. *HaHa! ... Shall we go shopping at the supermarket after work? ... There's a new series on Netflix. We could watch that tonight?*

I did, early on, go to McDonald's with her for lunch. That was fine, as a one-off, but I didn't want to get into a daily habit, so on the following days, I said my lunch break was at a different time, or that I had to work through.

In the evenings, she's always there, next to me, wherever I turn. She's polite, offering to help me prepare dinner and, later, to wash up – she assumes I'm the chief cook and bottle washer. I do it because I don't want Matt and her spending time together in the kitchen. She does everything a different way to me, which is just so annoying.

She spends ages in the bathroom, making Matt wait when he comes in hot and sweaty from work. He doesn't seem to mind. I do. Then we eat, and Matt and Lucy chatter away like they've both been holding their breath all day. I find myself getting ever more irritated.

She doesn't then excuse herself after we've rinsed crockery and loaded the dishwasher. She doesn't go to her room. Or go out. She sits with us the whole evening, going to bed when we do. Matt and I cannot even make love, even if I wanted to. I really don't like the thought of her hearing us.

I've had enough, and I want her to go but feel so horrid

about it. "Why?" I imagine her wailing if – when – I ask her to go. "Because ... because you're just always bloody here."

It's so rotten of me – the thing is, she hasn't done anything wrong, and I can't just ask her to leave because I'm irritated by her. Everything she says! Everything she does!

I have to have a good reason to ask her to go. And when I do, I will. It will be soon, I'm sure of it.

MY CHANCE COMES the next evening. During the day, I'm asked by Rachel, someone who's just started in my section in the office, to have a drink with them at a local pub that night. Matt's out for a few pints with Baz and his other football mates, and Lucy will be home alone. So I agree to meet Rachel at a café-bar on the seafront at eight o'clock.

She's a young woman who is really friendly but struggling a little with processing the forms. For some reason, probably because I say "hello" and "goodbye" and always smile whenever I see her, she turned to me for help. To my surprise, I am pleased.

The evening goes well, we share some chilli wraps and have a couple of halves of cider, and by the time we leave, she seems much more cheerful. I am too. I wonder, maybe, if we might become friends. I like her openness and jolly comments. She kisses me on the cheek as we go our separate ways. I hesitate; then I kiss her back

I am still happy and thinking about our conversation as I drive home and pull up a way along from our house. I notice immediately that Matt's small white van is parked outside. He is earlier than expected, as he normally stays at the pub with his mates until closing time.

I feel a sudden sense of dread of what might be happening indoors. Over the past week or so, I've been careful to be bright and cheerful. But I've kept a close watch. And I have never ever given Lucy much of a chance to be alone with Matt. I thought that tonight it would be safe to go out.

That's all now changed. They are both in there together, not expecting me back until later. The lights in the living room are on, I can see through the half-open curtains. The lights above, in her room, are off. I don't know what to think.

I switch off the engine, get out of the car, shut the door carefully and then lock the car behind me.

I walk across the street, it's all quiet and empty, open the gate slowly so it does not creak, and make my way up the path to the main door.

I slip the key into the lock, open it and step inside, breathing steadily. I wait, full of apprehension, for a minute or more. I can barely breathe.

Then I open the inner door to our home, oh so carefully and silently, and stand on the carpet at the bottom of our staircase. It's dark, but I dare not turn on the light in case it alerts them.

I listen but hear nothing. No noise from the living room. Our bedroom. Nor Lucy's upstairs. There is a light on, shining from under the living-room door. It's shut. I think they're in there.

There are several stairs that creak and groan when my weight is upon them. I'm not sure which they are, two or three, I think, somewhere in the middle. I must avoid these so I don't forewarn Matt and Lucy.

I lean forward, pressing the third stair up with the palm of my hand, ready to stop when I can feel a creak coming.

That one's fine, so I step onto it with first one and then both feet.

I do the same again, three stairs up. Again, no creak, so I move onto it. Three more up, and the stair is about to creak. I stop, try the one above; that's about to creak as well.

I test and move up two stairs to avoid them, then one more check and another, and I am up and onto the landing. I stop by the fire extinguisher, pause, still listening. There is the faintest burbling of the television on low. Background noise. To what? I am about to find out.

I stride quickly along the landing, turn the handle on the living-room door and am inside in seconds. They are sitting on the sofa next to each other. He is sitting upright, half asleep, and is coming to after my noisy entrance. She is fast asleep, slumped against him, her head on his shoulder.

"What's going on?" I snap at Matt as he blinks several times and looks towards me. "What the hell are you doing?" I gesture towards Lucy, who is coming out of sleep as he moves his body, gently pushing hers away from him. The casual way he touches her makes me rage.

"We ..." he says, gesturing towards the television. "We were just watching something or other ... can't remember what ... and I fell asleep ... it's been a long day." Then he looks at Lucy, sitting up bleary-eyed, and laughs. "Lucy did too." Like it's no big deal.

She is quicker to wake up and regain her senses and is now on her feet. She stretches and yawns, shakes her head and says, "Sorry, Soph," as she moves to go by me. For a moment, I am about to strike her, I am that furious, but she says, "Sorry," again, and I hesitate. Then she is gone, heading upstairs to her bedroom.

"Why are you even here?" I demand. "I thought you were going for a pint?"

He mumbles something about someone having to go home early because their wife has just had a baby – like I want to know that. Then he goes on about coming back and Lucy was watching something and offered him a glass of wine – from one of our bottles – and how "it would have been rude not to". Yes, sure it would.

"So you cosied up all nice and snug?" I say, not letting this go. I hear Lucy coming down the stairs, going to the bathroom. He shakes his head and mumbles something about it not being "like that at all". And I ask, "Would it not be more normal for one of you to sit on the sofa and the other on a chair?" He comes back with a comment about having spilled a drink on one, and the other not having a clear view of the television. I give up.

"Whatever," I shout at him. He gives me a bemused look as I turn to go, indicating I am being completely and utterly unreasonable. I don't know if I am or not.

As I go on to the landing, I see the bathroom door is open, and Lucy is standing there, clearly having heard what was being said, and waiting to speak to me. "Sorry, Soph," she says again, like a bloody parrot. "It wasn't anything."

"Sure," I respond, my voice full of sarcasm. Before she can say more, I am into our bedroom, slamming the door behind me.

I lie here, ignoring their whispered voices on the landing at the bottom of the stairs leading up to her room. I resist the urge to shout, "I can hear you!" even though I can't quite.

When he comes to bed five or ten minutes later, I roll on my side away from him. He knows better than to put his hand on my shoulder or hip. Instead, he whispers, "I'm sorry,

Sophie. I didn't think. I'll be more thoughtful in future. It wasn't, you know. She's going soon anyway, once she's found a place."

I suspect he expects me to say "that's okay", and then I'll then roll over and face him, ready to make love. He'd be lucky. I just make a slight grunting noise – I don't want to discuss it.

So we lie here a while, and I think perhaps, maybe, he is going to open up and talk, reassuring me about Lucy, that nothing's going on, he loves me more than anything in the whole, wide world, and that, if I am really unhappy, we'll tell Lucy to find somewhere else to live. Instead, his breathing slows, and he is soon asleep, snoring. Not a care in the world. Un-bloody-believable.

Upstairs, Lucy has music playing on her phone. I can't make it out, but it's boom-boom-boom annoying. I want to shout upstairs for her to "turn it down!" but I'm so torn now.

I'm not sure if I've uncovered something between Matt and Lucy or whether I am becoming increasing irrational.

CHAPTER ELEVEN

TUESDAY, 24 SEPTEMBER, ANOTHER MORNING

Over the next week, I start to believe I am truly going insane. Lucy is still here: at breakfast, then she texts me during the day, and sits with us every evening. She is endlessly cheerful. It drives me mad. There's still no mention of getting her stuff and moving out.

Matt, of course, is oblivious to her fake jollity. Sometimes he is so nice that I could just scream at him. "Don't you see? She's playing a game!" He smiles at her and laughs at the (feeble) scatological jokes she's picked up at work.

I keep calm, knowing that she's going soon. Once she's found somewhere else to live. At that point, I'll start easing off, taking longer to reply to her texts, saying we're busy that evening when she wants to come round, and so on.

Everything she says and does gets on my nerves more and more. I notice she has various things she repeats over and again. "Righty-ho" is one. "Bless" is another. The worst is "yes, no", which she uses all the time whenever she is asked a question.

She's helpful, or tries to be. Carrying crockery and

cutlery to and from the kitchen, putting them in the wrong place. She eats desserts with a teaspoon. She places cutlery upside down in the dishwasher. She rolls towels rather than folds them. It's all silly stuff. But it drives me nuts.

And she touches Matt over and over. When he talks about what he's done at work, she sits staring at him. Then pats his arm and laughs at the end of his (not especially funny) anecdote. Matt cannot do gags, and there is never a punchline, not that I can make out anyway. The story just tails off. Lucy also brushes by him and bumps into him with a breathless, girlish "ooh!" Really, it's too much.

It's more than all of that though. The jollity. The helpfulness. The fawning over Matt. There's something much worse, more devious.

I can't quite put my finger on what it is. There are inconsistencies. And lies. There are contradictions.

It's part of a plan, for sure. To make a home for herself here. She's perfectly friendly with me. Makes a point of it. But it's Matt whom she's after, I'm certain of it.

I've been keeping a notebook, which I keep hidden on top of a kitchen cupboard. I write down what she's said to me and to Matt, sometimes together, sometimes apart. When she's been speaking to Matt in the living room and I've been in the kitchen, for example, I ask him later what she said. He gives me an odd look but always tells me.

She'd told me her husband and children lived in Milton Keynes. "Bletchley," she said to Matt. I looked it up. They're close, but still, they're not the same place. When Matt asked about her family, she said her father was somewhere in Scotland. She's told me she didn't know where he was.

The thing that troubled me most was when she talked to Matt about her children; she gave their names and ages, and assuming Matt remembered correctly, she got the age of the boy wrong. A year out. Neither here nor there, maybe. But what sort of mother forgets the ages of their children, especially when they're young? It's not like they're thirty-six or thirty-seven. That inconsistency really bothers me.

She lies, you see. Lucy. Has done from our schooldays. I used to think it was funny. A man – with a huge beard, she claimed – snatched her rucksack and ran off with it. Her homework was inside. Two men followed her home down a country lane. She had to run and run and run, she shouted, to hide behind a tree. That's why she was so late home.

Everything she said was exaggerated, a huge drama. It was a laugh at first. Tall tales to get her out of trouble. She was always adamant everything was true. Later, she accused a boy at school – the first she had sex with – of assaulting her. That was more serious, with parents, the school and the police involved. She backed down eventually.

Now I realise that Lucy's claim was awful. But as a teenager at the time, it never bothered me. Lucy was the joker. I was her heavy, I suppose. Backed her up, bashed our way out of trouble with classmates like Emily and the boneheaded boys down by the pier. Now, though, I have the growing sense that Lucy is spinning an elaborate web of lies, and she is the spider, and I am the fly. I have to do something soon to set myself, and Matt, free.

TONIGHT, Matt and I lie in bed, and before we go to sleep, I think I have to say something about how I feel and what I want. At last. I should have done it by now. I know that. I'm not a little worm.

But I have been so torn; I've not been sure if my suspicions about Lucy are well-founded or whether I am simply overcome with so many negative emotions. Truth is, I feel inferior to Lucy in many ways, and I am jealous of her. And I could not bear for Matt to turn to me and say, "But, Soph, that's just mad!"

I think now though, with her getting on my nerves so constantly and her comments being so contradictory, I have to speak out and get this sorted once and for all. I don't want a baby with her. I want her out of our home. In fact, I don't want her in our lives. I'm not certain how to say that to Matt.

"Matt," I venture, switching on my bedside lamp and turning on my side towards him. He rolls towards me, all hopeful. He puts his hand on my shoulder, and I move it gently away. "We need to talk about Lucy. I think it's time we asked her to leave."

"Why?" he says, rolling back and then sitting up. He sounds more anguished than I'd have expected. I think he means, "Why does she have to go?" I hate him for that. But then he clarifies it. "I thought we were going to try for a baby again?"

I sit up too, and I reach out so that we are holding hands. I'm not sure what to say next, that she gets on my nerves and I don't trust her – especially not with you? I don't think so. He's such a soft lump, and she'll manipulate him and turn him against me if she hasn't already. I can't tell him that.

"I ... just can't ... not now. It doesn't feel right. I want to leave it a while and see how we feel ... maybe after Christmas." Garbled words and meaningless sentences. I should have phrased it better. But I can't create a situation where it's her or me. I just daren't.

He looks tearful – he wants to be a daddy very much. I

know that. I can see it even more in his face right now. He babbles, "I think ... I thought ... we were going to ... when Lucy was next ... you know, the right time? ... not long now?" A pause, then, "Have you told her?"

I'm pleased he's asked that last question; the decision has already been made. "Not yet," I answer. Then, as he wipes his eyes, I add, simply, "I love you, Matt."

"You'd feel differently if she were pregnant, I'm sure." He doesn't seem to have heard, to have taken in, what I just said to him. I repeat it, and he then answers automatically without thinking, "I love you too, Soph."

He rolls onto his back, making an odd glugging noise. I roll on my back as well. I need to press on. While he is accepting what I say. But I need to express myself better.

"I also think it's time that Lucy hurried up and actually found herself a place to live. I know she's not gone back to the caravan park to get her car and stuff ... I understand why, what with that man there, but there are other sites ... there are rooms in town ... she could sort a house share, maybe with that woman she works with? She talked about that."

He doesn't just answer "yes." Instead, there is another long silence. I can almost hear his brain ticking and whirring, clicking through his thoughts and what he will say. The caravan site story is so odd, she must have paid up front for a certain number of weeks, with plenty still to go, and her clothes remain there. And her car. Who leaves a car behind? I don't imagine it's a Rolls-Royce, but even so. It makes no sense.

"I don't think she's got any money?" he responds, half telling, half asking. His voice then picks up speed. "She ran out of her savings at the caravan park. They've let her keep her car in a space there, as it needs loads doing to pass the MOT. She hasn't got any cash for it."

That's a no then.

They've obviously been talking behind my back about this – that she has no money until she gets paid by the care home at the end of each month. A hand-to-mouth existence. It annoys me that they've had these conversations and he hasn't shared any of them with me. And I am angry that he has obviously said she can stay here forever. Make yourself at home; don't worry about Sophie. She doesn't matter!

"Okay," I respond, pretending to yawn, suggesting I've agreed and am tired now and need to go to sleep. He yawns too. There's so much more I want to say about Lucy going, let alone her contradictory statements and lies. But I am not going to have a shouting match now, not with her listening upstairs, taking it all in, revelling in it.

"She's no trouble," he mumbles in a tired voice.

I want to shout out, "Who's this, then? Saint Lucy. The patron saint of loveliness?" If only he knew. I am going to have to show him what's what about her. I lie here, steaming with fury, waiting for him to fall asleep. And he does within a few minutes, and I look at his sweet face – despite all of this, I love him so much. She's not having him. She's not.

When he is fast asleep, breathing long and deeply, I reach for my mobile phone on my bedside cabinet. I google Lucy's mother, adding in "Milton Keynes" to narrow the search. It's not hard to find someone in the UK these days, especially if they have an uncommon surname and you know roughly where they live. Within minutes, I have found her – and in the morning, I will take a day off work and go and see her and discover all the evidence I'll need to present to Matt.

Then Lucy will have no choice but to go and be out of our life – our marriage – for good.

CHAPTER TWELVE

WEDNESDAY, 25 SEPTEMBER, CLOSE TO LUNCHTIME

I'm parked by a long brick wall at the entrance to a close on a housing estate, just outside Milton Keynes. It's a chaotic-looking place, full of semi-detached and terraced houses squeezed in like jigsaw pieces, with bins lined up at the end of driveways and cars parked half on, half off the pavements.

I see Suzanne – Lucy's mother – straight away. She is out the front, on her driveway, on her knees, digging weeds from between paving slabs. I watch for a few minutes. She looks much the same as I remember: chocolate-brown hair in a bob, a bright yellow blouse, light blue jeans and brown sandals. She must be in her early sixties now.

Part of me wants to reverse the car, out and away back to Felixstowe as fast as I can. I was always wary of Lucy's mother – she had a sharp tongue on her at times. I was hoping I'd see Freya, the sister, who was always amiable. But I am an adult and can take care of myself. And if I leave now, I will never know the truth about Lucy. Taking a deep breath, I get out of the car.

"I thought it was you," Suzanne says, getting to her feet.

"I won't shake hands." She is wearing yellow rubber gloves with a screwdriver in one hand and a dustpan brush in the other. She was never a hugger anyway. Much like my own mother. Two peas in a pod, both frozen and not so fresh.

"She's with you, then. Lucy." She speaks in a weary voice.

I pull a yes face.

"I'm surprised," Suzanne says bluntly. "She hates you because of her dad ... you're still in Felixstowe?" Half question, half statement.

I nod, stunned.

"You'd better come in." She turns, leading the way back into the end-of terrace house, pulling off her gloves and shoes and putting them with the screwdriver and brush by the front door.

I take off my shoes too – she was always a stickler – and follow her into the kitchen, where I watch her putting on the kettle and reaching for mugs and teabags and sweeteners. I feel wrong-footed, all my prepared questions gone from my head as Lucy's mother takes charge. She gestures me towards a bar stool.

"I've not got long," she says, brisk but not especially unfriendly. "Pilates session. I need to shower and change. Traffic's always busy getting into the centre." She pauses while the noise of the kettle fills the silence. "She living with you?" she asks, going on as she sees me nodding yes. "Is she taking her medication?" I must look bewildered, as she continues, "Serotonin, her antidepressants?" She pours boiling water into the mugs and then adds, almost to herself, "She really ought to be in counselling still."

I don't know what to say, it's all taken my breath away. I look around and comment, "It's nice ... here ... your place ...

is it ... is Freya still living with you? Is she well?" I'm gabbling.

She looks at me as if to say "shut up", but replies instead as she fiddles with tea bags and a carton of milk, "It's the best I can afford. I manage. It's just me these days. Freya lives on the other side of MK with her wife." She doesn't expand on that, and I'm not sure what to say. I didn't know. It doesn't matter anyway. "You?" she adds before I can frame a polite comment.

She comes across and hands me a mug of tea and then sits on the stool on the other side of the bar, her mug between us. "There are biscuits in that tin there, if you want some." A little dig. I look but don't open it. When I was younger, I would often eat two or three at a time, and she would sometimes make a teasing remark about getting fat, which was quite cutting to a teenage girl.

Instead, I just say I'm married to Matt and work in shipping, and my family's all fine. I don't mention that my father has died or that I don't see my mother or brother. I don't think she's that interested, really. It's been such a long time. We both know why I'm here – Lucy. That's all.

"So what's Lucy done now? Why are you here? Has she stolen from you and disappeared? Is that it?" The questions are asked in quick-fire, rapid succession and almost take my breath away.

I take a mouthful of tea, swallowing it slowly, thinking how to reply. I'm not going to mention the whole surrogacy thing. I imagine her sardonic laughter if I did. I keep my response as bland as I can.

"Lucy's come back to Felixstowe. She works at a care home. She was living in a caravan ... a nice caravan ... she had a bit of trouble with a man there ... so she's staying with us, Matt and me, while she sorts herself out. It's all good."

She laughs, a nasty sound. "Why are you here, then? What is it, a three-hour drive? If it's all good?" The killer question. I don't know what to say. But I want to say, "I'm suspicious of her." Eventually, I do manage to speak. But I lie.

"I ... she ... she's, um ... missing her children." I sound so feeble and go to add their names, but, in my nervousness, they slip my mind. "They're in Istanbul," I add, the only place in Turkey that comes to mind.

Suzanne bursts out laughing, something close to wild and uncontrollable laughter. She spills her tea, getting up and going over to the sink to get some kitchen roll. As she mops up the spillage, she splutters out an answer. "Istanbul? Her ex is up the road in Newport Pagnell, if that's what you mean ... and she doesn't have any children of her own."

I must look confused. She talks more.

"Look, I'm pleased she's with you and you're looking after her ... and I don't know what she's told you ... but I doubt it's the truth. Lucy was ... wild when she moved here ... what with her father and all. She had so many ... affairs ... older men, mostly ... and ... terminations ... well, eventually, I threw her out." She takes a swig of what's left of her tea, finishing it. "Later, she hooked up with this Turkish guy, Ahmed, and we assumed ... we were prejudiced, really, back then ... anyway, it turned out he was a nice man. A widower. He had two children. Lucy looked after them for a while."

She sighs and goes on. "We reconciled. Freya made up with her too. She seemed to ... I mean, she always had mental health issues ... since before she came here ... and she was ... anyway, Ahmed got a job up the road ... near his sisters so they could help with the children ... and Lucy just walked out. That's not what she told you?"

I shake my head: "No." Then I say, "She told me ... I don't suppose it matters ... she implied he was a brute ... a monster."

"She always played the victim well." She gathers up our two mugs, taking them over to the sink, where she rinses them out under the tap and puts them on the draining board.

I think that's it, that it's time for me to go, but she turns towards me as I get to my feet, and she asks another question, "Has she borrowed or asked you for money ... actually, can she get at your money?"

I shake my head. An almost incredulous, "No."

"Is she friendly with your husband, what was it, Matt?"

I nod my head. A worried, "Yes."

"If I were you, I'd move her on as soon as you can. Do you know what I mean?"

I pull a face. "Yes. I do."

I stand there a moment or two, not sure whether to say something else or just turn and go. I'm so used to being polite. Not that it really matters. Lucy's mother never liked me. I didn't like her. We won't see each other again.

"What do you want, waiting here? Ahmed's address? You can have it. But she won't be there, and he won't welcome you with open arms."

I shake my head, then nod. "Yes, okay, I'll have it, please."

She opens a drawer, takes out an address book, and flicks through it, holding a page open to me. "Photograph it," she says. I do so, with my phone. Then she is putting the address book back in the drawer and turning away from me, conversation over. I leave, neither of us saying goodbye.

GOOGLE MAPS BRINGS me to where Ahmed and his children live; a long, straight street with Victorian terraced houses to either side. The road is packed with cars. It's much like where I live, just more cramped.

I find a space in a street around the corner, and walk back. Seventy-six is easy to find, with the number on a black and white sign on the wall by the front door. I walk up a path that is neat and free of weeds. The black and white tiles of the doorstep look like they've just been washed. It's a well-looked-after home. I ring the doorbell and step back, hearing an explosion of noise inside.

The man who answers the door – Ahmed, I assume – is a tall, handsome man in his early forties, I'd guess. Black tee-shirt. Blue jeans. "Fit AF," as Lucy would put it. A handful of children – four – aged between about three and eight, jump up and down excitedly around him. Beyond them, I can see down the hallway to the kitchen, where two women, washing up and drying, look back at me. I assume they're his sisters.

He smiles, laughing as he swats the children away cheerfully. "You're new!" he says. "I'll come and help you with it."

"New?" I must look puzzled. I add, "Help me with what?"

He replies, ever so slightly flirty, telling me I'm an Amazon driver with a paddling pool arriving today for the children.

I respond by telling him I'm not. "I'm Sophie Curtis from Felixstowe." I watch his face change, hardening, as he hears the word "Felixstowe" and realises this is about Lucy. He shoos the children away. Then turns to me.

"Whatever it is, whatever she's done now, I'm not interested." He pauses as he goes to shut the door, and adds, "Unless you're here to give me my money back?"

"Money?" I respond. "What money?" I'm not sure what else to say.

"I thought not. Another scam. What, she's dying of cancer this time? Shame on you." Before I can snap back, "Just wait a minute," he slams the door in my face. I hear him stomping back towards the children.

I stand there, dumbfounded, not sure what to do. I wait, half expecting him to return, to open the door and say, "Sorry, sorry, my mistake. Let's start again."

But, of course, he doesn't. I am at a loss how to respond. There's no point in knocking again to ask him to explain himself. It would just enrage him more.

I turn and leave, angry with myself for not being better prepared with my first response. I could have replied, "I might be able to help get your money back." Even though it would have been a little white lie, it would have been a way to begin the conversation.

I'm so twitchy as I turn right out of the street, now hurrying towards my car. I could scream out loud at the top of my voice. I'm so, so stupid at times. If I'd handled it well, if I'd been more prepared, I might have learned something else about Lucy.

I'm not sure, even now, exactly what to think. Lucy's mother's comments about Lucy and her affairs and the terminations are hard to take in. And the stuff about debts and, well, there was just so much negativity. And Lucy hates me? Because of her father? I wonder if that's the case. Maybe Lucy's mother is trying to wound me. Behind the smiles, is there a nasty and bitter woman? She always seemed scary when I was a child.

I click the car open with my key fob, get in and just sit there, for a moment or two, settling myself. I open my bag and check my phone for messages. The usual one or two from Matt. I text a chirpy reply, adding another little white lie – I'll be late, as I'm doing overtime and then going for a bite to eat with work colleagues. Nothing from Lucy.

I jump, startled, by a knock on the passenger-side window. A dark-haired woman, maybe forty, stands there, gesturing at me to open the door. She is tall and thin with a pink top and white skirt, hair piled high in a sort of beehive. I recognise her from inside the kitchen a few minutes ago. One of Ahmed's sisters, I assume. I lean across and open the door.

She sits down and begins chatting in slightly accented English. "I know Felixstowe. Where you live there?" She smiles at me, and I smile back, relieved she's talking to me and I can find out what I need to know.

"Ranelagh Road," I respond. "It's like where you live, really."

She pulls a face, indicating she doesn't know where it is, and then asks if it is "near the shops".

I respond, "Yes, next road back – it's just along from the Salvation Army building. Do you know it?"

She nods, then shakes her head, and I am confused.

"Are you Ahmed's ... sister?" I say, trying to take the conversation forward. She nods more certainly, but does not give her name nor ask for mine.

"Lucy is my ... lodger ... tenant ... she has a room in my house. I went to see her mother ..." (I'm not sure why I'd do that if she were a lodger, but still.) "... and she sent me on to see Ahmed here." She looks slightly baffled, so I go on, more assertively now. "You don't like Lucy, then?" I try to make it sound jolly.

The story comes out of her in fits and starts. She struggles with some words, and I make encouraging noises for her to keep talking. "Lucy is bad person ... She lie ... she steal ... she cheat on Ahmed ... She bad ..." (She waves her hands for the word.) "Stepmother."

I'm not sure how to respond.

After a few more similar comments, what she says next takes my breath away.

"She is bad. She told Ahmed she was ... with child ... she show him ..." The woman makes a gesture, clear and unmistakable, down by her legs and then waves a hand in my face. Lucy showed Ahmed what she presented to me – a white stick with a blue line on it. Maybe she'd kept it from her first pregnancy, inking in the fading blue in melancholy moments.

"Now ..." She goes on, anger in her voice, before I can speak. "Ahmed said he wanted divorce so she stole his money ... all money ... and gone. Ahmed find her and get money and get divorce." With that, she makes some sort of dismissive noise in her throat – I am of no importance – and gets out of the car, slamming it hard behind her.

I sit here, devastated, fighting back tears. All of it, what Lucy's mother said, must be true. Lucy hates me because I revealed the appalling things that her father was doing. She went off the rails when she moved away. Affairs. Terminations. Debts. She conned Ahmed into marriage. Now, she has come back to destroy me.

I am trying hard to stay calm as I think what I need to do. I will drive home as fast as I can. I will reveal all of this to Matt. I will tell him Lucy is a bad person, evil even. She is here to snare him, trick him into a relationship, and to leave me on my own. Then the two of us will stand together; we will tell her to leave. Now! Matt and I will get over this; we will put it all behind us. One day soon, we will be happy again.

As I start driving, and my mind churns over what's just happened, I suddenly realise why that woman came to the car. It wasn't for my benefit; it wasn't so she could tell me all about Lucy. It was to find out where I – and Lucy – live. And I foolishly told her. Ranelagh Road, Felixstowe. And I wonder what that means, and whether Ahmed and maybe his brothers are going to hunt her down and seek revenge for what she did. I put my foot down hard on the accelerator.

I FIND a space to park in front of our house, and I get out, noticing Emily is in her front room next door, lights ablaze, looking towards me. It's so weird. I ignore her and instead gaze up at our windows. The living-room lights are on. Above that, in the loft, the lights are off.

I guess Matt is in the living room, watching Sky Sports, most likely. Waiting patiently for me. Lucy is in bed, fast asleep, probably. She's been going in to work early these past couple of days. Maybe she's doing an extra hour or two for the money, I don't know. I wonder what Matt will say when I tell him what I've discovered about her. He won't be happy.

I walk up the path, putting my key in the lock of the main door. The curtain of the ground-floor window twitches, and it makes me jump. I get a glimpse of the man downstairs peering through, and I am angered by his sudden movement.

I blank him, entering the house and shutting the door behind me.

At the top of the stairs, I stop by the fire extinguisher, to turn and walk along the landing to the living room at the front of the house. I will stand by the staircase, listening for the faint sound of Lucy breathing deeply, asleep in the loft.

I will walk in on Matt dozing with his mouth wide open, making that gargling noise of his. He'll have a half-empty can of lager still gripped in his hand, in front of a boxing match or a Grand Prix or something loud and furious.

But I don't need to turn and go along the landing to hear Lucy and Matt. As I stand by our bedroom door, I hear them in there. Together. Her moan. The urgent creaking of the bed. His sudden cry.

I am beside myself with fury. And then it happens so fast. My temper taking control.

I reach for the fire extinguisher on the landing, kicking the bedroom door open, storming in, the extinguisher held up above my head.

She is on top of him, still moving up and down, naked, her back to me.

I hit her hard with the extinguisher on the back of her head, and there is a stunned moment as I hit her two and three times more until she falls forward onto him.

Somehow, Matt is already pulling out from underneath her, rolling to the side, shouting at me, pushing her to the side and yelling at me to, "Stop! Stop! Stop!"

I do, eventually, sobbing in anguish and heartbreak, as she rolls slowly off the bed, hitting her head on the bedside cabinet and sprawling on the floor.

I drop the extinguisher on the carpet as Matt climbs out of the bed, the sight of him naked and still aroused making me feel physically sick. I turn, hurrying, stumbling, to the bathroom, where I vomit into the sink over and again. I then sit, crouched on the floor, for several minutes.

When I return to the bedroom, now full of regret and rising fear, I see that Matt is dressed in his black tee-shirt and boxer shorts. He is bending over Lucy lying there by the bed, his fingers feeling for a pulse.

I stand, my hands to my mouth in horror, hoping, praying, that she is still alive. If she is, God knows what will happen to me. I scramble, my hands shaking, for my mobile phone. To call 999. If there is a chance, even the slightest, for her to live. But I hesitate.

Matt leans forward, his head close to her mouth, trying to feel her breath on his cheek. Even though I am not religious, never have been, I find myself saying quietly, urgently, "Please God, please God, please God, let her live, let her live."

Then, finally, he stoops and kisses Lucy on the forehead. Stands up, reaches across to the bed, where a small hand towel is in the middle of it. I realise, in a horrifying split second, why it is there and what he is going to do with it.

He lays the towel over her face. It's meant to be an act of respect. But the thought and sight of it revolts me. He looks at me. I stare back, waiting for him to speak first. He does, eventually, in a surprisingly steady voice. "She's dead, Sophie ... you've killed Lucy."

PART 3
THE WORM HAS TURNED

CHAPTER THIRTEEN

WEDNESDAY, 25 SEPTEMBER, LATE EVENING

I lunge at Matt, hitting his chest with my clenched fists. He does not stop me as I thrash away.

He just says, over and over, "I'm sorry, I'm sorry, I'm sorry."

What seems like minutes later, I begin to slow my assault, and he grabs my arms, pulling me towards him into a great bear hug.

"She said we had to do it now ... to get pregnant ... I thought that was what we wanted more than anything ... a baby."

I shake my head. I don't want to talk about that. Not now. Not ever. I don't even want to think about it. I am sobbing desperately, so full of conflicting emotions. Matt and Lucy having sex appals me. But it's more than that. I've taken a life. I've killed another human being. Lucy is dead, and I don't know what to do. We stand like this for ages.

Then he seems to come to a decision, half pushing, half pulling me out of the bedroom, away from Lucy's body.

I take one last look at her lying there, blood everywhere,

and I know the sight will haunt me forever. More than just the blood. And the stench of her death. It's that I have killed. I am a murderer.

As we move along the landing, I look down at myself, spattered with blood. Matt is too, his face anyway. In my anguish, I hadn't noticed before.

I pull away from him in disgust, and he pulls me back, but then lets go as I persist.

"I have to shower. Look at me! Look at me!" I can hear madness in my screeching voice as I gesture at my body.

He nods an okay, turning back into the bedroom to change his clothes, I assume, and to attend to Lucy. I don't know what he will do with her.

I am in the bathroom, shutting the door. I need to be alone. I don't want Matt in here, washing the blood off his face, hands and arms, or peeing into the toilet. He can go along the landing and clean himself in the kitchen.

I strip off my clothes, leaving them in a bloodied pile by the basin. And I go into the shower, washing my hair repeatedly and scrubbing endlessly at myself with my flannel and a nail brush. On I go until my skin is scuffed raw and it hurts and I am bleeding. I am as clean as I can be.

I take my blood-soaked clothes and hurry down the landing to the washing machine in the kitchen. I put them in on the hottest cycle. Even so, I will never wear them again. They can go to the dump. I go back to the second bedroom, where I have a chest of drawers and a wardrobe full of clothes. I slip on pants and a black tee-shirt and jogging bottoms.

As I do all this, my mind goes back over everything I did. Picking up the fire extinguisher, going in, hitting Lucy over the head one, two, three, four times.

In that moment, I completely lost control. I wanted to hurt Lucy at least as much as she hurt me with her betrayal. Did I mean to kill her? In those few terrible seconds when my temper took over, I did, yes. I am appalled by that.

I was so jealous. There was, I hate to admit it, a flame – more than that, a growing love – between Matt and Lucy. Glances and smiles when they thought I wasn't looking. I should have – could have – avoided this. I was, in truth, insanely jealous.

I could have forgiven her – and Matt – for having sex that one time. A practical act, at least so I thought. That should have been that. But it was the start not the finish of things between them, and tonight, as the saying goes, "While the cat's away, the mice will play."

When I heard them – saw them – reaching ecstasy together, my mind tipped into insanity. In truth, and the realisation hits me, if Matt had been on top, I would have struck him the same. And then her. I would now be standing here with two dead bodies in our home.

I would have killed Matt in the midst of my madness. The thought sickens me, knowing what I am capable of in the most extreme circumstances. As I hear him now, moving between our bedroom and the living room, I wonder if I could ever be forced into such a monstrous situation again. I fear what I would do.

I walk into our bedroom – I will never come in here again – and I see Matt looking down at Lucy's body. He turns and says in a surprisingly calm voice, "I want you to go to bed, to sleep, in the spare room."

I nod, unbelieving, as he goes on talking, "I'm going to take ... Lucy ... and put her in the van ... get rid of her. Somewhere she'll never be found. I'll be a while ... I have to ..." His voice, full of desperation, fades away as we both imagine what he will do with her body.

"I'm sorry," he says unexpectedly as we stand there looking at each other. He wants to talk again about having sex with Lucy. How she tricked him. Stupid, soft-hearted Matt. I'm not going to think, let alone talk, about that. I'll never forget it, but we have to move on to dealing with Lucy's body. Now. Right now.

"Okay," I reply, and I take one last look at Lucy's body sprawled on her back on the carpet. I cannot bear to look at her bloodied head, but stare instead at her body below that. She was always a beauty, far more than me. I run to the bathroom, vomiting up bile.

I AM CROUCHED over on the bathroom floor, in anguish at what I have done, trying to catch my breath and slow my thumping heart.

Matt is moving again, room to room, picking up this, taking that, whatever he needs to get rid of Lucy and her ... her body. I must try to think of her as a body. But I cannot. I start sobbing.

Then, suddenly, Matt is pushing open the bathroom door, gazing down at me. He's now dressed in his old working clothes. I think he will hurry over, lean forward and put his arms around my shoulders, comforting me. But he just says one word, in a sharp voice, "Hurry!"

I get slowly, agonisingly, to my feet and watch as he turns and moves away, along the corridor to the living room.

He is in one of his busy-busy modes, matter-of-fact, a checklist of things to do and the order in which to do them in his head. He has no thoughts or feelings for me at this moment.

I follow him into the living room, lit only by moonlight coming through the half-open curtains. He has brought the body and laid it in front of the sofa. It is wrapped in an old duvet cover, soaking through with blood.

I have my hands on my face again, horrified by all of this, not sure what to say or do. I just want the body gone so I can start cleaning everything, wherever she has been.

I go to turn on the room lights, not thinking, but stop as he shakes his head, *No!* Then he is across to the window, peering through the curtains before pulling them to.

"I've wrapped her up," he says, gesturing towards the sofa, "... and I've got her phone to destroy ... everything else I need, tools and stuff, is in the van."

I gag at the thought and just nod: okay.

"I can carry her down the stairs over my shoulder, out the front door and into the van, putting her into the back, and then I'm away to ... you know."

I nod again, swallowing hard. For some reason, I assume he means Rendlesham Forest, some thirty to forty minutes' drive from here. Whenever we've been that way, we've always joked that lots of bodies must be buried there. It's that kind of place. Creepy.

Matt's talking again. "But I need to go down and out, checking it's all clear, no one's about, then open the van door ... keep the front door open ... so I can come back up and take her straight down and quickly into the van, and off."

I nod once more.

"What I need you to do ... now!" he says, raising his voice to focus my attention. "Is to stand by this window while I go and open the van, and you look up and down the road and at the houses over there ... make sure nobody's at a window. Got that? You'll signal to me that it's safe."

I move towards the window and him, expecting he'll hug me quickly, telling me he loves me. But all he does – says – as he moves by me towards the landing is, "Don't pull the curtains back or put the lights on; just stand quietly and look."

I hear him going slowly, step by step, down the staircase, careful not to wake the man downstairs. Then he's opening the creaking main door and is out and along the path to the pavement. He walks to the back door of his van, reaching into his pockets for his keys.

I look at the houses opposite, checking for lights on, a shadowy shape at a window, or a curtain twitching in the night. Nothing. I look up and down the road, to the left, right, and left again. All is quiet. Unnaturally so. It's not usually like this. We've got lucky.

Matt now has the van doors open; he turns back towards the house, glances about, and then looks up at me, offering a thumbs-up. I look around again and put my thumb up as well. It's like we're playing a stupid game, and the thought revolts me.

Everything unfolds so quickly. I hear Matt running up the stairs, and I am alarmed at the noise he is making. Thump. Thump. Thump. Thump. Thump. Thump. He takes the stairs two or more at a time, his weight heavy on each step.

And he is in the living room, leaning down and lifting the body, putting it over his shoulder. I think he will say something loving, encouraging maybe, as he turns around, ready to hurry away. But he just goes. I imagine her head lolling over his shoulder, dripping blood all down his back and onto the carpet.

I watch from the living-room window as he comes out the main door and walks up the path, across the pavement and to the van. From here, he appears to have a roll of folded-over, wrapped-up carpet over his shoulder. Or maybe that's just wishful thinking. It's obviously a body.

In she goes, dumped into the back of the van. He glances round, nothing and no one in sight, and then he slams the van doors. I can hear them from here and cringe at his thoughtlessness. He turns, does that ridiculous thumbs-up sign again, and is then getting into the van, reversing a metre or so before driving away.

I stand for a minute or two, looking for signs of life, movements at the windows, in the houses over the road. A street light flickers along to my left, creating a stop-start effect, like an old-time, black-and-white silent movie. I see, along to my right, two teenage boys walking along, up and by my house, their drunken shouts signalling that all is as it was. Back to normal.

I realise suddenly that there is a draught from some-where, a chilling breeze, and that Matt has left the main door and ours open downstairs. I will go and shut them before I spend the next few hours cleaning and washing everything to disguise what has happened. I will have to put her clothes and belongings into bin bags and take them later to a charity shop, perhaps in Ipswich. It will be a busy night.

As I shut the main door, it creaks stubbornly as I push it closed. I turn to go back through our door and upstairs, trying to create a mental checklist of things to do. And then I hear it, a sudden noise, from this side or that, I'm not sure, as distracted as I am. It sounds like someone has knocked something off a shelf and it has crashed noisily to the floor.

I think, imagine, it may be a clock. From a windowsill. In the home of the man downstairs. Or next door, at Emily's. Whichever, it does not matter. It occurs to me that someone – one of them – has been standing by their front window. Looking out. Watching.

Seeing Matt coming to the pavement and the road with a body over his shoulder. Putting it into his van. Driving away. And I am now sick with worry and fear. That the police will be called, and they'll arrive here in the next few minutes. And the murder – the slaughter, which I committed – will be uncovered.

I STAND IN THE HALLWAY, listening intently to what's happening on either side.

Behind me, there is our door and the staircase that leads up to our two floors of the house. It was always my sanctuary; not anymore.

To the left, there is the door of the man downstairs' ground-floor apartment. To my right, the wall, beyond which is Emily's front room.

I move to the door of the man downstairs, putting my ear against it. I'm not sure what I expect to hear. Silence, maybe. The faint sound of him snoring? His bedroom will be below ours.

I don't want to hear any other noises, sounds of him moving about, woken by what happened upstairs and then watching from his front window. Seeing what he's seen, now pressing buttons on his phone – beep, beep, beep – and calling the police.

My mind plays tricks with me, imagining I can hear the pit-pat of footsteps in slippers. But I shake my head and listen again, and there are no sounds at all. He is fast asleep, I'm sure.

I'm about to move across to put my ear against the wall to Emily's front room. But then I hear it and jump. A noise, the tiniest of scratches against the man's door, so close to my head.

I find myself in shock. I'm breathing deeply. I feel shaken inside. He is standing on the other side of this door, our heads separated by no more than a few centimetres of wood. The scratch was the sound of his hands, one of his nails, against the door, as he's leaning there, listening to me.

I try to still my ragged breaths, my chest pumping in and out, in and out. He will surely hear me gulping in air. The noise smothering the sounds of anything on the other side of the door. I step back and away, as quietly as I can. Then I glance up.

The door has a peephole in it. The man downstairs is looking out through it, I'm sure. Watching me. Revelling in my distress. He has seen Matt load the body in the van. Heard me walk down to shut the main door. Come to stand next to his.

The sound I heard wasn't his fingernail against the door. It was the noise of him pulling back the cover of the peephole to look out, to see me. Smiling with grim satisfaction as he presses 999 on his mobile phone.

I don't know what to do. Run upstairs, pack a rucksack and flee? Perhaps get into my car and drive to the forest, searching for Matt? Or, and the thought fills me with horror, I could knock on the man's door, force my way in, do whatever I have to do. My God, how could I even think such a thing?

Something in me, another moment of madness, sees me moving to his front door, my eye against the peephole, looking in, staring him down. I put my hand on the door, pushing at it, thinking, *Come on, come on, let me in*.

I cannot see anything – no staring eye – through the peephole, just blackness because the cover must still be in place. And there is no movement of the door; it is shut and locked tight.

I raise my hand, my clenched fist, ready to bang on the door, to tell him to open it, to stand and face me, but then I hear another noise. The flushing of a toilet. In his apartment, near the back, as ours is, and I wonder if I am going utterly mad.

The man downstairs is not at the door. He has not been looking out. Has not seen anything. He's been in the bathroom and is now going to bed. Like any normal person would be doing at this time of night.

I stand there, feeling foolish, and then wonder what this – the killing of Lucy – means from now on. There will be outside threats, I'm sure. Her employer wanting to know where she is. And that friend of hers. Ahmed will turn up at some point. But the biggest danger is from inside my head, the guilt eating away at me and making me do mad and impulsive things.

Then I hear it, from next door, the sound of music coming from Emily's front room. I stand for a moment, taking a minute to recognise the tune. It's ABBA's "Does Your Mother Know" – and I'm not sure if she's playing mind games with me or if I'm just perceiving danger everywhere.

CHAPTER FOURTEEN

THURSDAY, 26 SEPTEMBER, GONE MIDNIGHT

The music from Emily's house has just been turned on, I'm sure of it. I listened so intently before and heard nothing. It's not *loud* loud, turned up to attract my attention. But I can certainly hear it, even the words, quite clearly.

Why would she turn music on – and that particular song with its taunting lyrics – in the early hours of the morning? Because she heard what happened, saw Matt with the body by the van in the road and, thinking she is so clever, is sending me a message, playing with me.

Then again, perhaps the old woman has only just gone to sleep, after Emily has been on her feet all day, running around, feeding her mother, cleaning up, helping her into bed. Now she's put on some music and is relaxing for half an hour before going to bed herself.

I stand, terrified that Emily has heard and seen everything – the attack on Lucy would have been noisy, especially so in the quiet of the night. Enough to rouse her and make her move to the wall, listening.

I take two steps to the main door, my head leaning

against the frosted glass, waiting to see the bright blue lights of a police car siren. Perhaps they will arrive in silence, the first sounds I hear being those of heavy boots stomping up the path.

I open the main door slowly, its creak seeming so loud into the quiet of the night. But there is no one there. They'd be here by now. Anyhow, I'm not sure Emily is the sort to call the police; she'd want to use the knowledge to her advantage, wheedling her way in with me, persuading me to be her best friend. *Or else.*

I am out of the house, down the path, turning right, up her path, and onto the small, paved patio, full of plants in pots, by her living-room window. I have to know, now, what Emily is doing.

If she has heard and seen what happened and all of this – the song and the lyrics – are to toy with me ... well, I don't know how I'll react. I'll decide once I find out. I'll knock on her door, tap, tap, tap. The thought of the only thing I can do to silence her terrifies me.

I stand by her window, moving close to look in. The curtains are slightly apart. Enough to see into her front room. I don't think, with the light on inside and darkness outside, that she can see me standing here, quiet and unmoving.

Emily is sitting in an armchair, gazing towards me. I jump, startled, and stumble forwards, my hands grabbing the windowsill, preventing my fall. I regain my balance and look again into the room. I think, for one second, that the noise of my hands on the windowsill has made her sit up, wondering what it is happening outside.

For so many endless seconds, I'm holding my breath, as we seem to be looking straight at each other. Me standing. Her sitting. I think she is about to get up, come to the window and look out, my face just centimetres from hers. I cannot change my position; such a sudden movement will only confirm I am here.

The madness inside me wants to tap gently on the window. Then, as she approaches, to move quickly and knock gently on the glass on her front door. She will come through and open it, and I will strike her down. But as my dreadful plan unravels in my mind, I realise I have nothing to hit her with. Dear God, what am I becoming?

I stand, watching, staring, unable to look or move away. And she just sits there, gazing back, a slight smile on her lips, ever so pleased with herself. Tormenting me.

I notice she has something on the armrest of her chair. A ball of wool and two knitting needles. I smile to myself, relieved at last. She's just knitting for half an hour before going to bed.

But then she picks up the needles, one last long look – a stare – at me, and she is up and out of sight into the hallway. She has seen me. Now she is coming for me.

I STAND on Emily's patio, unable to do more than turn towards her front door. Then I'm shaking and reaching down to pick up a ceramic pot by my feet. What else can I do?

I glance along the pavement and up and down the road and over at the houses opposite. All clear. I move fast to her front door, ready to push Emily back into her hallway, shutting the door behind me before I strike her.

But then, suddenly, the music and lights in Emily's front room are turned off, followed by the hall lights, and I hear her clumping heavily up her staircase. Thank God. I stand there on the doorstep, drenched in sweat, shocked at what I was about to do.

I put the ceramic pot on her patio, and I'm then hurrying back down her path, up mine, pushing the main door open and closed, through our door, moving quickly up the staircase and along to the living room. I slump on the sofa, gasping in air.

What I've done – did – to Lucy has unhinged me, my mind seeing threats where there are none. A lonely old man downstairs minding his own business. A sad woman next door finding a few minutes' simple pleasure when she can.

More than that, my overreaction – my mind imagining that the man downstairs and Emily next door are dangers to me – chills me to the core. It reveals I am capable of killing again to keep my secret, and my marriage to Matt, safe. That horrifies me.

I'm up and off the sofa, to the kitchen, under the sink, picking out a roll of bin bags. I must get busy; I must keep my mind off all of this.

I go from room to room, lights on, lights off, picking up everything that belongs – belonged – to Lucy. Separating her clothes and belongings into different bags. There's not much.

I'm back in the kitchen with two bin bags of clothes, whatever, by my feet, ready to go to the dump, charity shops, wherever, as soon as I can.

I stop for a moment, checking my mobile phone. I wonder if I should text Matt, *Sorted?* But something stops me, the sudden thought that maybe, sometime down the line, the police may check my phone and be able to access everything. Even deleted messages. I'd not want them to see that.

"Why," a police officer might ask, interviewing me under caution after Lucy was reported missing by her employer, "did you text your husband at one in the morning ... what was being *sorted?*"

I leave it, thinking that Matt will be deep inside Rendlesham Forest, doing whatever he needs to do. I cannot dwell on that, the utter horror of what's happening, so I go back to the cupboard under the sink, getting cloths and sprays and a bottle of bleach.

I begin in our bedroom, wiping and wiping at the fire extinguisher and then putting it back where it was on the landing, a constant reminder, at least for now, of what I have done. I'm then stripping the bed, taking my clothes out of the machine and putting everything in, again under the hottest cycle. Then I'm back, spraying and rubbing away at the bed, the bedside cabinet and the carpet, everywhere, over and over. I feel I'm moving so close to obsession.

I can't get all the blood out of the mattress and the carpet, so I turn the mattress over and move the bedside cabinet to cover the carpet for now, and then I go and make up the double bed in the spare room. It's where we'll sleep from now on, at least until this room has been redecorated and the mattress and the carpet have been destroyed, all of it replaced.

I go again from room to room, the landing, the front room, down the stairs, wherever her blood may be. I clean it all thoroughly, sobbing as I do. I even open our door and the main one, using the torch on my phone to see out, pretending to search for a lost key but actually looking for drops of blood on the path. There doesn't seem to be any.

At last, I put the cloths and sprays and the almost-empty bottle of bleach in another bin bag in the kitchen and sit there slumped on the floor, exhausted, my mind spinning in all directions.

I can't do any more for now. At some point, sooner rather than later, our bedroom will need to be changed, especially the bloodied mattress and carpet. Matt can put them in the van, take them far, far away in the dead of night, and bury them, maybe burn them, which would be safer. He can do something with the extinguisher as well.

And then what? We just carry on with our lives like nothing has happened? The thought horrifies me. I am a murderer. Matt is an accomplice. Even if we are never uncovered, we have to live with that for the rest of our lives. I don't know how we will.

What I did sickens me. My anger – what Lucy did, what Matt did – just took over, and I lost my mind for a time. Minutes, that's all. Seconds really, perhaps sixty or ninety. Not even that. If Matt hadn't done what he did, none of this would have happened.

I wonder about Lucy. She came back to Felixstowe and then tried to dupe me, expecting money from us to be a surrogate. If we had given her some, I don't doubt she would have vanished with it immediately. Instead, she conned her way into our home, lived with us rent-free, and, worse, set about stealing my husband.

She had sex with Matt tonight. I wonder, having seduced him, whether she wanted to turn him against me, eventually driving me out as she and Matt became the perfect couple.

Matt would have had – was having – sex with her willingly, if not enthusiastically. This was not like the first time, when – I think, or I want to tell myself – it was a practical, matter-of-fact act. This time, they were both naked, enjoying it, reaching ecstasy together. The ultimate betrayal. I must not think about it. I simply must not.

As I go into the shower, washing and scrubbing myself

once more, to get the stench of death off my skin, I feel my anger – my fury – towards Matt surging. If he hadn't allowed himself to be seduced, Lucy would still be alive. I would have had a chance to get rid of her by simply telling her to go, sending her on her way so I could resume my marriage.

I get out of the shower, drying myself. I then pick up my clothes from the linen basket in the corner of the room, taking them to the washing machine, ready to go into the next hottest wash. I dress in fresh pyjamas and a comfortable old dressing gown. When I sit in the spare bedroom, drying my hair, my feelings against Matt reach boiling point. This is down to him, all of it.

As I lie on the bed in the spare bedroom – this cold, anonymous room where our baby should have been, I imagine Matt and Lucy having sex at other times, behind my back, when I was at work, and having a drink with my friend Rachel. As our door opens and I hear Matt's footsteps on the stairs, I get up, grabbing a heavy, decorative paperweight from the windowsill, ready to confront him.

I AM STANDING at the door of the spare bedroom, the paperweight in my hand behind my back, as Matt gets to the top of the stairs. I look at him, in the semi-darkness, as moonlight streams through the skylight on the staircase to the loft rooms.

He looks frightened and exhausted and close to tears. I slip the paperweight into a pocket of my dressing gown. What the hell am I thinking and doing? He doesn't seem to notice. Thank goodness.

Then he is pushing roughly by, so I do not see his tears,

heading to the bathroom to shower. I go to ask him, "Do you want something to eat?" I stop myself, angry at my stupidity. My mind claws for normality in this horrifying situation.

I sit on the edge of the bed in the spare bedroom, listening to him in the bathroom.

I hear the shower go on, blasting hot water. I imagine his body spattered with blood as he rubs desperately at his hair, shoulders and stomach, down to his feet.

He cries out suddenly, in pain, maybe the water is scorching hot, but the noise is more one of anguish at what he has done.

I lean forward, my hands covering my ears, as I imagine Matt sobbing and shouting in his shame and revulsion.

I feel the same and wonder what we will do, how we will ever live with what we have done. It will be in our heads forever.

The chance to tell the police, to plead manslaughter on the grounds of momentary madness, has gone now that Matt has disposed of the body. It's murder.

We are in it together and will have to stand shoulder to shoulder to survive this.

Then Matt is back in the bedroom, naked, drying himself furiously with a towel. I glance away, lying down; then I go to ask him what he's done with his clothes.

He seems to anticipate my question, saying, "It all needs to be washed." He leaves the bedroom. I hear him in the kitchen, fiddling with the washing machine, and then going into our old bedroom to get dressed.

He comes back in a black tee-shirt and boxer shorts, gets into bed beside me and pulls the duvet across and over his shoulder. His back is turned against me.

I lie on my back, next to him, my mind full of questions.

Accusing ones, about his relationship with Lucy. Practical ones, about what he has done with her body.

"What did you do ... with her?" I ask eventually, as calmly as I can, my words seeming to float and hang in the air above us. I can feel him tense. Matt has always been a calm man; there has never been any anger or violence within him. But it feels now that he may snap under this unbelievable pressure.

"She's ... gone ... no one will ever find ... her," he says, turning over onto his back so we are both staring at the ceiling. I think that looking at each other would be too much to bear. He hesitated after the word "find", and I wonder if he was going to say "her body" or "her body parts" and then stopped himself.

Suddenly, unexpectedly, he rolls on his side towards me, then leans forward so his head is on my shoulder, and he hugs me. I feel his body shaking as I return his embrace. And finally, he says in a breathless voice, "It's over ... done with ... don't think about it ever again ... we have to start afresh in the morning ... pretend nothing ever happened."

Easier said than done, that.

CHAPTER FIFTEEN

THURSDAY, 26 SEPTEMBER, DAWN

It was a hellish night, at least for me. Matt was asleep, as he always is, before I was. I could scarcely believe it. I don't know how he does it. He lay there, breathing heavily and regularly – otherwise almost lifelessly – all the way through to the early morning.

It took me an hour, nearly two, to fall asleep, my mind full of so many emotions: shame, horror, guilt, worry, fear, mostly fear. My mind raced every which way, thinking how the murder might be uncovered. And all so easily.

When I finally nodded off for a few hours, I had terrible, nightmarish dreams about being chased through dense, never-ending woods by nameless, impossible-to-see monsters. I awoke at dawn and just lay here. Matt got up to shower at seven a.m. I felt I had not slept at all.

We do as we always do first thing in the morning. In theory, one of us gets to the shower first; the other makes breakfast. It's a standing joke, really. He always gets to the bathroom before me. Today, as ever, I make breakfast. It does not amount to much, it never does – orange juice from a carton, cereals, instant coffee from a jar, that's all.

It's really fifteen to twenty minutes when we sit down. Sometimes, we tell each other about our day ahead. More often, we stare into space, each with our own thoughts. Today, we talk. Matt has a new app that shows me where he'll be, fixing leaky showers or whatever. He finds it fascinating even though he's been more or less in the same place for weeks.

I think we have to talk about Lucy and the many possible consequences. I want to. Matt does not. He breezes through the app, showing me the screen although I barely look at it. I go to say something, "Lu …" but he waves his hands, *No, No*, and is up on his feet, mumbling something about having to get to work early. It's always been hard to get him to share his thoughts and feelings; this is going to be an impossibility.

"Wait," I say, getting up too. He looks at me as though I am, for the first time ever, about to offer to make him a sandwich and a flask of tea to take with him. I wasn't. It's not me. He usually sorts himself out, getting a coffee and a sausage roll at a baker's near to where he is working.

"The phone, what did you do with it?" When he left last night, he said he was going to destroy it. I need to know he did, that it's not out there, intact and buried with the body, ready to be traced. Beeping its *Here I am* signal. He shakes his head and replies abruptly that he smashed it and threw it piece by piece "here, there and everywhere". He seems affronted that I'd even ask him. I move on.

"Those bin bags," I say. "They need getting rid of now." I should have said I'd take them to charity shops or wherever later, but I cannot face it, the thought of old ladies picking through Lucy's clothes. The only chance I have of moving on from this horror is to get rid of everything fast and somehow pretend it never happened. "The fire extinguisher too."

"I'll sort them," he says, going down the landing to line everything up at the top of the stairs; then he goes to and fro, dressing in work clothes and getting his work bag and toolbox and what have you ready. He carries the bags downstairs in one hand, the extinguisher in the other.

It strikes me that, as Matt goes out to his van, the man downstairs and Emily may be by their windows, filming him on their mobile phones. More damning proof to show to the police.

It's madness, I know. I thought I had put that sickening suspicion behind me, but it's still there, just below the surface, ready to come up again, filling me with dread. I decide to confront it head-on. I go down the stairs after Matt.

He is already at the van, opening the back doors, throwing everything in, then hurrying by me to go up the stairs to collect his work bag and toolbox and, most probably, a bottle of water from the fridge. I go to the van, standing by the back.

I turn quickly, suddenly, looking first at Emily's house, each window, for signs of someone somewhere, a curtain pulled back, a mobile phone glinting in the sunlight, maybe a curtain twitching into place. But there is nothing.

As Matt comes out of the house, striding purposefully towards me, keen to get away, I look at the man downstairs' window for any signs he is looking out, filming and building a case against us. Again, there is nothing to see, and I breathe a sigh of relief. It's all my overactive, petrified imagination.

Matt puts down his things, hugs me briefly, one arm around me, and then puts his work bag and toolbox in the back of the van, shuts the doors and turns to go. "I'll get rid of all this today ... and that's the end of it." Before I can answer, he is getting into the van and driving away. I feel a huge sense of relief.

I walk back to the house, ready to have a shower, put on my make-up and head off to work. I'm going to start running again soon, but not today. I'll just sit down for a while before I leave; I'll have another mug of tea, calming myself.

I am comforted by Matt's "do-it-now" attitude, dealing with Lucy's body last night and her clothes and belongings and his clothes too this morning. Later, I will talk to him about the bedroom, especially the mattress and the carpet. I think he will cut out the bloodied parts of both and dispose of them somewhere on his travels tomorrow. Then, at last, I can start blotting out this horror.

Before heading to the shower, I walk upstairs to her room in the attic. I'm not sure why. It is stripped bare of her clothes and belongings. I open the windows and gather up the bedding to put in the washing machine. I will probably throw it away. Later, after work, I will dust and polish and vacuum everything, shutting the door and not coming up here again, at least not for a long while.

As I turn to leave, my hands full of bedding, I see it on the windowsill. Her keyring. I go across, picking it up and studying the keys on it. Two door keys for here. Two others – one for a door, the other for a car. The key ring is a small wooden circle with "49" on it. I walk downstairs and put her bedding in the washing machine and then wander into the living room, my mind going all over everything.

The caravan – "49" – and the car are kind of loose ends. I wonder if I should leave them be. Just keep out of it. But the thought of the car supposedly being abandoned – now that Lucy is never coming back to claim it – troubles me a lot.

The caravan park owner might report it to the police sometime soon, which will start to suggest that Lucy has disappeared. That could bring the police to our door. I can't have that.

I STAND HERE, frozen, staring into space, out into the road far below. My mind reels; I'm trying to make a possibly life-changing decision. Yet the world goes on around me.

Teenagers walk by on either side, shouting and laughing at each other. Cars go by too, pulling in and out to let each other pass.

Even up here, I can still hear the man downstairs bang-bang-banging. And someone is coming out from next door. I step forward. It's Emily, pushing her mother in a wheelchair. I stand still, thinking my terrible thoughts.

I don't know what to do about the caravan and the car. I have to decide though, and now – Matt will be gone all day, and I don't want to talk about it with him this evening. He'd be gung-ho, waving his hands dismissively: "Forget about them!" I need to give it some measured thought. My instinct is to leave them alone. Not get involved, leaving fingerprints and DNA everywhere.

Going to the caravan, entering, and looking around to see what's there is fraught with danger – the risk of being seen by the park's staff and being confronted, or at least remembered, worries me. "Why," the police might ask, "did you go to her caravan?"

What would I say?

And I don't know what I'd do with her car, if it's maybe parked in a space nearby. Where would I take it? What if I'm seen and recorded on CCTV? It might just be better to leave it where it is. Otherwise, "Why," the police would ask again, "did you drive her car away?" How would I answer that?

But doing nothing might be the worst thing. If – when – the police investigate what they'll assume is a missing persons case, they'll look first at the caravan. If Lucy has left, say, personal belongings behind – maybe a driving licence, even a passport – they'll wonder why. She wouldn't if she'd run off, would she?

If her car is maybe found a street or two away, they'll want to know why she would have supposedly left town without it. That would make no sense. Lucy wouldn't get a bus or a train out of town, leaving her car here. That would set off alarm bells, surely?

And at some point, there will be publicity locally. Posters up. *Have You Seen Lucy Yilmaz!* Stuff on Facebook. Instagram too. Someone, somewhere – the man downstairs, Emily next door – will contact the police, saying that Lucy lived here for a while, with Matt and me. That will immediately put us front and centre as prime suspects.

She went missing from here – so Matt and I have to make sure everything stacks up, including her caravan and car.

I have to remove anything incriminating in the caravan, any would-be evidence that might indicate she hasn't left town of her own choice.

And the car has to go – moved somewhere out of sight where it won't be spotted.

I text Priti, my line manager, a little white lie, telling her I feel ill – time of the month – and asking if I can work from home at least for the morning. They're always good about that these days.

When the answer comes – *Okay* – I am up, grabbing a pair of rubber gloves by the kitchen sink and putting them in my pocket. I need to be careful.

Then I'm downstairs and out the front door, heading for my car to drive to the caravan park. I'm not sure what I expect to find at number 49, nor what I'll have to do there. I just know I need to check it out and put my worried mind to rest.

IT'S a big caravan park close to an Asda supermarket and a petrol station, on a road down towards the docks. Whenever I've driven by, it's always looked busy, with plenty of holidaymakers and people in vans, picking up and dropping stuff off.

Today is another sunny day – surely the last of the sunshine before autumn sets in – and it's all quiet here. I left the car in the supermarket car park just up the road and walked along. I didn't want my car to be seen, perhaps recorded on CCTV, at the caravan park.

I'm now strolling, unnoticed, Little Ms Invisible, and following the numbered caravans towards 49 at the back of the park. I glance around. No one is about. Nobody is looking out of their caravan windows. I can slip in and out without being seen.

I get to the steps of caravan number 49. Then I take the rubber gloves from my bag and put them on, as if I'm going to do some cleaning. I feel kind of stupid, but it's also a sensible thing to do.

I take out Lucy's keys, wiping them on the side of my

trousers, a last-minute attempt to remove my fingerprints. I'm not sure why. It seems pointless. I'm incredibly nervous.

I put the key in the lock, turning it, and I step into the caravan. I stop dead in my tracks. I expected to be able to rummage around at my leisure. I expected the caravan to be empty.

But it isn't.

A man sits in the living area, white-haired and balding, his back to me, a can of lager in his hand. As he brings the can to his lips, he hears me coming in, and turns, then stands up, ever-so-slightly wobbly, to look at me.

He is in his sixties, closer to seventy, I'd guess, and has a haggard, lined face, but he doesn't appear unfriendly. Like a washed-up Winnie the Pooh. He is dressed in a grey sweatshirt and matching jogging bottoms. They are both badly stained.

I am already retreating, saying, "Sorry, sorry, wrong caravan," as I do. He smiles in a drunken, cheery manner and turns and sits back down heavily, resuming his drinking. I don't know who he is. I don't recognise him. He doesn't know me – and won't remember me either.

I stand at the bottom of the caravan steps, feeling foolish. I peel off the rubber gloves and put them back in my bag. Even if the man remembers me coming in, and I doubt it, he will simply recall the bright yellow gloves and assume I was a cleaner.

I wonder why he is there. The way Lucy talked, she gave the impression she'd be at the caravan park for a while, months, I'd assumed. Now, recalling what her mother said, I doubt that was the case. She took Ahmed's money and used some of it to pay cash to stay here, I think. If she'd intended to stay longer, it would've been far cheaper to have rented a room somewhere than pay holidaymaker rates on a caravan.

I suspect Lucy booked it for two or three weeks, maybe then expecting to somehow move in with me before she had to leave the park. The whole surrogacy thing played into her hands. After that, she pretended she'd been attacked and had to leave for her own safety.

I let out a long breath. I've been such a fool.

I turn to go, to hurry back to my car unseen, but a dark-haired woman of about my age, brisk and businesslike in a navy jacket, white blouse and navy skirt, is walking towards me. She looks angry. I look back neutrally. Her demeanour, assertive, even aggressive, changes, then softens. "Oh," she says, "I saw you on the CCTV walking to the caravan and thought you were someone else."

She has to mean Lucy. Of course, when we were younger, we sometimes got mistaken for each other. I think, from a distance, on a blurry CCTV, we still could. I hope she only saw me going to the caravan, not going in and coming out. I should just smile, make some excuse and walk off. But I don't. I want to know more. But if this conversation is ever reported, perhaps to the police, I'll need to say the right things to cover myself.

So I say, "Lucy Yilmaz?" Before she can reply, I go on, "I'm looking for her. She was renting a room. Just upped and left. She owes me money." Then I throw caution to the wind. "Does she owe you money too?"

She nods her head, replying without hesitation, "She paid a week at a time in advance. The last week she said she'd pay me for the next at the weekend. She didn't. She just vanished. I had a void I could have filled. I thought you were her, coming back for her things. I've a box of them in storage ... she can have them when she pays what she owes." She has a hard face, this woman.

I want to see, or at least know, what Lucy left behind. But to do that, I think I'd have to offer to settle the outstanding debt. But that would seem odd, wouldn't it? Given that she supposedly owes me money too. So instead, I ask conversationally, "Anything much in there?"

She looks at me, and it is an odd look. I think she is puzzled by me being here, that if I am simply someone who rented a room to Lucy, I wouldn't know that Lucy stayed in a caravan here for two weeks, let alone the particular caravan. Still, I don't think she saw me going into it. She must have been coming out of the office when I did. A stroke of luck. Anyhow, if I asked anything, it should have been, "Much worth selling?" I stand here, waiting, feeling increasingly tense.

"Dirty clothes and knickers, bit of make-up, a few magazines, nothing I could sell to cover what I've lost." She pauses and then turns and gestures towards some car parking spaces. "She's got her old Honda there. It's worth something. Not much. We can't get in it." A small smile crosses her face. "That reminds me, we were going to buy a clamp and put it on so she has to pay what she owes before she drives off."

I put my hand and feel the key to the car, but say nothing, just shake my head as if to say, "Oh well, never mind." Then I go to leave, but as I do, she coughs loudly, and I turn round to hear what she is going to say. She holds out her hand. "The key," she states, in a hard, cold voice, "I'm not stupid."

I reach into my pocket, turn to the side so she cannot see the key ring or the keys on it, and take off the car key. I hand her the caravan key and keyring. Neither of us speaks. She takes it from me. Not one word. I turn and walk away. This didn't go well. She thinks I am in league with Lucy. I'm not sure what that will mean going forward.

I RETURN HOME, ready to go to my computer, log in to my work account and start sorting through the backlog of forms. Nothing feels right, though.

My mind is still on my visit to the caravan park, the encounter with the hard-faced woman, and the existence of Lucy's car. I text my line manager, telling her I still don't feel well this afternoon, and that I'll do overtime to catch up.

Some part of me wants to go back and get the car, to hop in and drive it away. It's now or never, I think. Before it is clamped, which will almost certainly be later today.

As I drive to the caravan park and leave my car where I did before, I rationalise my thoughts. If Lucy is reported missing by her employer, that friend of hers at work, or even the caravan park woman, the police might suspect something bad happened in Felixstowe if her car were left here.

So I'm going to take it away – into Ipswich and leave it in a side road up by the railway station. It will look like Lucy has maybe driven there and got a train and disappeared into London. As so many people do, never to be seen again.

There is nobody about. I put on my gloves, hurry to her car, click it open and drive out of the caravan park without looking back. Simple as that. I gaze around the front of the car. Lucy was always messy. There are empty bottles of Coke Zero, screwed-up pick 'n' mix bags and parking tickets at the front.

As I'm coming through town, I pull over to take a proper

look at the car. On the back seat, there is a half-open, empty shoebox, a torn pair of tights, and an empty packet from a pharmacy. I reach across to read the sticker on it; it's from a pharmacy in Milton Keynes. Citalopram. I google it on my phone – Lucy was on antidepressants. Just as her mother said. This one has a different name, though, and I'm not sure if it's stronger. I guess so.

I rummage through the glove compartment and the spaces by the driver's and the passenger's seats to see what's there. It's mostly make-up wipes and tissues with lipstick on them. A small deodorant spray, half empty. It looks like a teenager's car, to be honest.

I put everything back as it was. Except for the pharmacy bag with citalopram on the sticker. I place that on the front seat next to me. When the car is discovered, the police will see that empty bag and draw their own conclusions. That a depressed Lucy has hidden herself away somewhere and taken her own life. It's wicked of me, I know, I know, but what else can I do?

I am about to drive off when I see Emily coming out of the supermarket over the way. She is carrying two plastic carrier bags of heavy shopping, which are obviously going to split at any moment. She stands on the pavement, looking across. I am about to duck down out of sight, but she has already seen me.

She'll come over with those straining bags when the traffic has gone, and stand by the window, expecting me to wind it down to offer her a lift home. God knows what she'll think of me sitting in an unfamiliar car in rubber gloves. What the hell would I say?

So I simply pretend I haven't seen her, dipping my head down and turning the key in the ignition. I start the car, rev it too hard, then roar up the road. I glance in the rear-view mirror. Emily stands there, watching me go. She must be baffled. She won't know it's Emily's car. She may one day when it's on the news and across local social media.

I drive the car, slow and steady, towards Ipswich, so careful so that I won't attract the attention of police cars that sometimes wait in laybys, monitoring the speed of passing motorists. I see there are CCTV cameras as I drive over the Orwell Bridge towards the railway station. I wonder if they can see my face clearly and how long they keep recordings.

I park in a maze of roads on a hill up above the station. I get out, checking the boot to see what's there. I do so unhurriedly like I am parking here and meeting friends at the station for a day in Norwich or London, maybe Cambridge. Other than a winter coat, a pair of boots and a water bottle, the boot is empty. I shut it, take off my rubber gloves, and walk to the station to go back to Felixstowe.

As I return home on the train, to then get a taxi back to my car, I wonder if I have left a trail of clues behind me. Emily, seeing me drive away at speed in an unfamiliar car. If she sees a *Have You Seen This Car?* appeal on Facebook, she may tell the police. They can then follow my journey on CCTV footage taken from around Orwell Bridge and the railway station. "Why," they will ask accusingly, "did you drive Lucy Yilmaz's car to Ipswich and get the train home?" How will I answer that and all of the questions that follow?

OUR EVENING IS TENSE – from the moment of Matt's arrival home – though we are both trying desperately hard to be normal.

As we eat and drink, little more than a ham salad and glasses of orange squash, he asks me how my day was, and I reply with what he wants to hear, "Same old, same old." I then add, "Yours?" And he mumbles a few non-committal words.

I don't mention Lucy or my visit to the caravan park, the car or my drive to Ipswich. Matt doesn't want to know; he's pretending our life is just as it was and will always be. It's changed forever, of course. But I will try to follow Matt's lead.

As we watch television, some new crime series from the US, neither of us really following it, there's something I have to say.

"Before you got back ... I started moving us into the other bedroom." He nods, yes, I noticed, as I add, "I can't bear ..." I don't complete the sentence as he shakes his head dismissively.

"But," I say. Surely he must know what I'm going to ask him to do. "The carpet ... the mattress ..."

He's up, an unusually angry expression on his face, before I can complete what I was going to say.

He heads out of the living room without a word, and I hear doors opening and slamming angrily as he makes his way to his van to fetch his toolkit. He's not meant to keep it there overnight, but sometimes he forgets to bring it in, or he can't be bothered. He's so blasé at times. Then he's back up, just as noisy. I hope it has not alerted the man downstairs to keep watch.

I sit on the edge of the sofa, listening to Matt in the bedroom, moving furniture, cutting carpet, cursing time and again, then pulling the mattress off the bed, dragging it to the door.

Half an hour or so later, without asking me to act as a lookout, I hear him clumping down the stairs. I move to the window, watching him throwing piece after piece of carpet – the whole carpet cut into maybe six smaller pieces – into the back of the van.

He stomps back up, still so angry, and I fear he is going to try to drag the mattress on his own across the landing, down the stairs, out the doors, up the path and to the van, for all to see. Bloodstains on display. I am alarmed a passer-by might rush to help.

I move quickly to the living-room door, to offer to lend a hand, so at least the bloodstains will be obscured by one of us as we carry it out. He is standing there, as if expecting me to come and assist. He knows me too well.

We carry the mattress down, Matt's body pressed tight against the side with the bloodstains, and we push and shove it into the back of the van. Like it's something and nothing.

I turn and glance round, and I notice Emily wiping the inside of her living-room window with a cloth. I make a gesture indicating the mattress sagged really badly in the middle – what else can I do? – but she does not respond. I'm not sure if she's blanking me because I didn't offer her a lift earlier or if she's just concentrating and hasn't really spotted us.

Matt is walking by, heading back inside. I follow him and wash my hands in the kitchen sink as he goes to the bathroom. We come back onto the landing at the same time. He's put his toolbox at the top of the stairs, ready to go.

We stand at what is now the door of our old bedroom. The base of the bed and the underlay on the floor both seem to be unmarked, although the underlay is very dusty. I will clean both thoroughly in the morning once he's left for work.

"Okay?" he says, and I nod to confirm it is. "Good." He adds, "That's that, then."

I guess it is for now. We can sort out decorating the room and replacing everything at a later date.

We sit and watch the rest of the new US television series, two episodes back to back, and we seem to relax a little, Matt especially, but we don't nod off as we sometimes do. Neither of us are that relaxed. I doubt we will be for some time. If ever.

Close to midnight, we go to bed, both of us instinctively turning away from each other to sleep. I could not bear to have him touch me. I think he senses that. But somehow, we have to put all of this behind us and try to live a normal life again. I don't know how on earth we can possibly do that. But we have to try. What else can we do?

CHAPTER SIXTEEN

FRIDAY, 27 SEPTEMBER, START OF THE DAY

Neither of us set an alarm on our phones for this morning – the first day of "being normal" – and we both overslept, me waking first at just gone seven thirty. Left alone, Matt would sleep on forever.

I nudge him awake before I head for the shower. "Your turn to do breakfast for once!" I shout as he comes to, all bleary eyed.

As he focuses on me standing there at the end of the bed, I say it again: "Make breakfast!" He sits up as I leave the room, calling, "I'm showering first," over my shoulder.

By the time I shower and get changed into my work clothes, Matt's already at the kitchen table, tucking into bacon and eggs. He'll shower and change after. It's his favourite breakfast, but I can't be bothered to do it first thing. I'll eat it though, trying to be normal.

I sit down opposite him, splurting tomato ketchup from a squeezy bottle onto the whites of my fried eggs. I like the yolks but need a bit of ketchup to eat the whites.

Matt seems cheerful enough but is all hurry, hurry,

hurry. He eats his cut-up pieces of bacon and eggs with a fork in his left hand, flicking through his phone with the right.

"I've got to get going," he says, shovelling the last piece of bacon and egg into his mouth together and swallowing them down with a mouthful of water from his glass. "Accident on the bridge."

The bridge – Orwell Bridge – between here and Ipswich is the main route in and out of Felixstowe. Whenever there is an accident, typically every week or two, the bridge is blocked and so are the roads for miles around. It's hell for motorists, especially with the lorries coming and going to and from the Port of Felixstowe.

"Have you got a route out?" I ask as he gets to his feet. He shows me Google Maps on his phone, and the quickest route is still over the bridge – it's showing as fifty-five minutes to get to the other side when it's usually less than twenty. I shake my head sympathetically as I stand up. He does not go to hug or kiss me as he normally would. He knows better than that after what he did with Lucy.

"You okay?" he says, gazing with his big blue eyes into mine. I nod, yes, I'm alright. We stand like that for a moment or two. "Really got to go," he adds, moving out of the kitchen.

I sit and finish my bacon and eggs, listening to him going from the bathroom to the bedroom to the bathroom for a brief wash and back to the kitchen to pick up his work bag. Then, one fleeting kiss on the back of my head, and he is gone, clattering down the staircase and out through our door to the main door. He creaks it shut.

I get up and walk into the living room at the front of the house. It occurs to me that everything we are doing now is just as it was before. Before Lucy. In a way. I hope it can get better. A doubt taps away at the back of my mind. The suspicion that I have overlooked something obvious that will lead to our downfall.

I stand by the window, watching Matt put his things in the back of the van. He turns to look up at me but is distracted by the postman he's friends with walking by on the other side of the road. He goes up that side and then comes back on this side, delivering the mail.

They know each other from football and banter, shouting across, laughing at what the other says. Matt waves goodbye to me. I wave back. The postman sees me and waves cheerily; then he carries on his way.

I turn to get ready to leave for work. I'm not going to wait for the post; nothing much comes in it these days, just bills and junk mail that goes straight into the kitchen bin.

Today, I'm going to try very hard to have an ordinary day, without my mind tormenting me and making me fear that everything is going to fall apart for us. It won't, not now. At least, it shouldn't, at least I hope not.

And the day, funnily enough, turns out to be just as dull and as mundane as ever, and I am, for once, so thankful for it. I sort out form after form in the morning, have my lunch in the sunshine, and do more forms all afternoon. Boring, boring, boring.

By the time I leave work for home, Matt and I are texting again about mundane matters. They are not warm and silly messages as they used to be, but we are at least communicating. I think, as I drive back, everything might, just might, turn out to be okay.

THERE IS a handful of post stacked neatly by our inner door. I go through the envelopes as I head back upstairs. Six in all. One is for "The Occupier", trying to sell double glazing from the look of it. Another is addressed to Matt and me from a local estate agent, probably asking if we want to sell our property. Not now, we're in negative equity.

As I go into the kitchen, I drop those two letters into the bin, unopened. Three of the remaining letters are for Matt. All look work-related. One, based on the stamped logo on the front, is from a supplier who always invoices by post like it's still 1955. The other two are from the tax people, most probably VAT and PAYE.

I sit down at the table and study the remaining letter. It is a brown, square-shaped envelope with a white piece of paper on the front, sellotaped on. *Matt and Sophie* is at the top of the paper, followed by our address. There is a first-class stamp stuck to the top right of the envelope, stamped *Ipswich*, which means it's been posted locally. Felixstowe, most likely. I think it all goes to Ipswich first and then back again.

I turn the letter over, to see if there is an address on the back – to show where it's been sent from. But there is nothing. It's a cheap, rough and ready brown envelope, probably one of a pack bought in Poundland in the town.

The white piece of paper is odd. Someone has gone to the trouble of printing on it. Then cutting round the edges to fit the envelope. The sides are torn and jagged with snip, snip, snips of nail scissors. I'd say it was maybe an offer or something from a local garden centre. Put together by Farmer Giles.

Matt and Sophie looks plain weird. Like a friend has written. But no one of our age uses the post these days except maybe for sending birthday or Christmas cards to elderly relatives. I don't even do that much. I mostly send messages with funny GIFs. A troubling thought sits at the back of my mind. I can't think what it is. But it's getting bigger and scarier, and it's rushing towards me.

I open the envelope and take out a white sheet of paper, similar to the paper on the front of the envelope. This is an A5-sized piece, torn in half from an A4 sheet and then folded over. The words have been typed on a computer and then printed off. I find myself breathing heavily as I read what has been written.

Dear Matt and Sophie

I know what you done last night. You killed her.
I WANT PAYING.
£500 CASH.
OR ELSE I TELL THE POLICE WHAT YOU DONE.
Put the money under the blue bin behind the library midnight Saturday.
DON'T FUCK ME OFF.

I sit back, stunned, at what is in front of me. Someone saw Matt taking Lucy's body to his van the other night. Maybe watched as he threw in those bin bags yesterday morning. The man downstairs? Emily next door? Someone over the road? It's certainly a neighbour, it has to be, watching in darkness from behind drawn curtains.

I study the letter again, the poor grammar and the use of capitals to emphasise key points. Is it written by someone unintelligent and uneducated, Emily maybe? Or someone smart, like the man downstairs, who is pretending not to be? Hard to tell.

The demand for £500 in cash hidden under a bin at the library at midnight tomorrow suggests to me that it is Emily. It's so ... I can't find the right words. Stupid, I suppose. Like something out of a cheesy black-and-white movie. A laughable demand. And yet it isn't. Not really. If I don't do something, they – whoever it is – will go to the police. Even a stupid person can send an anonymous letter with a photo attached. And that's it. The game is up. I feel my anger rising. I'm furious. And frightened. I'm feeling helpless, too. But, I tell myself, I won't let myself be a scared little nobody.

I'M up off the kitchen chair and down the stairs without thinking, pushing the letter back into the envelope so it looks like it hasn't been opened. I don't know why. I'm running on angry emotions.

I'm knocking – several times, louder than I should – on the door of the man downstairs. I stand there seething, furious that someone would try to blackmail us. It might be £500 this week. The same the next. It will be never-ending until we can no longer even pretend to afford it. Then they'll call the police anyway.

I wait, a feeling of fear and sickness rising up. It hits me hard. What if he did send the letter and I confront him with it, what then? I could be in danger. In my fury, I've brought nothing with me to defend myself.

He opens the door, this grey-haired, beady-eyed man in a white shirt, brown cardigan and grey trousers. He looks small and inoffensive. Like an old-time bank clerk with ledgers under his arm and a row of pens and pencils poking out of his top pocket.

Whenever we've spoken, he's always looked at my lips like he wants to kiss me. It's so gross. Now though, he glances down as I swiftly move my arm holding the letter behind my back. I do it fast. It makes me look guilty of something. He sees the gesture, and I feel like a naughty schoolgirl in front of the headteacher.

I look at him, knowing he has spotted the letter and, if he wrote it, that he may react badly. He might shut the door in my face, hurrying back into the gloom of his apartment to call the police. Or he could drag me in, slamming the door behind me. And then what?

"Yes?" he says, politely enough, in his well-mannered voice. I can't place where he's from, there's an accent and it's more north than south, I think. There's a touch of grit in it. He's looking at my lips again. It's disgusting.

"Is that my post? Did you get it by mistake?" he asks as I hesitate, thinking of the words to say, regretting my haste coming here. My stupidity, really. If he is the letter writer. More than that. Madness. I've put myself in terrible danger.

"There," he says, pointing to my hand behind my back as I stand here struggling to respond. It comes out as, "Come on, come on, I'm busy." I show him the letter, holding on tight to it, feeling deflated. More than that. I am frightened.

He stares at it, reads the front – *Matt and Sophie* – and then gestures for me to turn it over to look at the back. I do so reluctantly, and he can see it's been opened. I watch his face, wishing that I had something in my pocket, that paperweight or our fancy paper knife, for self-defence.

I expect him to look back at me, realising I know he wrote it and I have caught him out. And his face will change, harden, making his decision what to do. I take a step back, thinking how I will react.

But he simply seems nonplussed, not sure what to say or do. He shakes his head, the slightest of gestures, blows air through his lips as if to say: "Really? What is this nonsense?" He then says, "It's for you ... and it's been opened." He goes to shut the door.

"Sorry, sorry," I say, feeling so foolish. "I ... I thought." He looks me up and down, from behind the half-closed door.

"I don't understand. Did you bring me the wrong letter by mistake?" He looks at me in a matter-of-fact manner.

"No. I ... sorry ... I'm not sure what I was ..." I was about to say "thinking," but he gives me a look like he's talking to a madwoman and shuts the door in my face. I curse myself and my temper and hurry back upstairs.

MATT, when he arrives home half an hour later, is clearly determined again to act normal, to be as we always were, and to not mention anything about Lucy. Even so, his face looks sick with worry. He's not fooling me. I'm twitching too, of course.

As he comes in, I ask him how his day was. He answers blandly and then repeats the question back at me. I just reply, "Okay," and he turns and heads for the bathroom.

By the time he's out, I've two plates of sausages, beans and chips on the table, two lots of buttered bread on side plates and a bottle of Coke and two glasses good to go. He likes his comfort food. I'm trying to stay calm.

We sit and eat and drink in something close to silence, the sounds of us chewing and swallowing seeming so loud.

I cannot think of anything ordinary to say. I am going to try to leave the letter until we've finished our meal. It's in a pocket of my jeans. I'll take it out, unfold it and push it across the table to him. Then watch his face and hope he offers a solution. God knows what that might be.

Matt clears his throat once, twice, several times, and I think he's going to start talking. He glances at me, then looks away.

And so, we keep on eating and drinking. The longer the silence, the harder it is to break.

I could tell him about my day at work. Processing forms. He could talk about what he's done today. Unblocking pipes. We've done it a thousand times and more before.

So we don't. On we go, cutting sausages, scooping up beans, dabbing chips in ketchup. I swallow mouthfuls down with water, feeling increasingly tense.

Then he speaks, his voice sounding almost strangulated even though he's trying to talk normally, to chat. "They've ... um ... they're building a new service area ... um ... on the way to Bury." He stops, swallows with difficulty, and takes a gulp of water.

"That's good," I respond, continuing the inane conversation. I clear my throat, with a cough. "Will you stop for something on the way there or back?"

He smiles, although it comes out as more of a grimace. "Well, it will probably be two or three years. I doubt I'll be going there then."

It hangs in the air, a mutual thought: "I'll be in prison by then." I wonder if I will be too.

He looks at me encouragingly, seeming to know what I'm thinking, like he can hear my thoughts. I expect he's going to say, "We'll sink or swim together." But he doesn't. He pulls a rueful face and continues eating. I cannot hold back. I want to scream to the skies.

I reach into my jeans, take out the letter and pass it to him. I can't wait any longer.

"We need to sort this," I say simply. "It's urgent."

He looks alarmed and then drops his head down, knife and fork by the side of the plate, the letter close to his face as he reads.

He's so still. Like he isn't even breathing. He sits lifelessly. The letter shakes slightly in his hand.

Eventually, his head still down so I cannot see his face, he passes it back to me. I hesitate but take it and watch as he brings his head up. He looks stunned and terrified in equal measure. Somehow sick as well.

He speaks, at last, almost groaning. "We should have given ourselves up straight away ... we might have had a chance ... if we had come up with a story ... or even told the truth." He takes a long, shuddering breath. "It's too late now."

"What should we do?" I ask him, in as calm and as measured a voice as I can. "What can we do?"

He thinks, and I wait as patiently as I can for his reply. I clasp my hands together tightly.

He shrugs, raising his hands, palms upward, to say, "Who knows?" But he says, in a despairing, questioning voice, "Pay up?"

I nod and reply, in a reluctant voice, "We could ... but they'd want more ... and more ... it would be never-ending."

"Don't pay up, then," he retorts, then adds, "And they'll tell the police, and we'll end up with life sentences. What else can we do?"

We look at each other properly, and we both know the

only reply to that question. "Who do you think it is?" I ask. "The man downstairs? Emily? Who else can it be?"

He looks at the paper, turning it over as if the answer is written on the back. "It's not them. They both know ... knew ... Lucy's name. They'd have put *You killed Lucy*. There wasn't anyone in the road. So it has to be someone on the other side, looking out. I don't know anyone over there. I guess they must know us." I nod; me neither, at least not to talk to. I see familiar people coming in and out. And we've had wrongly delivered post with our names on the front pushed through the letterbox late at night once or twice.

He goes on. "And it's someone young ... and stupid. I mean, £500! Someone older would have just gone to the police ... they wouldn't get involved for that sort of money. It's so ridiculous."

He picks up his plate, the meal only half eaten, then reaches across for mine. I pass it to him. As he stands up, he says, "I've got this quiz with the lads later ... can't not do it ... I'll get some cash out then and the rest in the morning."

I nod in agreement.

"I'll get to the library early tomorrow, before midnight. Put the money under the bin and then hide nearby. When they turn up for it – surely to God they must realise I'll be there ... they must be a teenager or something – I'll confront them, see what they know, and see if I can bluff it."

He breathes heavily. "I'll only, you know ... if I have to ... if I have no choice. It won't come to that, I'm sure. What did they really see? It was dark. Half lit. She was well covered. I was just dumping a roll of carpet. It'll be fine, I'll sort it." With that, he nods with certainty. I do too, although I'm not so sure. Not at all.

CHAPTER SEVENTEEN

FRIDAY, 27 SEPTEMBER, MID-EVENING

We've been trying so hard to be normal, or at least to act normally. But of course it's completely impossible after what we've done.

Nothing can begin to heal until we've dealt with the blackmailer.

I don't know how that can be resolved without doing what we did with Lucy. I can't bear to think about it.

Matt has gone to his quiz. He hesitated before he left, asking if I'd be okay on my own, like I was a young teenager being left without a babysitter for the first time. I told him to go.

I'm sitting on the window ledge of the living room. I'm flicking through a book, a pamphlet really, by a local author about walks from Felixstowe all the way up the coast. I'm looking for new places for when I start running again. I must do that soon. Running's part of my normal, everyday life.

It's hard to focus, to keep my mind on the pamphlet, with all these thoughts in my mind. I seem to spend more time looking out to the road than I do reading.

There, it's gone again.

A sudden flash of light.

Into my face.

I noticed it thirty seconds or so ago. I thought it was a reflection from the beams of a car's headlights, with two cars passing by each other, one driver flashing and pulling over, the other flashing back and driving through.

But that did not feel right. The brightness and angle of the possible reflection. And it reminded me of something. I'm not sure what. I've been sitting here, still and quiet, in the same position. If it had been a car's lights, it wouldn't happen again.

But it just has. And I realise what it reminds me of. Lucy and I running around as teenagers, flashing a torch at bedroom windows on the housing estate where we used to live. Flashing the torchlight again when someone came to the window. Then running off.

Someone nearby, opposite me, has a torch. Aimed this way.

More than that, though. It's something closer to a laser beam.

And they are trying to shine it into my eyes.

I turn my head, so many ideas racing through my mind. It may be teenage boys most likely, up to mischief. I just happen to be sitting opposite, my eyes a target. It's a nasty bit of fun for them.

But I've lived here for years now. As has everyone in those houses on the other side of the road. I've often sat here at night when Matt's out, curled up like a cat, reading a book or scrolling through my phone. It's comfortable.

And that's why I wonder if it might be the blackmailer, taunting me, knowing I cannot respond. That I can't go over and threaten them, that I have to stay here, putting up with this.

I move slightly to the side and wait for the next flash of light.

It comes, another thirty to forty seconds on.

And I see the window that it's coming from. Opposite-ish to the left.

I get down from the window ledge, pulling the curtains to, then standing there, thinking. They – whoever it is opposite, blackmailing us – thinks they are oh so clever. That they can do anything. Mock me. Laugh at me. Have fun at my expense.

They are wrong. I will not hide away like a frightened little rabbit. I will not be cowed. I will stand tall and strong and give as good as I get.

I know who lives in that house. Two gay men in their mid-thirties. I see them from time to time. I used to say hello in passing. But I stopped. They always blanked me.

They won't now, that's for sure.

I pick up the letter. Grab that paper knife from the sideboard.

I'm down the stairs and out through the front door.

I'M ACROSS THE ROAD, to the pavement on the other side, and on to the gate of their terraced house within seconds. Then I stop, taking deep breaths, calming myself, realising once more that this is madness.

What would I do when they opened the front door, standing there with a knife in my hand? It would end badly.

I turn and go back across the road, indoors and upstairs

and back to the living-room window, looking out, waiting again.

There is no one there now, flashing a light at me. I stand, thinking what to do. I'm still angry. Then their front door swings open. They are both standing there, and I think for a moment they are coming across for me.

But they are not. They embrace, and one of them – it's difficult to tell them apart, they are both tall and slender and dark-haired – sets off for a jog. The other one waves him off.

I've no time to change into my running gear. He'll be gone and out of sight. But I am wearing a black tee-shirt and leggings – a jogging outfit at a glance – and my running shoes are at the top of the stairs.

I'm out and after the man over the road. I can see him running away. He's a jogger. I'm a runner. I can catch him easily. Whenever and wherever I want.

I suspect he's heading for the Grove, where there's a car park, football pitches and woods. Deep, dark woods. I've seen him there before a few times. He ignored me.

Not this time. I'll confront him about his beam of light. And if he's been writing letters. I have the letter. And the knife. Not that I intend to use it. Unless I have to.

I see the man over the road turn at the top of Ranelagh Road, on to Hamilton Road, our high street.

By the time I get to it, he has turned right towards the roundabout that leads to the medical centre and on to the woods. I'm closer to him now, though.

Then closer still as he goes by the medical centre and disappears on the path into the woods. I am almost upon him.

I follow him along the path lit only by shafts of moonlight through the trees. He is ahead of me, concentrating on putting one foot in front of the other.

I hold back, running in step with him, wanting the only sounds he hears to be his own laboured breath and the thump-thump of his trainers hitting the ground.

When he stops, leans against a tree, draws in breaths, I will be upon him, standing there, confronting him face-to-face. Two or three minutes on, that's what he does.

He dips his head down, his hands on his knees. As he brings his head up, he sees me standing in front of him, and he reels back gasping, literally gasping, in horror.

"What's your game, then, what's your game?" I was too busy following him to prepare the right words to say. "Why do you keep flashing that beam in my face?" would have been better.

And I should have spoken in a calmer, more mannered tone. I sound angry and breathless, spoiling for a fight. He thinks so too, judging by the terrified look on his face.

"You're ... across the road ... you live upstairs from Martin," he states, his breath jagged, his words stop-start. "What are you doing?"

"You ... sat there flashing your torch in my face ... what was all that about?" I say the words less angrily now, more hesitantly as I get the sense I've made a mistake.

"We flash Morse code messages to each other ... us and Martin ... some nights ... just being silly ... we're all in the ..." He stops, anger rising in him now. "They weren't to you! Christ."

I realise I have made myself look so foolish. My emotions getting the better of me, yet again. I put my hands up in a placatory gesture, starting to back away. "Sorry, sorry."

His courage rises as I turn, and he shouts after me,

"What the hell do you think you're doing anyway? Running after me? Pouncing like that? You're mad. Fucking mad." I turn and leave, apologising profusely again and again.

As I run back home, blinking away tears of frustration and anger, I begin to think that I am. Mad. Lucy. All that's going on around me. The blackmailer. I'm tipping over the edge, and I wonder what will come next. I hope my apologies are enough to placate the man I've just confronted; I imagine he'll tell the man downstairs – Martin – but hopefully not the police. I'm struggling to catch my breath, my whole body coursing with the fear that that's exactly what he will do.

CHAPTER EIGHTEEN

SATURDAY, 28 SEPTEMBER, THE MIDNIGHT HOUR

Matt returns home not long after midnight, Friday night into Saturday morning. In just under twenty-four hours, our fate will be decided. He is exhausted and edgy. He says he has some cash and will get the rest in the morning. He does not mention the pub quiz. They usually come "about halfway", which really means "second from bottom, just above an old man and his dog". Not that it matters anymore.

It's another sleepless night, with even Matt turning restlessly, dragging the duvet on and off. He falls asleep close to two a.m., but continues rolling, muttering angrily to himself. He is in torment. It's not like him.

I go and lie down on the sofa in the living room and grab a few hours' sleep before Matt wakes me, moving about at seven o'clock. After a quick breakfast, he hugs me, and I let him before he leaves for a day's overtime. We need the cash, although in truth it doesn't seem to matter so much right now. "It'll all be over soon." His final words. I doubt it.

I text my line manager that I'm going to do some extra hours from home today to catch up on my workload. A message pings straight back from Priti: *OK, well done, thanks!*

I'll do some work. But what I want – really have – to do is to sit by the living-room window all day, watching the other side of the road. If I wait long enough, someone over there will give themselves away. A twitching curtain, a glance up and across as they leave their house.

I will then know who is blackmailing us. And I will go across and speak to them. I know I'm not a warm and persuasive person, but I will do my best, and it is far better than Matt would do later tonight. Their life – and ours – depend on it.

There are comings and goings between nine and ten o'clock. The gay men who see but studiously ignore me. A white-haired old lady, some way along to my left, shuffles out along her path, pushing a trolley towards the town. I doubt Miss Marple's our blackmailer.

Next, a teenage boy of maybe eighteen, in white tee-shirt and jeans, comes out of the house almost opposite. He shrugs a rucksack on his back and wanders away, without looking across.

A little later, a couple of about our age comes out of their house down to our right, and they move to their car. She looks up and around at the sky to see if it might rain, perhaps. I lean back so I cannot be seen. It's a sunny day, no sign of rain. It might be them.

By lunchtime, with no other movement from the houses over the road, I go to the kitchen and get a cloth and a spray from under the sink. I then walk downstairs, out through our door and the front door, and to the pavement, where I stand by my car. I clean the windscreens, front and back, and the windows.

Really, I am looking at the houses over the road. My car is parked roughly where Matt's van was the other night. I want to work out who could possibly have seen what Matt was doing.

Allowing for lampposts and trees and scaffolding on two houses further along, I believe there are five – just five – houses that could possibly have offered a clear view of Matt at his van.

To the far left is the old lady's. I watched her come back an hour or so after she left. She walked slowly up the path, painfully so. She never turned towards me. It's not her, I'm sure. Next door to her is where the gay men live, and I don't believe it's them either.

In the middle, the teenage boy lives with his forty-something parents. His father is a short, nondescript man who always seems to wear the same grey suit. I think he works in an office at the docks. I've seen him there at times. We both pretend to not know the other. I don't see much of his wife, who is thin and busy, busy, busy in her manner. Whenever I have seen her, she's been going out early and coming back late. Maybe she works in Ipswich or Bury St Edmunds or even London. Anyway, it could be the father or the son, perhaps.

Both of the last two houses on the right – ones that could have seen Matt the other night – have For Sale boards outside. One is vacant; the old man there died, I think. I haven't seen him for months. The other is occupied by two men, one older, the other younger. I think they are father and son. I see them on odd occasions. We do not speak or even smile or wave. It could be them.

The afternoon passes slowly as I do a little work on my laptop, but still keep watch from the window ledge. Matt texts a couple of times. *It'll be okay!* and *Don't worry, we'll be safe!* I send back smiley-face emojis but really wish he'd stop. What if the police were to look at our phones? I delete the messages.

There are people coming up and down the street all afternoon. It's quite busy. But they are going to and from the town. No one notices me other than a group of three boys, one of whom spots me and shouts up coarse words, gesturing for me to lift my top. I turn away, going to the kitchen to get a glass of water.

By late afternoon, I have had enough. I thought it might be the couple who looked up as they left the house, but I'm not convinced – they'd not have been able to see Matt clearly. I can't imagine it's the old lady. That leaves the parents of the teenage boy, probably the father, or the teen himself.

I give up. What a waste of time. I feel tense and angry with myself for expecting to resolve it like this. I go to move off the window ledge, to put some sort of salad together for our tea for when Matt arrives home. I think we have some lettuce and a few tomatoes at the bottom of the fridge; a few slices of chicken at the back. That will have to do.

As I move, two things happen at once. Matt arrives in his little white van, earlier than usual. There's no space in front of our house, so he pulls up outside where the teenager and his parents live. I doubt the father will be happy about that. We generally all try to keep to our own places when we can. He'll now have to park round the corner.

As Matt parks, the teenager appears, on his way back from wherever, maybe the cinema in Ipswich. Matt doesn't see him as he gets out of the van, looks up and smiles, waving cheerily at me. The teenager looks at Matt, then across and up at me. For a moment, no more than a second or two, we look into each other's eyes. Then he has turned and gone.

I can't tell whether the teenager just noticed Matt and looked over to see who he was waving at. That's possible, likely even. But he held my gaze for a fraction longer than he needed to. And I wonder if he is the blackmailer. Maybe, just maybe.

Before I can do anything, Matt is in the house and bounding up the stairs, like an excited puppy. For me, the evening and what lies ahead fills me with dread. I don't see how it can end in any way other than it did with Lucy. Unless I can get to the teenager first.

"Here," he says, "for you." He pulls a bunch of carnations, bought I suspect at half price from a petrol station on the way home, from behind his back. It's so inappropriate at this time. Like cut-price, wilting flowers will cheer me up, fixing anything. He goes on, "And I've got the rest of the cash out, so we're good to go." He kisses me on the cheek, and I let him, before he turns for the bathroom.

I must hurry. I cross to the living-room window, working out what I am going to say when I go over to speak to the teenager. To try to somehow resolve matters without bloodshed. What can I possibly say?

I turn to shout at Matt, "I'm nipping out. I won't be long!" but the words stick in my throat. The teenager's father has just returned, parking along the road and walking to his house. As he gets to his path, he looks towards me, then stands there staring.

I'm uncertain if he's thinking, "WTF are you doing, sitting there watching everyone all day?" or if it's something more sinister. That he's challenging me with his gaze. I step down and away, not looking back. I'm not going to go across.

Not now. It will probably go badly, like the encounter in the woods last night. I am badly spooked.

MATT IS RELENTLESSLY, infuriatingly upbeat all through the evening as we await our fate. He chatters away, makes silly comments and even pulls funny faces, all in a desperate attempt to pretend everything is normal. That he did not have sex with Lucy. And that he's not, in all probability, about to kill someone later tonight.

I try to smile and respond to his comments, but I am distracted at best. Is it the teenager blackmailing us? Or the father? Perhaps both of them. I don't know what to do. How could I ever have thought of strolling across and starting a conversation? "Excuse me ...?"

By the time we've eaten our salads, loaded the dishwasher and completed a few household chores, we are sitting next to each other on the sofa in the living room. Neither of us put on the television as we usually do. We sit here in an almost unbearable silence for what seems an age. At last, I decide to speak.

"So what exactly ... are you going to do?" My voice croaks and cracks in the middle of the sentence.

He sighs and then shakes his head. He doesn't want to talk, no doubt, after so many run-throughs in his head all day. But I need to know.

Eventually, he takes me through it step by step. "I've £500 in cash, twenties mostly." Like that matters. He thinks, then adds, "It won't be the last of it, will it?"

I shake my head.

We sit there, side by side, locked in our own thoughts.

I think we both know that our savings, such as they are, will be gone within a couple of months if we have to keep on paying.

And, of course, we will. At some stage, sooner rather than later, we'd have to say no, and then what will happen? Matt talks again.

"I'll leave at eleven. Get there before him. It's definitely a him." I don't comment as he continues, "Just in case he arrives early to watch for me."

I nod, that's a good idea.

"Once I've put the money in an envelope under the bin, I'll tuck myself out of sight somewhere and keep a lookout ... even if it takes all night."

I nod again.

"When he comes to get the money, I'll step out and talk to him and see if he really saw ... Lucy ... or he's just bluffing." Dear God, this is Matt, the skilled negotiator.

I have to reply. "But ... if he's bluffing ... why are you even there?" He looks unsure. "You'd just ignore the letter or go to the police." I'd laugh if it weren't so desperate. "The fact you're there means you did it!"

Matt is not an angry or violent man, but as I turn to look at him, I can see strong emotions in his face. I expect him to shout at me for the first time in as long as I can really remember, but he swallows and, after a moment or two, replies quietly.

"I have to speak to him, don't I ... kind of get a sense of things. I mean ... I have to try ..." His voice tails off. I think of suggesting I will go instead, but Matt, who likes to think of himself as a gentleman at heart, would insist he should do it. Besides, if it came to it, the teenager would probably be stronger than me.

Again, we sit there for a while, lost in our own troubled thoughts. I think, hand on heart, we are both coming to the same horrific conclusion.

Matt reaches out, and we hold hands. He keeps squeezing mine to reassure me. To be honest, it doesn't. And it hurts. He's stronger than he thinks.

I rest my head on his shoulder, and we sort of snuggle ourselves into what should be a comfortable position. Matt is stiff and tense. I don't seem to be able to breathe evenly.

"I'll do everything I can not to have to … you know." He sits up, pulling in on himself, like he's been wounded. "I mean, how … what can I do, though?"

I think hard, looking for a solution. There is none that I can see. "Shall we give ourselves up?" I ask in as calm a voice as I can.

He takes his time to reply. "Maybe, when it happened … it would have been best. We might have … I don't know. Walked free. But … what's been done since … we'd go to prison for years."

The clock on the wall turns slowly towards eleven o'clock. We lie back, our eyes shut, thinking what to say and do. In truth, there is nothing, and we both know it.

Then Matt is getting up. Before he goes to get his jacket and his wallet, he says, in a voice breaking with emotion, "I'll wait for him to say what he saw … then tell him he's wrong … Lucy's gone back home. And I'll go to the police if he doesn't stop." He lunges at me, hugging me tight.

I hug him back as hard as I can, like this is the last time I will ever see him. It won't work, of course. His plan. Matt is not the sharpest knife in the drawer. He'll bungle it, and it will come down to who is the stronger, him or the teenager. If that's who it is, of course. I think it has to be.

It's not just the act itself, the absolute horror of it. It's worse than with Lucy, really. This is premeditated. With Lucy, it was just a terrible, instinctive act. It could be called manslaughter. Maybe? I just don't know. But this is planned. It's definitely murder. There is so much else that can go wrong too, of course. CCTV around the library. Passers-by. I watch Matt go, and suddenly I can't stop crying. I think this is the end of us.

I CHECK the clock on my bedside cabinet. The red numbers show it is 2.37 a.m. Matt has been gone for close to four hours now. I watch as the numbers move to 2.38 and then 2.39 and 2.40.

The longer he's been gone, the sicker I feel. I'm full of fear that everything is falling apart. The thought that Matt has uncovered the blackmailer, killed them and is now burying their body makes me want to gag.

Even worse, I wonder if the blackmailer has fought back, pinned Matt down and called the police. Or maybe Matt was seen committing the murder and has already been arrested. I lie here waiting for the police to start banging on the front door.

I'm so restless that I get up and walk into the living room, crossing to the window, pulling back the curtains, looking out into the moonlit road. It's meant to still my mind. It doesn't.

I see something scurrying along the pavement over the road, under the white-haired old lady's gate and up the path and out of sight. A cat, I hope. Even so, I'm spooked by it. I've always hated rats. Big, fat rats.

What the hell are we doing, killing like this? Where will it stop?

I look to my left as I see the lights of a car, moving so slowly, maybe checking the numbers of the houses. It is a police car. They are coming for me. A minute or two, no more.

I wait, unmoving, to be certain. The police officers won't be able to see me behind the curtains. They will if I make a sudden movement or the curtains twitch.

If – when – the car stops outside my home, I will take my chance, grabbing my running shoes from the landing, my debit cards from my bag in the kitchen, then down the outside staircase, somehow clambering over hedges and fences, running away. To where? I've no idea.

The car slows, stops, just below the living-room window. The moment is now. When I go on the run, to wherever, until my cards are blocked. Then what? Homeless and on the streets?

The car rolls on by, accelerates, moves to the end of the road. It's just a random patrol. I feel myself drenched in sweat, my mouth dry, about to be physically sick. I feel vomit rising.

I make it to the bathroom, gagging and drooling into the sink. I put my head under the tap, drinking in cold water and splashing my face until finally, I return to bed, exhausted.

I'm still lying here, watching the numbers click to 3.59, 4.00 and 4.01, and I'm close to despair. My mind is always so negative in the early hours. It crosses my thoughts that Matt has upped and left me.

My mind plays with this idea for five, six, seven minutes, until I hear the key in the main door, our inner door then creaking open and footsteps coming up the stairs two at a time.

The bedroom door swings open, and Matt is standing there. I sit up on my elbows as he speaks, rushing his words: "It's done ... sorted ... we won't hear from him again ..." I go to respond, asking a question, "Who?" and, "What did you do?" but he's already turning, going out of the room, adding, "I don't want to talk about it."

I lie here, trying to take it all in. I hear Matt in the bathroom, crying. Then showering. On and on. More crying – sobbing, really – as he dries himself, then goes along the landing to dump his clothes by the washing machine in the kitchen. He is there for so long I wonder what is happening. I imagine him on his knees, distressed. I don't know what to do.

Finally, he comes quietly into the bedroom, pulling pyjamas from a chest of drawers, dressing, and climbing into bed next to me. I cannot bear it and pretend to be asleep. He sighs and sobs to himself, breathing heavily, and as we lie there long into the night, he whispers the Lord's Prayer time and again. Somehow, I don't think that will help us now. We're doomed. I know it.

PART 4

UNDER SIEGE

CHAPTER NINETEEN

SUNDAY, 29 SEPTEMBER, A NEW DAY

After a sleepless night, both of us twisting and turning silently in endless torment, I awake to find Matt is not in the bed. I wonder when he got up and where he's gone.

I check the clock on the bedside cabinet and see it's coming up to seven thirty. It's a Sunday morning, and we usually lie in, often making love. But not since Lucy. And not today. Perhaps never again. Now that I'm listening, I can hear Matt moving about the kitchen. I get up, have a shower, clean my teeth, dab on make-up, and change into fresh clothes. Weekday habits, really. I make a decision to run today. Time to myself, really – to think.

I sit down at the kitchen table as Matt brings across a tray – two mugs of tea and two plates of toast and marmalade. "Sorry," he mutters. "I couldn't face … you know … meat."

I flinch.

I notice he's already dressed and good to go to work. I think he's been crying. He mutters something about being asked to go in today for a few hours to do something or other, "when it's quiet". I nod in agreement.

"We've got to carry on as we were," I state simply. What else is there to say – or do?

He nods, sits still for a moment, then leans forward, head down, sobbing his heart out.

"We have to be really strong for each other," I add, trying to disguise the tremor in my voice. I reach out my hands and put them on his shoulders. "Come on, you're meant to be strong ... for me." A long wait.

He sits back up reluctantly, wipes his face with his hands and mumbles, "I know, I know, it's just that ..."

"You did what you had to do." I try to comfort him. "You wouldn't have if you'd had any other choice." I'm not sure what else to say.

"It's just ... it's just ..." His voice comes to a shuddering halt.

"Do you want to talk about it ... what happened?" I don't want him to. I don't want to know any of it. But it's better that he confides in me than a chippy at work or Baz at football. Either of them will go to the police, they'll have to. And I know Matt's stupid enough to do that.

"He ... the boy over the road, Riley Thomas, I spoke to him once ages ago ... said he saw me with ... a body. I told him he was mistaken. He said he'd go to the police then. He pulled a knife on me. There was a struggle. I ... I killed him ... I had to ... it was ... life or death. I ... I ... it was him or me. Honestly. And ..." He stops speaking and draws in the longest, shuddering breath.

We look at each other in desperation, and I am thinking what to say to calm him down and get us back to something like normality, when there is a sudden buzzing noise from the landing. Someone is pressing our doorbell at the main door, and it's buzzing up here.

"It will just be an Amazon driver leaving something or other," I say. "They sometimes buzz to indicate they've left a package on the doorstep. It's usually for him downstairs."

Matt hesitates, waiting for the driver to go away. The buzzer goes again. Buzz. Buzz. Buzz. Buzz. Four times.

We look at each other. He looks as sick as I feel. I don't think it is an Amazon driver. It's someone else. And they want to speak to us as a matter of urgency. It will be to do with Lucy or, maybe, the teenage boy, I'm sure of it. God help us.

WE SIT HERE, the world forcing its way into our life when we are at our most vulnerable.

Buzz.

I have not thought much about Lucy this past day or so. My mind has all been on the letter and the blackmailing teenager. I think it's been the same for Matt.

Buzz.

I can't believe this will be about the teenage boy. His parents would only just have noticed he was not in his bed. They'd assume he had stayed round a friend's, surely? Teenagers do that all the time at weekends. It will be a while before they worry. There's no reason they'd be buzz-buzz-buzzing on our door. Why us?

Buzz.

"Leave it," Matt says. He tenses, holding his breath.

I nod, and we both sit here, waiting to hear the delivery van starting up in the road and being driven away.

"They've gone. Whoever they are," Matt concludes,

standing up. I look at him, not sure what to do. The buzzing, again and again, worries me.

Bang.

For Christ's sake, they're now banging on the glass panel of the main door. "Ignore it." Matt sounds irritated. "They'll give up eventually."

Bang. Bang. Bang.

It doesn't bloody sound like it. That they'll leave. They sound determined to speak to us. Whoever "they" are.

Bang.

I hear the man downstairs opening his door. Annoyed, obviously. Then the main door. There is a conversation. Raised voices, although I can't make out the words.

There is more noise – a thump, thump, thump on our door at the bottom of the stairs. Matt and I look at each other helplessly. We'll have to answer it.

Another door slams shut. The man downstairs is going back into his home, angry and trying to make a point.

"You go?" I say to Matt. He needs to open our door before the thump-thump-thump is repeated, louder and longer. They're not going away.

He nods, moving quickly, out and down the stairs. I hear him opening the door.

Then a woman's high-pitched voice, loud and worried. Matt's response is quieter, more measured and reassuring.

She speaks again, her voice insistent. I move closer to the staircase so I can hear her words clearly. "Can I come in, please, and speak to Lucy?"

A pause. I hear him say a hesitant, "Yes," stepping back, moving aside, and I listen to her footsteps hurrying up the stairs, followed by his. I step out and smile at her, a forced smile, of course.

I have no idea who she is, nor what this visit means. But it alarms me, the mention of Lucy. I sense that it is the first twist in the unravelling of what we've done.

I BECKON her through into the living room. She stands before me as Matt heads off towards the kitchen. A young woman in her mid-twenties, I'd guess. She is tall and thin and has Disney tattoos on her neck, shoulders and arms. Like she's a walking advert for the local tattoo studio.

"Jo. My name's Jo," she says in a distracted manner, wanting to get the introductions out of the way. "How do you do?" she then adds, a strangely old-fashioned phrase in contrast with her appearance: black vest top, ripped jeans, big black boots.

"Sophie," I reply, shaking her outstretched hand lightly. I don't know when I last shook hands with anyone. She has a strong, tough-looking face. But it's not hard or threatening. There is kindness there, and I guess what she's going to say before she speaks.

"I work at the care home with Lucy, and I've just got back from visiting my grandparents ... last night ... my nan's got dementia ... she didn't know ... anyway, Lucy ... someone texted me to say she's not turned up for the past couple of days. She was meant to do an extra-long shift yesterday. Is she ill? Is she in bed?" She pulls out a big bag of chocolate buttons from her pocket; it's obviously a present for Lucy, possibly for the two of them to share.

She looks at me quite openly, not suspicious at all. She knows Lucy and I are – were – friends, I guess they talked, and she is aware Lucy lives – lived – here. I hesitate as I hear

Matt walking back along the landing towards us. I want him to hear what I say so we both tell the same story.

"Lucy …" I wait until Matt is in the room, behind her. Then I think quickly. I can either be specific – Lucy's left and gone back to her husband – or vague; she just packed up and left, we've no idea where. That's what I say, adding, "We came in from work, Thursday, and she was gone!" I make my voice sound incredulous.

She looks surprised and, uninvited, sits down on the sofa. Like we're going to have a long conversation. A discussion. She assumes we are automatically friends because of our friendships with Lucy.

Matt asks if she'd like something to drink. He says he's "making a brew". He's such an old dear at times with his pots of tea and plates of chocolate digestive biscuits.

She asks for a glass of water, and Matt suggests a Coke Zero, and I could scream at him. Don't go through every type of fizzy drink we have!

But she insists, "No, water's okay." And so he goes back to the kitchen to fetch a glass for her.

"I don't understand," she says, although it sounds more like a question than a statement. "Why would Lucy disappear like that, without a word?"

I am formulating a reply, to mention Lucy's husband and children, maybe suggest one of them has had an accident, but she goes straight on. "She was so happy here … her job … and you … and me … and she was having your baby!" So, I think with a jolt, Lucy maintained that lie. To get paid time off work, knowing her, I guess.

"Well …" I reply, hoping Matt will be back soon and not contradict anything I'm about to say. "She wasn't actually pregnant."

"She was! She was! She told me so. She showed me the stick!" I look at her face, and there's something about her – the staring eyes, the manic way she is speaking – that suddenly frightens me.

Then Matt is back in the room with two glasses of water for us. For God's sake, Matt. He hands them over and gestures he's going to the kitchen to get his stupid mug of tea. He's making me so nervous.

"She was definitely pregnant." Such emphatic words. "And she was looking to buy a place here – over by the docks – and I was going to rent a room from her ... I live with my parents at the moment. They're alright but, you know ... old farts." She tails off, sipping water from her glass.

Matt is back again, with his mug of tea in one hand and an opened packet of chocolate digestives in the other. He sits in an armchair, leaning forward, putting the packet on the coffee table. No matter that he was meant to be going to work. He takes two biscuits and says, "Help yourselves." He's so jovial. I don't think he realises the potential dangers of this conversation.

I think of saying that Lucy had told me she had a blue line when she did a pregnancy test and that, next time, it was gone. But I look at her face – the certainty of a zealot – and fear that it will lead to an argument.

"I imagine she's gone back to her husband then ... and her children ... she must be missing them."

Matt nods, chewing on a biscuit, and then says that Lucy said as much to him.

At this, this Jo woman is on her feet, and I can feel the frustration and anger in her as she raises her fists and leans forward, screaming inside. "No, she wouldn't!" She almost spits out the words. "Not without saying! She's vanished without a word to anyone – she'd have said something to me!" Like they're best friends forever. As Lucy and I once were all those years ago.

She goes on, and I sense our world is about to collapse in on us. "I've been calling her on her mobile – and it just goes to voicemail. I've texted her so many times. She never responds. It's just not what she'd do – ghost me." She gives me the strangest look. "I think … I think this is really, really weird," she continues. "Something's happened to her. Something bad. She just wouldn't … she wouldn't …" She stumbles and chokes on her words. I look at Matt, not sure how to respond. Before I can, she sobs out one last sentence. "I'm going to call the police, report her missing."

MATT LOOKS HOW I FEEL – terrified at this sudden turn of events. The moment the police are involved, they will come here to talk to us, which will put us in great danger.

I don't know what they'd do. Question us. Interview us under caution if our stories did not match precisely. And Matt would screw things up for sure. He'll contradict himself. Then they'd be back here, sealing off our home, searching, obtaining her DNA, digging in the garden even.

Matt's little white van. It comes to me immediately. They'll do a forensic examination of that and will most likely find Lucy's DNA in it. The teenager's too. Matt will not have cleaned it thoroughly. He can't even dust the sideboard properly. Then what? We're arrested and charged with a double murder.

Before I can speak, I see Matt putting down his tea carefully, almost in a mannered way, and getting to his feet. For a frightening moment, a split second, I think he is going to move across and silence her.

I shout, unthinking, "No-oo-oo."

He sits back down, startled. I can't tell what he was going to do – perhaps he was just planning to take her empty glass to refill it. Surely he must recognise the life-changing significance of her comment though.

She is already reaching for her back pocket, to take out her phone and make the call now. Here. In front of us. But she stops and stares at me. I have to say something convincing and fast to stop her. Otherwise? What other choices would we have.

"Her mother's dying ... she told me before she left. Sorry, Matt, I should have said." I look at Matt, and he gazes back with a blank expression on his face. A contradiction of what I said before. And an obvious lie; clearly, I'd have told him. I could kick myself.

I go on, trying not to gabble, attempting to say the right things – believable things. "She got a text late at night from her stepfather."

The woman might know that's a lie depending on the conversations between Lucy and her. But what can I do?

"And she went off straightaway, saying she'd be back soon and not to tell anyone ... I don't know why ... work, I suppose. She swore me to silence." I shrug. I'm flustered, realising that what I'm saying makes little sense. I hope this woman doesn't question me.

She does. Looking baffled, she states that she thought Lucy's car had "packed up".

I reply, "No, she used it to drive to Milton Keynes." I don't add anything, the more I say, the risker it is. I look back at her with as much equanimity as I can muster.

She looks disbelieving and then confused, different thoughts colliding in her mind. She says, "Okay," reluctantly and then asks if Lucy's been in touch since.

"No," I reply. "I think her mother's in end-of-life care." I then add, "And Lucy was having issues with her phone battery." But wish I hadn't.

There is the longest silence. We all stand here, a frozen tableau, waiting for her response. Her life-or-death reply. My mind goes over all I've said – about just vanishing to missing her husband and children through to a faulty phone battery – and I know full well it's simply not believable. It's nonsense. But I had to say something.

One, two, three seconds more and I think Matt is about to lunge at her. I'm looking at him, begging and pleading him in my mind not to do it. He won't look at me. He's about to kill again. I go to say something, anything really, to break the silence. But my mouth is dry. It's too late. But then she responds.

She slips her phone back in her pocket, with an "Oh, well." Like it's something and nothing. And she says, "Knowing Lucy, she's gone off with a man for a few days in a hotel." She laughs, and I try to as well, but it won't come. Matt looks from her to me and back again, not sure what to say. He looks queasy.

Then she is up and leaving, with a "nice to meet you" and a "must be going", as she'll be "late for work". I follow her out and down the stairs. Through our door. The main door. To the pavement. "Tell her to text me when she surfaces." We stand there awkwardly for a moment. The back of my top sticks to my back with sweat. I am wishing her gone, *now*, hoping that will be the end of it.

But she asks me for my phone number, and I hesitate,

not wanting to give it to her or, if I do, to give the wrong one, a digit out. But it would make things worse – odd if I refuse, and it would only encourage her to come knocking again if I give her the wrong number. So, after a pause, I reel off my number, and she notes it in her phone.

And that's it, for now. I watch as she walks along the road to my left and around the corner to, presumably, her car. I wonder if I will hear from her again. With my phone number, I'm sure I will as the days pass without contact from Lucy. Worse, I wonder if she will mull over our conversation, spot the contradictions and decide to call the police after all.

CHAPTER TWENTY

SUNDAY, 29 SEPTEMBER, AFTER BREAKFAST

Matt leaves a few minutes after the woman. He looks strained but does not comment on what's just happened. He doesn't seem to think it is significant. A quick hug, a peck on the cheek, and he is gone. I watch as he reverses his van, pulls out and is away up the road.

I'm going to go for a run, so I hurry about, having a quick tidy and getting my things together. I have to try to get back into my usual routine as soon as I can.

I pop back into the living room before I go, just to pick up Matt's cup and the two glasses, to put them in the sink in the kitchen. As I do, I glance out the window, wondering idly if Matt's space will still be empty when he returns later. It is now and then but not often.

I swallow hard. There is a police car parked where Matt's van was a few minutes ago.

I lean forward to see if there are police officers in the car. They're not there. Nor are they on the pavement or walking up a path. Perhaps they have parked here to go into town to get takeaway coffees. I doubt it. They'd park closer.

I know where they are. They have crossed the road, walked up the path and knocked on the door where the teenage boy lives. Lived. And so it begins.

The teenager did not come home last night. Maybe his mother waited up for him until one or two o'clock to make sure he returned safely. Then roused the sleeping father to say he was not back.

A brief conversation, one worried, the other tetchy, wanting to go back to sleep. "I'll call the police," the mother would have said. "Don't be stupid," the reply would have come. "He's stayed over a mate's."

They'd have agreed to wait until morning. Then rung the police at the nearby Martlesham headquarters. "He's never done this before!" Now, a while later, the local bobbies on the beat have been told to call in on their rounds. It's nothing at this stage, but they have to follow procedures.

I crouch down by the window so I can see out, but I know I am unlikely to be seen. I watch and wait. I want to see the police leave and get a sense of what's happening.

I imagine, as he's a teenager, the police will be working with the parents to put a missing persons report together. Then they'll do whatever the police do behind the scenes. I can't imagine they'd do much more than say kind and reassuring words just yet. He's a teenage boy, a lad, doing what lads do on a Saturday night.

It's agony waiting. I knew this was coming. But not so soon, not now. I feel a trickle of sweat running down my forehead, along the side of my eye.

People pass on by, in and out of town. I want to get up and go, just ignore what's in front of me, but I can't. I have to watch the parents and the police as they leave.

I can't help but think this – the missing teenager story –

will be all over Felixstowe and everywhere in the next twenty-four to forty-eight hours. Facebook posts. Newspaper front pages. Instagram. Posters on lampposts all across town. I don't do social media, as I'm a really private person, but I know it will be huge on Facebook.

I'm now drenched in sweat. Beads of it run down my face and drip onto my top. The back of my top is sticking to me. But still I wait. I have to.

Then, at last, the door of the house opposite opens. Two police officers emerge, putting on their hats. One older man, one younger woman. Both smiling, chatting, encouraging.

Behind them stand the parents of the teenager. The thin middle-aged woman is at the front. She is nodding and agreeing with the police officers. The shorter man behind is distracted and looks troubled, separated from the others.

I watch as the police officers stop halfway down the path, and both turn back at the same time; it seems rehearsed. They say something – nice and encouraging, I imagine – and the middle-aged woman smiles and thanks them and turns towards the house.

I watch as the husband steps aside as she reaches the front door. She brushes by him without a word and disappears into the house. He stands for a moment looking at the police officers as they cross the road, just out of sight of me. He wants to call after them, say something else: "He's a teenage boy, doing what they do at that age."

Then he steps back inside and shuts the door. I imagine them going about their day separately, sitting in different rooms, one watching television, the other reading a book. Or maybe one will go out, and the other will stay at home, waiting to hear.

I must go for a run. I have to try to put all this out of my mind as best I can. I get to my feet, deciding to change my clothes and wash my face and neck before I leave.

As I stretch my arms and aching body, I glance down out the window. The two police officers are at either side of their car, talking to each other. She looks up and sees me.

I instinctively step back, then turn and walk away out of sight. I try not to think about her spotting me. I hope she thinks nothing of what she saw. It worries me – as every little thing will do from now on.

RETURNING HOME AFTER MY RUN, I receive a text from my line manager, asking if I can maybe come in for few hours. This does not happen very often, but, occasionally, there is a lot on, forms backing up, a busy schedule, and she wants us to get ahead of ourselves.

I text back, *Yes, sure* and then add, *Half hour?* It gives me a chance to shower and change. I don't mind doing overtime like this, as the money always helps. We like to have enough in the bank to last a couple of months if need be, but we sometimes struggle with that if we have to buy something unexpectedly. We had to get a new fridge-freezer recently. Priti texts back a thumbs-up emoji.

I'm still in a flap about everything – even after I have showered and dressed and put on my make-up and sat down in the living room to calm myself. I keep looking out the window, drawn to it: I must seem such a snooper. The two gay men come out of their house, walk along, again ignoring me. I guess, at least I hope, they did not report me to the police. I suspect they will tell all the neighbours they know though; I've seen them talking to the teenager's father before. They seem friendly.

I arrive later than I said I would be at the office, still upset about being seen by that female police officer. She'll think it strange, me watching like that. She may even mention it to her older, male colleague. When the police come knocking door-to-door in the next day or two to ask about the teenager, they'll question us more closely than anyone else.

I make up some story about my car not starting as my line manager comes across to speak to me, and I say I will stay until we get everything done. She smiles and pulls a silly face – "whatever" – and I sit down at my desk and turn on my computer.

I have to focus on the endless checking and passing on of forms, let my mind be lost in the tedium of the work. It will be hard not to have my thoughts wander, especially at those moments when I'm waiting for forms to come in.

This morning, not all of us in the section are in the building. We are short-staffed anyway; at least, the workload has increased by about thirty per cent in recent months, and there is a recruitment freeze, so it's just the four of us in the section, Monday to Friday.

The best – a young man in his earlytwenties who is quicker than all of us – is not here. Neither is an older woman who is terribly slow anyway. She's more trouble than she's worth, truth be told, as she has to keep asking for help. So it's just me and Rick, an older man in his fifties. Widowed, I think.

The time passes surprisingly easily – form after form after form, two or three conversations with my colleague, and a short break where I check my phone – nothing from Matt –

and I listen to my colleague talking about his battles against slugs on his lettuces.

Over a short lunch, sitting on a bench outside the building with a bottle of water and a packet of crisps from the dispensing machine by the lifts, I check my phone again. I scroll through all the Felixstowe-related pages on Facebook I can find. Most of it is neither here nor there.

But there is a just-added mention of the teenager on one group page – a photo of him and a *Have You Seen ...?* comment and explanation that he went out at eight o'clock and never came home. *Where Is He? Help!* It scares me. The parents are acting so fast.

There are already a dozen comments – some, what look like older folk judging by their names, commenting that he's *out on the town* and *sowing his wild oats* and *LOL!!!* Younger ones are more alarmed and helpful, suggesting, *Ask Adam* and *We'll spread the word around* and so on.

Rick and I have both agreed to work until four o'clock. He's already run out of things to say about lettuces and other vegetables in his garden, so the afternoon is quieter. Between forms and during my break, I check Facebook time and again. The appeal has spread now to different groups, and comments are growing in number every time I look. In fact, it's snowballing.

The comments are alarming. I had expected that they would mostly be of the *He'll be back soon* and *turn up when he's ready ... like a bad penny* variety. But they are not. It's all *It's not like him!* and *He's a lovely boy, so caring.*

I've the sense he is in some way vulnerable and that his family and friends, the whole town, will soon be up in arms about his disappearance.

As I am leaving, nipping away quickly as Rick pops to

the toilet, Matt texts, and my heart plummets. So much for not putting anything in writing anywhere that the police, maybe, just maybe, might see one day. *Have you seen Facebook? Riley Thomas!!!*

"Why," the police might one day ask, "did you message that?"

Talk later, I reply, nothing more, and then delete the thread on the way to my car. I must ask Matt to do the same. How many times! He's so dumb. I'm not sure, if our phones are checked, whether the police can uncover deleted messages. I imagine so.

I leave work, driving straight home, my mood worsening on the way. When I arrive, I cannot breathe properly. There are now posters of the boy on lampposts up and down the road. His parents are certainly wasting no time.

MATT and I are scratchy with each other through the early part of the evening, getting back, showering, eating. Eventually, over our meal, we settle into a tense silence. We both have our phones in our hands and keep checking Facebook, other social media and the local online newspapers. We show each other what we see. I'm pretty sure police forensics could follow this digital trail, too, and question us about it. But we need to know what's happening.

It's still mostly on Facebook, but there are literally hundreds of likes and shares and comments. The teenager seems to be the nicest, kindest, sweetest boy who ever walked the earth. It's at odds with the image I have of a blackmailer who pulled a knife on Matt and would have killed him.

I think some of these comments are from people who didn't know him. I sense it's soon going to roll into an army of armchair detectives with their various observations. Teenage activists will be putting up posters and searching the train tracks and beach coves for him. On it will go, swirling all around us.

As we sit down later in front of a turned-off television, I tell Matt again not to put "anything about anything" in a phone message, email – everything. He looks surprised, like he'd forgotten, and then nods, taking out his phone and clicking through, removing all of it.

"And delete your browsing history too ... imagine if the police looked at your phone and saw you'd be following the case so closely, so much." He goes to retort, but I add, "I know he lives opposite – lived – but even so ..." We both delete. What good it will do, I don't know. Not much, I suspect.

"We need to go over ... what's happened," he replies finally. "So we can double-check we've not missed anything obvious." I nod, and he says, "You ask questions ... you're better at this than me ... Miss Smarty-pants."

"Right, okay, the teenage boy ..." I can't name him, making it personal. I take a deep breath and ask one question after the other.

"Was there anyone in sight ... however far away ... when you ... killed him?"

"No, of course not." He shakes his head, annoyed that I think he could be that stupid. I let it go.

"What about CCTV?"

"Not that I could see. I checked carefully when I got to the library. If there had been any, I'd ..." I cut him off.

"So you got him in the van, then, what, drove him somewhere ... and that went smoothly?" I don't really want to ask in detail. The van – the bodies in the van and their DNA there – troubles me so much. I'll come back to it. "And you destroyed his phone, scattered it, like you did with the other one?"

"Yes, but I'm not going to tell you more," Matt replies. "In case, you know ..." He means if we are ever interviewed by the police. I can't tell what I don't know. "It's done with ... it's been done properly ... he'll never be found ... nor his phone, trust me."

I bite my tongue.

"So his hair, skin, DNA, Lucy's too, could be in the back of the van ... direct from them ... and maybe even coming off your hands and the clothes you were wearing at the time ... into the front of the van? A hair from his head on your top and then falling onto the driver's seat?"

He sighs and misunderstands my question. "All the clothes went through the washing machine ... and we got rid of them." He hesitates. "Is hot washing enough to get rid of any ... DNA?"

I shrug, indicating I'm not sure. It's not what I meant or asked. And then I repeat the question about their DNA being somewhere, anywhere, in Matt's van.

"I hosed it all down, inside and out, inside the back where ... they were ... at the car wash up by the supermarket at the school. Would that be enough?" He doesn't mention the front of the van where he could have been unintentionally leaving their DNA from his hands and clothes. I shrug again, indicating we need to be a hundred per cent sure.

I google on my phone, imagining Matt somehow had DNA on his hands afterwards and then touched it everywhere. The best I can find are contrary statements about the likelihood of DNA being recovered from clothing or where it has been. Some state yes, others no. I say, "Possibly, it's all so contradictory. This last one states, 'Despite washing, DNA may still be recovered.'"

I google again to see if DNA is likely to be still inside the van, and there are so many cases where the DNA of people murdered and disposed of via a van have been found inside the vehicle. I read out one or two, pull a face, then read on. "Fire seems to be the only way to really destroy evidence, to get rid of traces of DNA ... and even that's not a hundred per cent foolproof."

Matt shakes his head and sighs. He's starting to realise – as I do – what he's going to have to do and as soon as possible.

I google once more and come across an article that states, *"The study found that DNA can be transferred from surfaces within a car to locations beyond the car by a driver."* So, whatever we do, Matt could still perhaps have transferred the boy's and Lucy's DNA anywhere, into our home, for example. I cannot think about that. The boy's DNA on the banister on the landing. I do not say anything. I feel nauseous. Obviously it would be catastrophic if his DNA were discovered here.

CHAPTER TWENTY-ONE

SUNDAY, 29 SEPTEMBER, INTO THE EVENING

Matt is crying. I am too. Thing is, we're two halves of the same person. We know what the other is thinking. We're frightened. I lean over, my head on his shoulder. We comfort each other.

We both know we are trapped. The net is closing in. Someone, sometime, will report Lucy missing to the police. Maybe her employer. Or her work friend. Her last known home was here. Opposite the house where the teenage boy lived.

A rookie police officer will say, "That's a coincidence, guv. Two people going missing from houses in the same road. Near enough opposite each other."

"No coincidences in police work, Constable," the senior officer will reply. They'll turn to the other officers in the room.

"Go and interview the people from the houses ... anything that doesn't add up ... bring them in for questioning." The most senior officer will give the order. And that will be the beginning of the end for us.

I sit up straight, saying, "If the police come here, want to talk about Lucy, we're done for. They'll know something's odd immediately. You can't lie convincingly. They'll separate us, pull our story – stories – apart, get us contradicting each other."

Matt sits up too, wiping his eyes. "You just say you came in from work that night and she was gone, vanished. I'll say exactly the same. Nothing else. Just stick to it."

"They'd ask so many questions. Did she leave a note or text or message me, us. What do we answer? They'll not believe she just went without a word. That Jo woman will say she was having a baby ... our baby! Christ, what will they think? She supposedly also walked out on her job, which she needed ... and what if they really question that woman and she repeats everything we said to her."

Matt shrugs, saying it doesn't matter; we simply stick to the same story and all will be well. He's so naïve. I don't think he's even thought things through like I've been doing.

He just says, "They'll think she's gone home." Then adds, in an authoritative voice, "Nothing to see here; please move on."

I can't keep the exasperation out of my voice, with so many thoughts tumbling through my mind and straight out of my mouth.

"What do we say when they ask why she was living with us? Do we mention the surrogacy thing? Or not? What if they bring in forensics and look at that bedside cabinet where she hit her head ... I've cleaned it, but what if there's still something there? Just a single hair. What if they go inside the front of your van and find her DNA there? Or they find the body, and your DNA is all over it?"

He simply looks nonplussed as I go on.

"Then they discover her car up by Ipswich train station. Why did she leave it there if she was going home? It drives perfectly well. Easier to drive to Milton Keynes than get the train and dump your car! What if my hair ... my DNA is all over it? What if I'm on the CCTV at the station, showing I'm going home? Questions, questions, questions. How do we answer all of them, every single one, correctly ... and the same?"

He sits, thinking, aggravatingly silent.

"They'll ask us so many questions about when she was here, just stupid things, trying to catch us out, say the opposite of each other. The bottom line is, why would she vanish into thin air?"

I stop, breathing heavily, pausing before I go on. I'm close to shouting now.

"What about the teenage boy? I mean, they're not going to think that's just a coincidence. Lucy here. Him there. Are you on CCTV recordings in town the night she disappeared, driving to the library, pacing up and down? Have they got recordings of you driving out of Felixstowe and coming back hours later? Is there DNA in the van? If there's anything there from either Lucy or the boy, that's it, game over."

My voice is rising in anger, and fear too. "What will you say when the police ask you if you had sex with Lucy?"

He turns and looks at me, his eyes all glassy from my relentless questions.

"If they find her body, they'll find your stuff in her, traces of it."

As I wait for his reply, I imagine what the police officers will ask. "So you're telling us that Lucy Yilmaz left your house without warning?"

Matt will nod, sticking to his story.

"And that you have never seen, spoken to or met with Riley Thomas, across the road from you?"

Matt will nod again, his body still, his hands clasped in his lap, trying to look relaxed.

"So could you explain why the DNA of both Lucy Yilmaz and Riley Thomas have been found in your work van?"

And Matt will stare blankly at them, not knowing how to respond. "Uh ..." he'll go. "Uh."

As he sits here now, looking at me. I can see his mind clicking through his thoughts, oh so slowly. Click. Click. Click. I wait to see what he says.

"They won't find the bodies."

I turn to him, not wanting to know why. I mouth the word, "No?"

"No," he replies emphatically. "Never." There is a slight smile. It's a chilling sight – and thought. He goes on. "And look ... if the van gets torched, that will destroy all the evidence ... realistically ... they won't find complete DNA among ashes." He looks triumphant. "No bodies. No van. No evidence."

I grimace at him. I'm not sure it will be as simple as that.

MATT GOES STRAIGHT ON, talking about destroying the van right now, this evening. I agree he has to. There's no time to waste. No matter how well he's cleaned it, there may be a flake or a speck of something that will reveal telltale DNA. I doubt he cleaned it as thoroughly as he suggests. We go over everything about destroying the van. I ask him lots of questions, and he answers one by one until I'm satisfied.

We agree: the van has to be set on fire and left as no more than a smoking shell. There may be CCTV footage somewhere of the van going here and there, to the town centre, to wherever Lucy and the boy are buried, and back, but that's not proof of anything. Matt couldn't sleep, we had an argument, whatever. There won't be any DNA evidence left to uncover in it. That's the thing.

Now here we are, just before midnight. Matt's going to drive the van to an out-of-the-way place off a layby in a quiet, wooded road five miles out of town on the way to Ipswich, set it alight, and then walk home through fields and woodland to the village of Trimley St Martin.

I'll meet him there in my car. We'll report the van stolen the next morning. Joyriders. To not do so would arouse suspicions. That bit scares me. Are joyriders going to steal a small white van rather than a boy-racer type of car? Would they bother torching it? I doubt it. I have to stay steady. We have no choice. I swallow my fear.

Matt hugs me as he's about to leave. Long and hard. Like he's never going to see me again. I hug him back, fighting my conflicting thoughts and emotions, and then step away.

"You've got everything?" I ask briskly, and he pulls gloves from the pockets of the dark hoodie he's now wearing. Then a box of matches and a lighter from the other. He smiles, like he's a clever boy, then puts them back.

I kiss his cheek, goodbye. He keeps a can of petrol in the back of the van, has done for years since he ran out of fuel late at night coming back from an emergency plumbing job in Great Blakenham in the middle of nowhere. I only hope a canful is enough to set fire to the van. And that he can light a match or flick a lighter properly and not set himself alight. He's that clumsy.

He looks out the window, down into the road, making sure it's all clear. He then moves quickly by, patting me on the shoulder, and is away. I listen as he goes down the stairs, out our door and the main door, shutting them both behind him.

I am at the window, watching him get into the van, when I see a police car to my left, at the top of the road, coming slowly along. I think it's just out and about on some sort of midnight patrol, but it slows as it gets to the house opposite, and I feel, suddenly, I am under surveillance. I step back quickly.

I have to text Matt, somehow tell him, *Don't go! Let the police car go first! Don't be seen!* But I stand here helplessly behind a curtain. If he pulls out and they follow him down the road, the officers will almost certainly remember it when a report comes in from us the next morning that the van's been stolen. They may later remember Matt as the man getting into the van. We could not dare put in a report. But it would be so suspicious if we didn't.

Then I'm hurrying down the stairs, through the doors, along the path. Too late, Matt has pulled out in the van and is gone. The police car rolls by me, both young male officers looking my way. The driver smiles politely towards me. They'll both remember me, a wild-eyed woman in a panic.

I watch the car following Matt's van down the road to the end. Matt's van goes left. The police car goes right. I should leave it at that, go back inside, wait fifteen minutes or so before driving my car to Trimley St Martin. I must stop worrying.

But I can't. I sense that Matt and I are now in appalling danger. If he torches the van, then runs off across the fields – all as planned – there is a chance that the flames from the van will soon be seen from the parallel A14 road and be reported immediately to the police.

And as the news is radioed to police cars in the area, the officers who just passed by me will hear it. And they will think of Matt, the van, and me looking deranged and desperate. And they will come knocking on our door with questions we're unable to answer.

I have to get to Matt, to stop him before he sets the van ablaze. What was the best thing to do is now, due to a sudden twist of fate, the worst. I am grabbing my keys, down the stairs, running to my car. I have to hurry.

I'M DOING SEVENTY, eighty miles an hour along the A14, keeping a watch for police cars in laybys, behind me and on the other side of the road.

To the left, across fields, I can see where the wooded road is and find myself holding my breath, hoping I can get there before the explosion.

At the very least, I have to get Matt away from there as police cars race to the scene. Before he sets light to the van if I can.

I see a police car in my rear-view mirror. I'm in the inside lane. The police car is on the outside lane, behind a lorry.

I slow my car to keep within the speed limit. But it prevents the lorry moving into the inside lane to let the police car go by.

I accelerate again, sick with worry. The lorry heaves and groans its way behind me. I wait for the police car to drive on by, ignoring me.

Over the fields, I see lights on the wooded road. Few cars use it, especially at this time of night. It's Matt, it must be.

If the van goes up in flames now – I expect a loud boom as the petrol tank explodes – there's nothing I can do to help him.

The police car in the outside lane will turn on its flashing lights and accelerate up to eighty, ninety miles an hour. It will get to Matt before he's barely had a chance to start running away.

The police car goes by me. I don't glance across. I don't want to be seen. Make eye contact. Be recognised.

I wonder if it might be the two young officers who drove by our house twenty minutes or so ago. If they look across and notice it's me, it will stick in their minds.

Then they are gone, off and into the distance. There's no explosion. Not yet anyway. I breathe a sigh of relief, realising I'm soaked in sweat.

I'm coming up to the turning on the left that takes me down and around to that wooded road and the laybys. Matt will be just beyond one of them, tucked behind in a wooded clearing.

As I signal, the lorry behind me blasts its horn, the driver holding his hand down so it goes on and on. He's angry I got in his way.

The lorry accelerates, and all I can see and hear are blinding lights and a deafening noise. I swerve, coming close to spinning off the road. Somehow, I right the car and move towards the wooded road.

It is long and wide, with trees to either side. A quiet, almost eerie place. I drive along slowly, my body still shaking from the lorry almost forcing me into an accident.

Then I see Matt's van in a layby far ahead of me, just

before the wooded road turns right on to another road into Ipswich.

The road ahead, the other side, coming towards me, is empty of traffic. But there is a car behind me now, having just come off the A14 as well. It keeps a steady pace, and I cannot tell if it is the police or not.

I slow my car to thirty miles an hour and keep close to the side in case the car wants to overtake. I've seen boy racers hurtling down this road before, roaring and hooting as they go.

The car behind me does nothing. It tucks in at the same speed as me, keeping a steady distance, neither getting closer nor falling behind. It seems to be tailing me.

I accelerate a little, to thirty-five miles an hour. It does the same. I slow back down to thirty. So does the car. I'm sweating again now, fearing that, somehow, we've been uncovered.

As I approach Matt's van, I see him coming round from behind the back, looking up and down the road. Dear God. He looks like a cartoon villain. He's so obvious.

I cannot slow and stop, as I'm frightened of the car behind; I'm scared to draw the driver's attention to Matt and what he is doing.

Matt realises it's me and watches open-mouthed as I drive past. I shake my head furiously at him and watch in my rear-view mirror as he stands, staring after me.

The car behind pulls out, and I cannot see what it is as it sits, for several agonising seconds, in my blind spot. Then I recognise it.

And it is gone, this AA repair van, to the junction at the top of the road as it turns towards Ipswich. I pull over, sit for a moment or two shaking uncontrollably, and then I do a three-point turn and head back to Matt.

"Leave it, Matt, leave it," I shout, winding down my window as I slow the car. "It's too dangerous. The police are everywhere. They'll be here before it's burned out. Come home, come home now."

He is already running towards me, petrol can in hand, and I'm thinking, *No, no, not my car, you idiot, go back and drive your bloody van home.* God, he's so stupid at times. But he's shouting back at me, scared and desperate.

He wrenches the rear door of the car open and throws himself and the can in behind me. I struggle to keep the car steady, swerving to the left and the right, as he drags himself up, pulling the door shut. All I can see in the rear-view mirror as I accelerate away are plumes of thick black smoke rising from the van.

CHAPTER TWENTY-TWO

MONDAY, 30 SEPTEMBER, THE MORNING AFTER

Matt muttered, stumbling over his words, something about trying to set the petrol tank alight ... didn't work ... set the seats on fire ... so much smoke ... the van will blow eventually.

He made me pull over after a few minutes so he could put the petrol can in the boot. I didn't know why. I was too shaken to ask. I guessed it was because, if we were for some reason stopped by the police, he wouldn't be sitting there smelling of petrol with an empty can on his lap.

I drove home as fast as I could, waiting to hear the sounds of police sirens and maybe the noise of a loud explosion behind me. But I didn't. Perhaps vans only explode like that in Hollywood movies.

We didn't talk about what happened – about the van – when we got home. We were both too shaken up by everything and, I think, scared of the possible consequences. We seemed to go on to autopilot, showering, putting our clothes in the washing machine, getting changed and going to bed.

Matt fell asleep before me. I just lay there worrying into the early hours and beyond.

It – the burning of the van – was a terrible mistake. Done in the madness of the moment. As I lie wide awake, I wonder whether the police will have got to it early. Perhaps seen the number plate. A report being sent on to visit the owner, Matt, in the morning. The fire brigade may have turned out too. Another report filed, no doubt. More paperwork leading, eventually, the police to our door.

Then again, it was in an out-of-the-way place with little traffic at that time of night. The van could have burned itself out, not to be seen until the morning rush hour when some motorists use that road as a quieter, less busy route to Ipswich. Someone then would report it to the council, who I believe are responsible for dealing with abandoned cars and the like. If so, I try to convince myself, maybe, just maybe, the police might never be involved much beyond a basic report.

But the plumes of smoke and the subsequent fire will have been seen from that main road, the A14.

The thought nags at me through fitful sleep until dawn. I could not shake it from my mind.

Every time I began to drift off, I imagined I was being chased in the night by a shapeless, terrifying monster.

Matt's up before me at just gone seven o'clock and is brisk and busy-busy-busy, unnecessarily so. He's showering and getting dressed for work and leaving toast and a mug of coffee on the kitchen table for me. As I sit down, he tells me he's in a hurry, got to get to work early, will grab a coffee on the way. I assume he'll report the van.

Nothing's been said, but we know he's going to use my car today, and for a while. I'll work from home or maybe walk or run to work. It's about as close as going to the pier and back. It's no big deal. I decide to work from home today, be on guard for the police, and so I text Priti to okay it.

Matt is worried, I can tell, realising too that what we did, in the heat of the moment, was foolish and may come back to haunt us. I know him well enough to realise why he's going early – he wants to drive down that wooded lane to see what's what and draw his own conclusions.

I don't think he wants me to know that – but he has always been so transparent to me. He takes the weight of the world on his shoulders, as he did with getting rid of Lucy and the teenager, to protect me. I'll not ask. I love him for what he does.

As he turns to go, I stand up and hug him. He hugs back, but it's a brief and light touch. He may become emotional if I hug him too long or say sweet words. I let him go. I'm about to remind him to put in an insurance claim – it will seem strange if the police turn up and ask and he hasn't done so. But I see his tense and nervous face and simply kiss him goodbye on the cheek. I wonder what the day will bring for us.

I'M RUNNING AGAIN this morning, between Matt leaving and me working from home – trying to get back to some sort of normality. It's tough – my mind is filled with guilt and swirling thoughts of being uncovered at any moment. I'm going to act as normal as I can until, eventually I suppose, everything becomes normal again. A new normal.

I worry most about being locked up for years and years. That thought makes me feel so ashamed. Just thinking about myself. But I can't bring Lucy and the teenager back, and going to prison won't resolve anything. It's not like we'd ever do anything like it again, is it?

I have two favourite runs that I alternate, one along the seafront to the pier, the other the opposite way to the woodlands at the Grove. This morning, it's the pier. I'm wearing my earbuds and listening to funny podcasts, like I used to do.

As I turn a corner into Ranelagh Road on the way back, I'm laughing at something that someone's said in the podcast, proper laugh-out-loud laughing. For the first time in ages. It makes me feel better for a split second.

I'm so full of laughter that I forget for a moment about everything. I'm not looking where I'm going and run straight into a middle-aged man. He stumbles back into a bush, then steadies himself.

I see to my horror that it's the teenager's father from over the road.

I put my hand to my mouth, stifling my laughter. He looks upset, not expecting anyone to be smiling or laughing when his son is missing. Maybe he's just angry because I ran into him. I stop, taking out my earbuds, trying to think of what to say.

"How are you?" I blurt out. He takes a deep breath, somehow seeming angrier now. Maybe I should have just said "sorry" and run on, not engaging with him at all. I want to keep him at a distance. I don't want him to have me on his mind, on his radar, creating the sense that I'm odd, and suspicious. "Any news?" I add, trying to ease the uncomfortable situation.

He shakes his head, replies, "No," and then glances at my face, assessing me. He adds, "You're from over there, aren't you? With the plumber."

I nod and introduce myself, us really, as Sophie and Matt. He replies – his name is Mike, and his wife is Greta.

The questions – all in a desperate tone – then come tumbling out uninvited and without pause: "Did you know Riley? Ever speak to him, you or your husband?"

I shake my head as he goes on, his eyes desolate, his hand twitching at my arm. I don't pull back, as I don't want to offend him.

"Where were you on Saturday night? What were you doing? Did you see ..."

I laugh again, a disbelieving laugh, that he's questioning me, and Matt, as suspects. This time, he's not angry at my laughter, but suddenly embarrassed, realising how inappropriate his questioning is. I don't think he meant to be quite like that. He's so overemotional and distraught that he's beyond rational thought.

"I'm sorry," I say. "I'm so sorry."

Then he's talking again, gabbling away with me as his confidante. "The police believe Riley's just run off, that he'll come back in a week or so. Teens do. Sofa surfing, they say. But ..." He searches for the right words. "We've not had an argument or anything ... not really ... there's no boy ... partner ... his friends haven't heard a word." He stops suddenly and sobs.

There is a horribly awkward moment where he half turns towards me, perhaps expecting a hug. I can't do that. Certainly not with a stranger. And part of me loathes what I am doing, standing here pretending to be kind and caring. But I put my hand out and rest it lightly on his arm. He rolls his eyes upwards towards the sky, in utter despair. And then he says in a crackling voice, "He's been mu ... murdered. I know it. I know it … I feel it here." He puts his hand on his heart.

He's then sobbing and shaking his head and in a world of his own, this broken man. I look towards his house, hoping his wife may be at the window so I can gesture to her to come out. But there is no one there. I gaze around to see if someone is in the road I can call across. But there is nobody in sight. I have to do or at least say something, inadequate and useless as I am at this sort of thing.

I turn away from him slightly, indicating I have to go, I'm in a hurry, things to do. But I can't just run on, leaving him like this. It's rude. And it would seem heartless. I have to say a few words of sympathy. "I'm sure … you know … when I was young, my friend and I went off for a few days without telling anyone … up the river to Sutton Hoo … our parents were furious with us when we got back. I was grounded for weeks."

He looks at me now through tearful eyes. I have said something miraculous. It's like, because I have engaged with him, shown compassion and understanding, I am now his saviour. "Really?" he says in a brighter voice, then adds, more doubtfully, "I'm not sure Riley would go to Sutton Hoo. He likes music festivals." He's not thinking; he's taking my words so literally. He stands there, thinking. This is going to be a drawn-out conversation.

"Look, Mike, I'm sure it will be okay." I pat him encouragingly on the arm. "I've got to get to work. But keep me posted; let me know what happens, okay?" As I turn to go, he says something sounding positive that I don't quite catch. I keep going. I should not have said that last sentence.

As I'm walking across the road, he shouts, "Thank you." Then again, as I don't respond, "Thank you!" I turn and raise my left arm towards him, in acknowledgement. I smile at him, and he smiles back. And I hate myself even more, being so encouraging when all along I know the truth of the matter.

His son is dead by my husband's hands.

Then I'm on the pavement, away to my home, wondering if speaking with him was a good or bad idea. I guess it might help me to keep tabs on what the police are doing about Riley. Then again, I suspect this heartbroken man might become a constant nuisance.

I WISH, when I bumped into the teenager's father, that I'd simply shouted, "Sorry!" and kept running. I started work on my laptop on the living-room sofa after I'd got back, showered, put on make-up and changed into fresh clothes. Each time I stopped for a break in the morning, I felt drawn to look out our living-room window. I was half expecting the police to arrive about the van. I'd not answer, wanting to talk to Matt and agree on a story before he speaks to them.

I saw the man sitting by the window of his front room every time. I guess he's signed off work with stress or something. It's poignant in a way; he is waiting for his son to walk up the path. "Dad, I'm home!" My heart bleeds at the thought.

When I walked to the Tesco Express at lunchtime to stretch my legs and get something to eat and drink, he waved at me. I pretended not to notice. But he waved more wildly and opened the window to call out. He updated me on what the police are saying and doing – someone high up is about to call him, so he's sitting, waiting, by the landline phone. It took ages for me to extract myself as he went through so many possibilities; I then ignored him on my way back from the supermarket.

He's on my mind after that. I kind of understand why he's latched on to me. I had a cousin, Lee, who died of meningitis when he was seventeen. His father once told me that nobody spoke to him about Lee after his death, not at work or anywhere. One or two people even crossed the road to avoid him.

I wonder if that's the same with the teenager's father now, with some people assuming his child is going to be found dead somewhere and not wanting to say it out loud. But because I've been perhaps the only person to talk to him, he's sort of latched on to me.

My cousin Lee's parents separated soon after his death and then divorced a year or two later. Losing a child must be unbearable. I wonder if the teenage boy's parents are handling this in different ways. I see her coming and going, while he just sits there waiting.

As I'm coming out for an afternoon run – I've had enough of forms by three o'clock – he's not at the window as I turn to pull the main door closed behind me. I'm sighing with relief inside – he's getting on with his life and leaving me to mine. I feel mean about my feelings. Even so.

But as I walk to the pavement, I see him hurrying down his path towards me, gesturing at me to come across. My heart sinks. He's been sitting there, and he came straight out when he saw me on my doorstep.

I fix a smile on my face as he gets to my gate, although I'm tense and on edge. I feel sorry for him. This needy, desperate man. I feel ashamed as well. But I don't want to encourage him. Nor do I want to risk letting anything slip. I should not be engaging with him.

"We're going to go to London in a few minutes." He sounds positively excited. "They, the police, think it's a good idea." He swallows. "They believe Riley's gone off ... he'd had an argument with Greta about ..." He stops and swallows, sounding so emotional. Then goes on, "... London. Riley wanted to go to the O2 to see ..." He waves his hand; he can't remember who it is. "It's tonight, so they're hoping ..." He struggles on. "... he'll be there. We're going to go down and put up posters. And ..." He bursts into tearful laughter. "... There's only one main entrance where everyone comes in and out. So we're going to stand and wait until we see him."

He steps forward suddenly, grabbing and hugging me tight. He hugs so hard I can't catch my breath. He has his head on my shoulder, and I can feel his hot breath on my neck. I feel really uncomfortable. I put my arms around him and pat his back briskly, two and then three times. I pull away from him, the smile rigid on my face.

"Thank you," he says, wiping his nose with the back of his hand. I wonder if he's left a smear of snot on my tee-shirt. "Thank you for being so supportive."

I nod and smile, although I've really done very little other than bumping into him and being as polite as I can.

"We're going to find Riley, have a Frankie & Benny's meal – he loves his Frankie & Benny's; they still have one at the O2 – and we'll go to the concert with him, if we can find seats, and then come home." He says all this excitedly, and I almost expect him to add, "And we'll all live happily ever after." But instead, he just stands there bubbling and frothing with happiness.

I pat him on the shoulder as I go by him and shout, "Best of luck!" over my shoulder as I start running. I don't add,

"Keep me posted," as he will, come later tonight, have had his hopes dashed.

But it is, I am ashamed to say, good news for Matt and me. With the belief that he is alive and is heading for London – where all sorts of terrible things might happen to a teenage boy on his own – the focus will be there not here.

As I run, I feel my hopes rising. It may be assumed, not so very far down the line, that something awful has happened to him in London. And he can rest in peace wherever Matt has buried him for years and years. Perhaps for ever.

MATT ARRIVES HOME JUST after six o'clock, and I have a supermarket pie and peas meal ready for him, after he's showered and changed and sat down across from me at the kitchen table. He likes a meaty pie smothered in thick gravy.

He's calmer now, steadier. I ask if he's driven by the van, and he nods and replies, "Yeah, twice, it's okay." He does not add to that, and neither do I, assuming maybe it's now burned out and is waiting to be removed by the council.

I go to ask if he's put in an insurance claim, but something in his expression, suggesting he does not want to talk about any of it, stops me. I assume he will when he's ready. He has to, really. He then says he's off to see his mate Baz for a pint and a chat. He leaves amicably enough with a hug and a kiss, with both of us trying to act normal.

I spend the evening flicking between YouTube and Netflix, trying to find something to watch, to concentrate on, even a ninety-minute rom-com to see through to the end. But

I hop from one thing to another, losing interest within a few minutes.

I know, when I go for my run in the morning, what is going to happen. The thought makes me feel sick. The teenager's father will be watching from his window and will hurry over when he sees me; he will be desperate to tell me about tonight.

Not that I need to be told. They waited at the O2 before the show, bubbling over with hope and expectation. Then came home long after the show had ended and the arena emptied, their dreams scattered to the winds. He'll hug me, heartbroken.

Matt comes back just after eleven o'clock, shaking me awake by my shoulder. "Time for bed, Soph," he urges. I often nod off in front the television when I am on my own. But not when Matt's there. He always goes first. I don't know why.

There's something about Matt, his facial expression, the way he walks – the fact he is tunelessly mumbling the words to some song or other – that makes me think he has got good news of some kind. I don't ask. It can wait until he's ready.

As we go to bed, he puts his hand on my back. I say, "Not now," thinking, *Not ever*. He moves away a little so he's not pressing against me. We lie like that a while until he falls asleep. I then slip out of the bed.

I sit, into the early hours, on the window ledge in the living room, watching through the thinnest crack between the curtains. Waiting for the parents of the teenager to arrive back. My morbid fascination, I suppose.

At some point, as I am struggling to stay awake, they pull up in his car. The wife gets out of the passenger side. She shuts the door and walks up their path, putting the key in the lock and going indoors. She leaves the front door open. He sits in the driver's seat for a moment or two. I think he is crying. He then follows her. A few metres apart – the whole world, really.

Still, I sit and watch. The lights going on in one front bedroom and then another – this couple ripped apart by grief, now seeming to sleep in separate rooms. Lights in the left bedroom then go off, the ones in the right bedroom staying on. A living nightmare.

I stay where I am for half an hour or so, just thinking, so full of shame about what we have done. Lucy and the teenage boy. Riley. I should call him by his name. Not "the teenager" or "the teenage boy". But saying "Riley" makes him seem too real, a flesh and blood person.

I go back to bed and move close to Matt, who is lying on his back. I snuggle up to him, and he turns and puts an arm around me. He stays asleep, but I am awake, feeling so sick, and I know I will be for some time yet. Eventually, I move away from Matt and lie on my back too. I am still in torment.

Matt seems fine in the morning, getting up and ready and going off cheerfully enough. He doesn't say anything about any good news, and I wonder if maybe I was mistaken, that he'd just had a pint or two of a new beer or something. I still feel I may be sick at any moment. Other than that, I'm going to try to act normal today, starting by walking to work in the sunshine.

CHAPTER TWENTY-THREE

TUESDAY, 1 OCTOBER, JUST AFTER ONE

I get an hour for lunch at work, twelve thirty to one thirty. I'm fed up with my job and have been for years. I'd leave, but I don't know what else I'd do. Shipping. Admin. The docks. It's all I've ever known. It pays well enough, I suppose, for what it is, and other than the occasional need for overtime, I get my evenings and weekends free. One day, I'll get up and go and do something more fulfilling, but with the hell of everything else going on right now, the familiarity and the routine are strangely comforting.

There is a room where you can sit and eat your packed lunch and chat with work colleagues. But I only take in a bottle of water and bananas and apples, and I see enough of my work colleagues all day. They're mostly young and laddish but friendly enough even though they make me feel old. They talk another language and laugh at things I don't find funny. There's a TV in the room, but it's always on a news or football channel. I'm not interested in either.

When the weather's nice, I sometimes go to the seafront to have my lunch. I sit by the Ferris wheel and watch the world go by. It's where I am now, on a bench, listening to the excited screams of young mums and toddlers going up and round and down again. A white-haired man, in his eighties I'd guess, gets up from the next bench and hobbles away. The joyful noises don't bother me. In fact, I like them.

I rummage through my bag, so many packets and bits and pieces, taking out my bottle of water and a banana. I put them beside me on the bench. I will eat and drink in a moment, here in the sunshine. For once, despite the horrors that still swirl around me, I feel alright for a few minutes.

But I have a slight headache, so I dig deeper for the packet of paracetamol I keep at the bottom of my bag. I find it. The packet is empty. I sigh, flicking it into a bin close by. I must remember to get some more when I go shopping.

I eat my banana and drink my water, relaxing in the sunshine. I shut my eyes, listening to the hubbub of happiness all around. Something is troubling me, though. I'm not sure what it is. I finish my banana, putting the skin in the bin and the bottle of water back into my bag.

Then I see it, tucked to the side, unopened. Noticed only by my subconscious.

A packet of tampons. With everything going on, all of that has slipped my mind. Next to the packet is a pregnancy testing kit with one or two sticks still in it.

I've missed my period, I'm sure of it. What with the stress of everything.

I dig deep into my bag again, pulling out my phone, clicking through to the calendar, which I've forgotten to complete in recent weeks. The whole of September is a blank. So I scroll back to August and note my period dates, start and finish.

I'm late. By more than a week, maybe two. I count on my

fingers. I'm usually pretty regular. But I have been later than this at difficult times over the years. When my father died, I was so late that I convinced myself I was pregnant.

The word *pregnant* sticks in my mind. I can't be. Surely not. But I roll my thoughts back over recent weeks. We did it once or twice. I work out when, looking at the calendar, counting the days. Supposedly, we did it at what should have been my most fertile time. Not that I've ever been fertile. And not that I'd have noticed anyway. We'd given up.

I'm up, bottle in one hand, bag in the other, hurrying towards the toilet block that's a few minutes' walk along the promenade. My heart is in my mouth. I don't know why. It can't possibly be. Not like this. Not out of the blue. Not after everything. I'm being stupid. But it has happened like this with other women I've talked to. Three or four miracles among the couples I know, so maybe it's more common than I would have thought.

As I enter the block and hurry into a cubicle, crouching over the toilet, I take the kit out of my bag. I open it with shaking hands. I can't believe I'm doing this, peeing on the stick, getting my hopes up one last time. To be dashed yet again, breaking my heart into a million fragments.

Moments later, I am peering at the stick in the murky light, angling it for a better look. And I am suddenly sobbing as I see a blue line, faint but unmistakeable. Against all the odds, I've proved everybody wrong. I am pregnant. I'm going to be a mummy.

I ITCHED and twitched and fidgeted all afternoon, doing

my stupid, brain-dead work. I just wanted to text Matt, *We're having a baby!!!*

But I knew I should tell him in a magic moment, not when he was bent over a toilet, unblocking it with a plunger.

I thought instead I'd get home early and make his favourite meal. But when I got back, it all seemed too much effort, so after he texted me he was leaving, I went into town and bought fish and chips.

I got as far as putting salt, vinegar and ketchup on the fish and chips on plates on the kitchen table. A bottle of Coke and two glasses next to it. No alcohol for me for a while. My hands shook as I put the cutlery on the table.

I managed to disguise my feelings as he returned home, came upstairs into the kitchen, and saw what we were having for tea. He hugged me and asked if we'd be having treacle sponge and custard for pudding. A favourite with this meal. I laughed, the little stick behind my back, and replied we had Neapolitan ice cream in the freezer. He likes that well enough.

He went for a quick shower, and I stood there in the kitchen, beside myself with joy, literally unable to stand without jigging about. I wanted so much to go and bang on the bathroom door, shouting "Hurry up, Daddy!" But I just had to see his face when he realised what I was saying. So I waited – such an agony – until he sat down at the table, picking up the longest, fattest chip and dabbing it into a big blob of ketchup. So here we are.

I go to say, "I'm pregnant," but I just manage, "I'm ..." choking on the word *pregnant*. I feel overwhelmed.

He looks across at me with his big gormless face, chewing his stupid fat chip, and watches as I put the little white stick in front of him. Then point at that faint blue line.

I watch his face change from puzzled to bewildered to overjoyed. And then he is up on his feet and around the table and putting his arms around me. I hug him tight.

And we just, I don't know how to describe it. *Dance* is the wrong word. We begin by jumping up and down, and then, eventually, we slow and lurch from one foot to another in an odd shuffle until, finally, we rock backwards and forwards in each other's arms.

Pure and utter bliss. This is, quite simply, the best moment of my life. Better than anything. Meeting Matt. Marrying him. Our honeymoon night. Everything. All of those wonderful moments combined don't come close.

I wish we could stay like this forever. And we try, God knows we try. After a minute or two, we slow our happy rocking and steady ourselves. And we hug each other tighter, swaying slowly from side to side. Matt hums a sweet and silly tune in my ear.

"How?" he asks at last, in a crackling voice. We stop moving and lean back, looking into each other's faces. "How on earth did ..." His voice tails away. He is crying now.

I lean forward and kiss his tears, then lean my head against his. It takes me a moment or two, more than that if I'm honest, to find the words. "It's a miracle. Truly, a miracle."

And then we kiss, almost tentatively at first, and then it gradually becomes more passionate, more needy, more intense. At the same moment, we stop and step back and turn and make our way, hand in hand, to the bedroom.

PART 5
A CHANCE OF HAPPINESS

CHAPTER TWENTY-FOUR

WEDNESDAY, 2 OCTOBER, A FRESH START

After we have made love, we lie on our backs, staring at the ceiling, in a state of perfect bliss. Matt was so nervous, worried that he might somehow harm the baby. I laughed and said the baby was still a tiny speck and perfectly safe. Even so, he was gentler than usual, which was sweet of him, and we took our time taking our pleasures.

Then Matt told me he loved me, and I replied, "I love you too." We hadn't said that to each other after making love for a long time. It had become such a practical thing, trying for a baby. Almost just another bodily function at times. And then we had given up trying as such. And we both felt a mix of feelings – sadness, bitterness, regret – about that, I think. We haven't made joyous love – rather than needy love – for a while. Until now. All is right in the world again.

"I can't believe it," Matt says suddenly. "I just can't. All this time. After everything." He reaches out and lays his hand on my tummy. "Mummy!" he then adds, and I reply, "Daddy," in a shaky voice, and that seems to set him off again, crying to himself. So I roll on my side towards him, and we look into each other's eyes.

"You'll be a wonderful daddy," I say to him, running my fingers through his hair. He replies that I'll be a marvellous mummy. I rest my forehead lightly against his face, and he kisses it. "We'll be the best parents in the world," I add. "Just the three of us, me, you … and Max." I laugh, pulling away, knowing he hates the name Max. At school, there was a heavyset boy called Max who once sat on Matt's face and broke wind simultaneously.

We both sit up.

"Max!" he says with mock indignation. "Max? How do you know it won't be Fiona!" He knows I loathe that name. There was a prissy girl at school called that. He laughs, and I do too. Then he adds, "Who knows, it might be twins?" And we both say, at the same moment, "Max and Fiona!" And laugh so happily. I fall back on the bed, and Matt lies on his side, facing me. There is a moment's silence as we are both thinking the same thing.

"Go on then," I say, laughing. "Get on with it … do it again … a bit longer this time please, Mr Curtis." He laughs too as we roll back into each other's arms.

This is a fresh start. Matt and I and our baby are going to be a little family. I can't wait.

We will put what Matt did, Lucy, the boy – Riley – and everything else, including the van, out of our minds. Put our heads down and keep going, making sure this joy lasts forever.

THE NEXT DAY goes really well. I can't stop smiling to myself, so much so that one of my work colleagues asks, only half joking, if I've been drinking. I replied, "No, I'm just really, really happy." He didn't ask why – not that I'd have told him!

Matt sends me silly messages and pictures of newborn babies that make him laugh – one with a startled look, another with lots and lot of black hair and, my favourite, one with what looks like spiky punk hair. I reply with so many emojis, mostly bulging pink hearts.

If the rest of my life could be like it is today, I'd be the happiest woman in the world ever. I love Matt. He loves me. We are having a baby who will be the most precious thing in the whole wide world to us. Our love will embrace us all.

I stop off at the supermarket on the walk home from work, still insanely happy, picking up vegetables and noodles and stuff to make a stir-fry for our tea. I want us to be as upbeat as we can be from now on. Getting ready for our little family-to-be.

Looking around as I arrive home, I am relieved that the man over the road is nowhere to be seen. I can do without him pouring misery over my happiness.

I do a double take, though. There is a small white van parked along the way that looks much like Matt's. Like Matt's did, I should say. For an instant, my brain assumed it was Matt's. I shake my head at my stupidity as I walk up the path and into the house.

I open the main door, step inside and put the key in the lock of our inner door.

There is a commotion behind me. The slamming of a van's door, footsteps running along the path. I turn as a man pushes his way inside the main door.

Before I can speak, he bundles me over, face first on to the staircase, kicking our door closed behind him.

I think, for one awful moment, that he is going to climb on top of me as I lie here, his hands around my mouth, silencing my screams.

But he is pulling me up on to my feet, then pushing me up the stairs, following me.

I turn on the landing, and we stand face-to-face. I see to my horror that it is Lucy's husband. What the hell does he think he's doing?

I am spitting mad. I open my mouth to yell at him, "How dare you?" But he is already speaking. And I am cowed by his sheer size and threatening manner.

"Where is she? Lucy? Where?" Somehow, I sense he's been parked outside watching all day, expecting to see Lucy coming or going. "Tell me!"

He realises she's not here. Otherwise, he'd be pushing by me, going room to room, checking.

"She's gone," I say as calmly as I can. "Left ages ago. Why do you think I came looking for her? Duh." I'm angry. Scared too. This isn't the sweet-natured man I saw with his children. I think quickly. "She owes me money. So if you find her, tell her to pay me back." I'm on the front foot with him now, on the offensive, just wanting him to go before Matt comes home and this escalates into a fist fight or worse.

He stands there, frustrated and furious. He doesn't meet my eye. Won't apologise. This fierce, strong man. He's unable to back off and simply leave. "You know where she is," he states, his voice flat and menacing.

"Just go," I say quietly. "For God's sake. Go now. Before my husband gets back." I know, as I say the words, that the last sentence was a mistake. Instead of taking it as a warning, he'll interpret it as a challenge to his masculinity.

Before he can respond, threatening me further, we both turn, hearing Matt's key in the main door. Now Matt's into the hallway and through our door, bounding, head down without looking, up the stairs.

Lucy's husband is pulling something from his pocket. As Matt gets to the top of the stairs and starts to realise what's happening, Lucy's husband jabs at him. Matt is stunned, stumbles back and falls halfway down the stairs, banging his head on the wall.

I clutch at my tummy; I don't know why. Lucy's husband looks my way, and for one ghastly moment, I expect him to lunge at me with the knife too. Instead, he just snarls, "Tell her I'll be back. With my brothers. I want my money, all of it."

Then he's down the stairs, stepping over Matt's body, and he's gone, running away like the coward he clearly is.

I should run downstairs to Matt, but my legs don't seem to work. I should, at least, think straight and walk to the living-room window to make a note of this man's number plate. But I can't even do that. How can I report it anyway? It would be one more thing to bring police to our door. What would I even say?

Does any of it matter? I wonder as I stare down the stairs at Matt, willing him to move, to make a noise; why doesn't he groan or show some form of life? But he does nothing. He's just lying there. I hold my tummy tight and watch his inert, silent body.

CHAPTER TWENTY-FIVE
WEDNESDAY, 2 OCTOBER, EARLY EVENING

Sitting on the stairs by Matt, I'm cradling his head in my hands and then reaching down his body, his chest, his stomach, to feel for blood on his black tee-shirt or trousers.

I lift up my hand, and there is blood on it. I look closer, pulling up his tee-shirt, and there is a slice of red, a thin cut, to his side, on the hip. It's bleeding and will need seeing to professionally. For now, I gently press his tee-shirt back against it.

Lifting my head up, I see Matt moving his head slowly, shaking it, stirring, coming round. I wait, close to tears, as he regains consciousness, then pulls a pained face. "That hurt." He gasps, blinking hard.

"You've been stabbed." A stupid thing to say.

"I know. I twisted. I thought he'd missed me. Who is he?"

"He didn't miss," I answer. Another pointless comment. "Lucy's husband," I add.

"I need to get up. Stand up."

"Wait," I reply. I don't know why.

But he is already on his feet, grimacing and groaning. "My head hurts. I'm going to throw up."

And my phone is suddenly beeping, an incoming call. I shake my head. For God's sake. Not now.

"Get it," he says, turning and tentatively taking a step up the staircase. "Might be important." Like this isn't.

I pull my phone out of my back pocket, glancing at the screen. It's the care home woman. Jo. I thought she'd gone and left us alone. Christ, I can do without her.

I slip the phone back, helping Matt up to the landing and into the bedroom, where he sits on the edge of the bed, holding his head.

"I feel ill ..." he mutters. "And this is painful ..." He clutches at his side, wincing, and then feels with his fingers. He stares at the blood on them, his expression nonplussed.

My phone tings this time, indicating a message has come in. I ignore it. I need to talk to Matt about going to hospital.

"Sort it, Soph," he snaps, his voice edgy. It's not like him. I guess he realises how close he was to being fatally stabbed.

I check my phone, and it is, inevitably, a message from Lucy's work colleague.

Call me asap. News about Lucy!!!

I ignore it for now, although the last three words alarm me.

I say to Matt, "It's nothing, just work stuff. I'll do it in the morning."

We sit there for a moment, and then he says, "Shine your phone light on my hip. So I can see it properly."

I shine the light, and we both look at the knife wound. It's a small, sliced cut at the top of his hip. "You could report that to the police ... normally," I add in a wry voice.

He kind of laughs, but it is a mirthless sound. "Yes." He thinks a while. "It will need to be patched up."

"He could have killed you." I sound angrier than I'd have expected. "If he'd stabbed you in the chest."

"I ... I don't think he meant to stab me. He just wanted to scare me, make me get out of the way. I wasn't as fast to move as he expected. It's not really a proper ... it's just a slice." He tries to laugh, but he is in pain. After a while, he goes on. "I'm just bloody ... two left feet, me. My head hurts." He sounds dazed and confused.

We sit there a while. Then he says he's alright. I say he can't possibly be. Not yet. He goes to get up, saying he's going to walk to the community hospital a couple of roads away from us. "I need to get this stitched up and come home and sleep it off." I tell him to stop, sit down; we need to agree on a story first. He waits to see what I come up with.

I'm worried that the doctors and nurses at the hospital are legally obliged to report a knife wound to the police. We can't have them turning up on our doorstep with their questions about how Matt got hurt and then, inevitably, asking about the teenager over the road. Putting two and two together. They'd make four, for sure.

Googling on my phone, I search for *NHS, knife crime, reporting*, and there is the usual mix of conflicting articles and comments and extreme, opposing opinions. From what I can make out, doctors and nurses are supposed to report knife crime to the police, but they don't always do so. We have to assume they will.

"So," I say to Matt as he turns and looks at me, expecting a perfect story. He isn't going to get it. "You say you were cutting vegetables in the kitchen ... the doorbell went ... you ran downstairs with the knife in your hand ... tripped ... and cut yourself."

He nods, and I think he has the same thought as me, as the nurses will have: a likely story. I say I'll drive him there. Sit in the waiting room while he's being seen. But he shakes his head, saying, "No, drop me, but don't come in; it's too dangerous ... they'll question us both ... we'll say different things."

We both nod in agreement. I'll collect him when he calls.

I go to the bathroom for a soft towel for Matt. I probably should have done that in the first place if I'd be thinking straight. He stands up carefully, pressing it against his side. We check we have our phones. Make our way carefully downstairs to the car. As we get in and I signal we're pulling out, a police car drives up behind us. I ignore it, driving away but watching in my rear-view mirror as it pulls into the space I've just left. They're going to the teenager's house, I hope, not ours.

I'M BACK HOME, sitting on an armchair in the living room, the palms of my hands flat against my tummy. I should be thinking sweet dreams about our baby and our life together. But I'm not and never will be.

I feel nauseous, waiting to hear from Matt. I wonder if they will report him to the police. Or even, maybe, there could be a police officer there at A&E in attendance in the evenings. Who knows? What will Matt say?

We are trapped, completely and utterly. The woman from the care home has messaged again, insisting now, *Call Me!!!*

Lucy's husband and his brothers will come back soon, threatening violence. The police car is directly outside, two officers in with the teenager's parents. What if they then come across here?

Everything overwhelms me. I dip my head down and weep, for all that has happened.

For Lucy, who did not need to die. For the boy over the road, who had all his life ahead of him.

But mostly, if I am honest, for us and, more so, for our sweet baby. I don't see how we can ever be a happy little family. Do we even deserve it?

My phone beep-beep-beeps. It is the woman from the care home. I answer it – if I don't, she will just keep on, and eventually she'll come round.

She doesn't ask how I am, just dives straight in, asking if I have heard from Lucy. I say no. She takes a deep breath, both pleased and excited by what she's about to tell me.

"Two things." She sounds breathless. "There's this man here, nice old boy, Ron, who Lucy was friendly with. She was his favourite. He says he's had money taken ... and he has accused Lucy."

I stifle a groan. I know instinctively where we're heading with this.

"We thought we'd settled him down ... he's in the early stages of dementia, really ... but he told his son when he came to visit ... and he's a solicitor and a bit of a ... well, you know what they're like ... and he's said he's going to report it to the police. I don't know if he will or not, but if Lucy contacts you, perhaps you can warn her?"

I nod, knowing she doesn't really care about my response. That's not all, either. There's more. There's worse. Much worse.

She continues, her voice almost bursting with self-importance. "Her dad turned up this afternoon, looking for her!"

I cannot breathe, realising suddenly that Lucy's mother and father must be in close contact, and everything I said to her in Milton Keynes will have been relayed back to him. Lucy's not been in touch. He's come to find her.

My lies to this woman – that Lucy has gone back to Milton Keynes to care for her sick mother – are about to unravel.

"It was really weird," she says. "He said Lucy hasn't gone home, that her mother isn't ill, and there is no stepfather!"

I can't speak, what can I say, how do I answer any of that? She's found me out.

"So Lucy told you a pack of lies ... I told you, Sophie, didn't I?" There is triumph in her voice. "She's holed up in a hotel somewhere, probably with a married man."

I told you so. I told you so. I told you so.

Thank God, though, thank God. She assumes Lucy lied, not me. I can scarcely babble an incoherent response. "Yes, okay ... that's not good."

Before I can ask about the father, what he said he planned to do, she is being called away – she must be at work – and says to me, laughing, "Tell Lucy to stay disappeared!" I fake a laugh, more of a groan really, as she abruptly ends the phone call.

I wonder if – when – the police will now turn up at our door, looking for Lucy. I don't doubt they will soon confirm Lucy's last-known address being here, from the care home when they follow up on the solicitor's report.

And Lucy's father is back in town. I imagine the care home woman would have told him that Lucy's been staying with us here in Ranelagh Road. It won't be too long before he arrives.

And Lucy's husband, of course. He thinks I know where Lucy is, and he will soon come back with his brothers to get that information out of us. I imagine them storming our home, holding us hostage, demanding to know Lucy's whereabouts. We are surrounded by danger, and it's moving ever closer.

I get up and walk to the bathroom, lifting up the toilet seat and bending over, vomiting what is in my stomach two, three, four times until it is empty.

Wiping my mouth, I go into the kitchen and pour water into a glass from the draining board. I gulp it down, trying to get the foul taste out of my mouth.

I clutch my tummy, my baby, and wonder what the effects of all of this stress and trauma will be. I am filled with dread, the fear that, somehow, I will lose my baby before the pregnancy is properly established. I recoil at the thought.

My mobile phone tings as I walk across the living room to look out the window. The police car is still there, the officers in the teenager's house. I wonder what that means – I have an irrational moment where I imagine they have found his body and have come to tell the parents. Surely not. But the thought won't go away.

Done! Matt has texted. *No police!*

I could curse him for putting that and sending it to me. He just doesn't think. I text back that I am coming now, and I grab my keys and head down the stairs and out. The man over the road has his door open and is saying goodbye to two police officers. He waves at me, and for a second, I think he is going to gesture at me to come across.

The two police officers glance over, and I am pretty sure

that the younger of the two, the woman, is the same one who saw me watching the other day. I wave and then look away, pretending to fiddle with my keys. I cannot take much more of this.

By the time I pick up Matt and come back, the police officers and their car have gone. The man over the road has disappeared inside. Matt witters away about not having to wait for long ... the nice nurse who believed his story ... fixed his wound ... booked him in to change the dressing ... lovely, lovely, lovely ... it all goes over my head as I walk up the path. I worry his visit will be on the records somewhere, if not actively reported. That report may prove to be the final straw.

MATT SHOWS me his dressing on the landing. Once I have shown sufficient interest and touched it lightly and he's winced and made a dramatic whooshing noise, he goes to change into his pyjamas while I put the kettle on.

I move slowly around the kitchen, my sorrow and fear close to bringing me literally to my knees. I can't go on much longer. My spirit is close to breaking. My body too. Oh, my dear sweet baby, what am I doing to you?

I turn to Matt as we sit side by side on the sofa, holding mugs of tea. He seems somehow pleased with himself – smug – as though he's come home from a world war with a chest full of medals. I touch his arm to gain his attention, and he looks at me, smiling goofily.

"I can't ... do you think we should turn ourselves in?"

"What? What?" He sits up, a look of incredulity on his face. He cannot comprehend what I am saying.

"It's ... Lucy's been reported to the police for stealing from an old man at the care home." I don't mention the husband or the father.

He shrugs and gives me a "so what?" look. He doesn't take in what I've implied. It's all coming at us fast; it's rushing to our door.

"The police have been over the road again ... they'll be here soon." I can't explain myself clearly.

He puts his mug on the coffee table, takes mine and places it next to his, and then turns to face me.

I stand up, so angry with him. The patient look on his face. The patronising "little lady" comments he's about to make.

"The baby," I say, in anguished tones. "Our baby. They're going to find out what we've done. We'll lose our baby."

"They won't," he replies, his voice forceful and adamant. "There's no evidence. No DNA. No bodies. Nothing."

"No ... no bodies," I stammer. "There are no bodies to be found? Nothing?" I can't believe what I'm hearing.

"Nothing." He holds out his hands, palms upraised, like he's just performed a magic trick and fooled everyone.

What he's implying sickens me. I think suddenly that he's dissolved the bodies in acid. I know sometimes he's had to use it at work. I gag instinctively.

He stands up and hugs me and says, "It's all okay, it's all okay." I hate the condescending tone of his voice.

"I can't stand it anymore. Lucy's people keep coming here. Him over the road. The police. I'm going mad." I go on, my voice trembling. "I'm not bringing our baby up here. It's so claustrophobic. I can't bear it. Everyone watching us all the time. All of this ... it's unbearable." My voice rises; it's sounding irrational, close to insanity. "It's too much. I'm going to lose this baby." I'm holding my tummy again and screaming at him. "And then we're going to prison."

I am stepping back, my head up, eyes rolling. I feel faint. Matt catches me as I'm falling to the floor.

The last thing I hear is him saying, "Don't, Sophie, don't say that, don't." And then, as I pass out, "I love you, Sophie. I love you."

CHAPTER TWENTY-SIX

THURSDAY, 3 OCTOBER, THE MORNING

I have the worst night of my life, worrying endlessly. But not about Lucy or the teenager, none of that. I am resigned to what will happen, come what may. The police will arrive at some point, and Matt will fumble his answers, and we will be done for.

I fear for my baby. Not that she will be taken away from me – from us – but that she will not even survive what I'm going through right now. The stress and tension. I say "she" because I know the baby is – was – a she. I don't know how. I just do. It's an instinct.

By morning, I am convinced that my baby has already gone, and I have nothing left to live for. I cannot continue anymore. I keep up the pretence of being okay until Matt has gone to work. He shouldn't, but he does. With his lumpy head. And patched-up hip. Mr Tough Guy. Then I lie on the bed, in ruins.

I do not message my line manager to say I am ill or to ask if I can work from home today. I'm past caring.

I fall in and out of troubled sleep. The buzzer on the

landing goes twice during the morning. But not on and on. I ignore that too. And the man downstairs drilling and banging like there's no tomorrow.

I just lie here staring into space, convinced that my life is at an end. Like my baby's.

I think, idly, about taking my own life, before the police come to the door, and how I could do it painlessly.

I imagine Matt's face as he finds my body here in the bed when he comes home. The horror as he cries out in agony and falls to his knees. Having to deal with the aftermath: telling people, going on, waiting for the police on his own.

I could not do such a thing, I know it. Not to Matt. I just couldn't.

But what future is there for us, Matt and me? Even before Lucy came back, things between us were strained.

The pressure of wanting a child – such a simple thing for so many people, even the most awful ones – was beyond us. And although we clung together through all of it, the strain was tremendous. We weren't thinking straight when we brought Lucy into our lives. Our fatal mistake that led to all of this.

And then we had our unbelievable, happy moment, and now, suddenly, it's gone.

I have one last pregnancy test stick left in the kit in the side of my bag. I'm going to use it to see if I am still pregnant. I can't sit here waiting to have a period to show if I am having my baby or not.

Not, I'm certain of it. When Matt comes back in from work, I will show him the stick without the blue line and tell him I've lost the baby – "see, I'm not capable" and that this – us, what we've done, this unholy mess – is over.

What we do then will be up to Matt. We could have one

last night together before taking tablets and alcohol and slipping away in our sleep in each other's arms.

I lie here on the bed, trying to still my mind, sending my appalling thoughts into a huge white void of nothingness. Trying to find inner peace. It is elusive, my mind continually returning to the horror of here and now.

I hear cars coming and going in the road outside – police cars. It is my imagination, overactive and fearful. I try to blot out the sounds from around me. Emily and her mother are shouting at each other next door. I need to be at peace, at least for a while.

My phone tings on the bed next to me. I take no notice of it. It goes again. I ignore it through the afternoon, five or six times in all. It will only be the woman from the care home. Or maybe Lucy's father if she gave him my number. Or the police. I'm not ready for any of them.

Then it beeps and tings over and over again. It's something urgent. I have to deal with it now. It's Matt, the last message reading: *News! I'm coming home.* I reply, *OK*, and then google for any news of Lucy and the teenage boy. On Facebook, his friends have organised something to be held at the Triangle – a community space in the middle of the town centre – tomorrow. That can't be Matt's news; it will be something else. If he's coming home now, it's terrible. He's going to want us to run.

I SIT HERE in the living room, scratching at my arms as I wait for Matt to return. *I'm coming home, I'm coming home, I'm coming home* reverberates around my mind. What does he mean? Why? What is this awful news?

He hasn't texted me since my reply, and I don't want to text him again – our messages need to be nothing but boring and irrelevant. Just in case. I keep googling on my phone to see if anything has happened in and around town, but nothing comes up.

I wonder if it's to do with the van, perhaps he was somehow seen setting it alight – a young couple in the woods maybe – and the police have come for him. I think on. That makes no sense. They'd come here, not his place of work, which they wouldn't immediately know.

I check all over Facebook, and God help us, there is a photo of the burned-out van on the page of a local Ipswich group; I doubt anyone could tell what the van was, let alone find any DNA in it. There are lots of inane comments. *You can't park there!*, for example. And *Won't pass the MOT!* I ignore the rest.

The longer I sit here, the more worried I become. There is always the fear that, somehow, he has been arrested. Or it will be the police who arrive, not him. I see, over the road, the teenager's father at his window. He raises his arm to me, without smiling. I wave back.

Then I see Matt pull up in my car over the way, and he's out, looking up and waving at me and running across the road all in one go.

He's through the doors and bounding up the stairs, two or maybe even three at a time. I wonder, suddenly, if he's about to shout, "Hurry, hurry, they're onto us; we've got to go."

But he comes into the living room, all breathless and excited, and it's clear that he's about to make some sort of announcement of great importance. I've no idea what. I can't tell which way.

He takes my hands, leading me to the sofa so we are sitting side by side, looking at each other. His words come out in a rush. "Baz," he says. "I've been talking to Baz."

I must look puzzled – what's Baz got to do with anything?

"North Stand Baz? From football. He's the one with that finca, that house he lets out; it was his parents' retirement place, in Spain."

He gulps excitedly and goes on, "He was saying it's empty until half-term but that he might cancel that booking because he wants to do it up, extend it or something for next year's season … put in a pool … they want to spend more time there too. Him and his wife, Sarah."

I'm ahead of him already, my hopes rising.

"So I've talked to him and said, you know, you're pregnant and … we want to take a break … until you've reached three months … so, look …" He laughs out loud, a delighted sound. "We can fly out and stay there … whenever we want … in return for some painting and plumbing and stuff … I can do all that." Before I can respond, he is leaning across, grabbing me and hugging me tight. "We're going to be safe."

My mind fills with questions. Our house. Jobs. Earning a living. The oddness of our sudden disappearance. Our baby. I have to tell him about that, our baby, when he draws breath. He's so thrilled.

He sits back suddenly, wiping his tearful eyes with the back of his hands. "I've worked it all out."

I sit and wait and listen.

"We can't afford to sell the house … we'd lose on it right now … so we send the keys back to the building society and walk off … say one of us has had a mental breakdown or something. Me, if you like. We've got money for the next month or two's payments set aside, so that will start us off in Spain."

He presses on before I can comment. "It's between Barcelona and Tarragona, in the north. His place. Out of the way. There's a bus that goes nearby a couple of times a day. And Baz has an old car there that he uses. We'll stay a while, DIY for board and lodgings. Lie low."

I can't work out if this is brilliant or stupid. Still, I need to say about the baby. But he's so excited.

"Then ... this is it. I've got this great idea, listen. Later, we'll move somewhere where are there loads of ex-pats ... Benidorm or Arenal, somewhere like that. Where we won't be noticed ... anonymous. We'll rent a caravan or something, buy one, maybe. Mobile, not static. And I'll do plumbing and odd jobs for Brits for cash. Kind of build up from there."

It's madness, of course. A pipe dream. Believing that we can simply up and disappear like that. It will look so suspicious. The police can probably track us down in Spain somehow too. And what happened to Lucy and the teenager will always be there, casting long dark shadows over our shoulders.

And what will I do in Spain? Can we just move there, register for hospital services, lead normal lives, run a business without registering it? I don't believe we can. And we don't speak the language. And then there's the baby. Or not.

But I see, really see, Matt's shiny, excited face – he looks like a child who has come up with a way to cure all the world's woes. And all to save me. Us. Our baby. I can't bring myself to tell him about the baby and that, really, it simply won't work. It's too bloody stupid.

He is hugging me again, so thrilled by his silly plan. And yet I find myself hugging him back and saying, "Yes, yes, let's do it." I think, if nothing else, it will get us away from here and all of this unbearable tension.

We can leave like we are going on holiday, make it all seem believable. We can stay there, in the finca, for a month or so. Keep a check on what's happening here if we can get a mobile signal. Decide what to do from there. It will be better than here. Anywhere will be better than here.

A FEW MINUTES LATER, I am sitting on the toilet in the bathroom, my legs slightly apart, peeing onto the stick. I am so full of fear, the thought of having to tell Matt the dreadful news, bursting his bubble, ruining everything.

I am not religious, but I find myself saying in my head, "Please, please, please," in case someone up there somewhere might somehow produce that blue line I am desperate to see. Like some sort of magic trick.

I wait a moment. I cannot bring myself to look down. To let my heart break and shatter into a million tiny pieces. How will I tell Matt, stand there and watch his face crumble as his world caves in?

Whatever, we will go to Spain together, and try to build a new life. We can keep watch from there on what's happening in the local media here.

Even if it all blows up and this Baz reports us to the police, telling them where we are, perhaps we can get out in time.

Rent a caravan, buy a bag of tools, Matt going out and about doing odd jobs for ex-pats, being paid cash in hand and keeping one step ahead. I imagine different scenarios. How they'd work. Maybe I'm fooling myself, but what else can I do? You have to hold on to hope.

"Are you okay?" Matt is tapping on the bathroom door. "Are you alright in there, Soph?"

I'm in a trance, playing out scenes in my head, planning our survival. That's all it is though, survival. It's no life, really.

"I'm good," I shout back. "I'll be out in a minute. All good." Off he trundles.

The reality is, we'd be forever on the run, at risk of discovery at any moment. Neither Matt nor I speak Spanish, and we'd stick out like sore thumbs among the local Spanish people. We'd have to stay on the coast where all the ex-pat Brits live. And that would bring its own risks.

Matt would be fixing a leaky pipe for a British couple, head down under the sink, and they'd exchange glances – they've recognised Matt from online news or a British newspaper – and one would hurry off to call the police while the other kept him engaged in a lengthy conversation.

If it's just the two of us, I'd not want to go. Living hand to mouth. Always looking backwards. Ready to run again at any moment. That's no way to live. We might as well stay here and take our chances.

I glance down at the stick still between my legs, and I am sobbing within seconds, great big breathless sobs where I can hardly catch my breath. So loud that Matt must be able to hear me from the living room or the kitchen.

I hear his footsteps on the landing, hurrying towards me. "Soph, Soph, I've got our flights from Stansted to Reus, day after tomorrow first thing. That gives us tomorrow to sort everything out. Is that enough time? Shall I book, Soph, shall I book them now?" I don't think he's heard me sobbing.

I stare at the pregnancy stick. That faint but precious blue line. And I stop my sobbing, and smile and call out tearfully, "Yes, yes, book!" He doesn't seem to notice the tears in my voice and simply bounces away, all Tiggerish. And I am happy. So, so happy. We will go to Spain as a couple and become a family there. It will be hard, maybe even impossible, but I'd do anything for my baby. Anything.

CHAPTER TWENTY-SEVEN
FRIDAY, 4 OCTOBER, ONE LAST DAY

Today is going to be manic, as we hurry to get everything sorted before we fly from Stansted to Reus tomorrow morning. There's so much to deal with. I text Priti to say I'll work from home again, if that's okay. It's a courtesy; she's always fine about it – even yesterday when I didn't message her.

Over breakfast, we make lists of what we each need to do, and Matt hurries off with his list on his phone. He goes to work so he can arrange things with Baz, and to pick up some cash that's owed to him. We'll have to convert that to euros at the airport. The worst rates, I know, but still. Needs must.

I've written letters to our families and friends. Not that we're close to anyone. It's just us against the world. I'm now writing a letter to post to the building society about our house and mortgage and walking away; I also need to get as many euros as I can and, later, tell my line manager I'm going. I also have to pack two twenty-kilogram cases.

As I leave to go to the post office to post letters and to get euros and a jiffy bag for my letter and the spare keys to the house, I stop at the main door just as I'm about to shut it and walk up our path.

Over the road, at the teenager's house, a police car is parked, and I watch as the front door is opened, and two police officers – an older man, a younger woman (her again) – come out, leading the boy's parents down the path towards the police car. Like some ghastly parody of a funeral procession.

My heart is in the pit of my stomach. I know what this means. I can't move. I just stand there watching. The father is a step or two behind the male officer, his head bowed so I cannot see his expression. The mother is next, her head up, and she has a look of utter devastation on her face.

The male officer opens the passenger door at the back of the car, and the father gets in and shuffles across the seat to the window closest to me. The mother sits next to him. The father looks across at me, and I can see that he is crying. He does not raise his hand or anything; he just looks over. I bow my head slightly towards him. He does not respond.

I can see beyond him, to the mother. She's sitting up straight, her head high and looking forward. She is alone, compact and self-contained, and does not even acknowledge her husband. I watch as the police officers glance over at me, exchange a word or two, then get into the car and drive away.

At that moment, the spell is broken and I hurry away into town with an even greater sense of urgency. It may be nothing much, I suppose, the police taking the parents of the teenage boy in, it may even be for questioning, the suspicion that they may know more than they are saying. Whatever it is, we need to be gone as soon as we can. Part of me wishes we could have flown out today, early this morning, but there is so much to do. And I know Matt wants to get the money he's owed. We'll need that.

I post the letters, get the euros and a jiffy bag, and use a cash machine to check the balance on our account and go back home to finish my letter. The curtains at the window of the man downstairs twitch as I come up the path. For one awful moment, I think he is going to open his door as I come through the main door, and start a conversation. He does not. But I note he is still watching, and I wonder what he has seen. And heard. And knows. Far too much, I fear.

At home, I finish the letter to the building society, writing about mental health and depression and having a baby and negative equity and voluntary surrender. I throw everything into it. I don't know what they will do with the house and our belongings and bills. At this moment, I honestly don't care. We have to get away as soon as possible. Matt. Me. And our beautiful baby-to-be.

AT LUNCHTIME, I leave the house again to go up the town to post the jiffy bag to the building society. It makes me feel ill, doing this, but what else can we do? We've set our course, and we have to follow it where it takes us. It occurs to me we could leave the house without returning the keys, just stay quiet, but at some stage the building society will pursue the matter and send in debt collectors. I don't want to leave the impression we've vanished, that we've run off into the night.

There are no signs of anything happening over the road. I don't think the police officers have returned the teenager's parents yet. I wonder if they are being interviewed under caution. I'm thinking more and more that it may well be that the police suspect one or other or both of them of wrongdoing.

I remember the man stumbling over the phrase, "He doesn't have a ... partner," and it occurs to me suddenly that the boy may have recently come out as gay. Perhaps the police have been told that by a school friend, and they've wondered whether the father and son argued about it – a reason for the boy to disappear either by the son's own choice or at the father's hands.

I post the jiffy bag and wonder, as I leave the post office, if it's a really stupid mistake. Part of me thinks it is. It's just ... so wrong. But it's also too late now.

My phone tings, a message from Matt. *Took ages! All good! Be home at 5! You good?*

At least he's not put anything incriminating. At last. It took him long enough.

I reply, *Good to go! Xxx*

As I walk back home, I notice a bunch of teenagers at the Triangle, the centrepiece of the town. Brass bands play there on Sunday mornings, that sort of thing.

There's about two dozen of them, half male, half female, roughly. There are two teenage girls handing out leaflets. Most people just walk on by or take a leaflet and glance idly at it before dropping it into the next bin. I can see, as I approach, drawn to them, that the leaflets are A4 in size and have a photo of the teenage boy on them, headed:

RILEY THOMAS – MISSING.

I go up to them, and they fuss and gush around me because I've stopped, handing me a leaflet, telling me about him, "so sweet" ... "so kind", and I cannot think what to say, how to reply, as more teenagers come across, surrounding me.

They seem to want me to do something, offering a handful of leaflets to hand out, but I shake my head, feeling embarrassed, shamed, really, and mumble I have to go, I'm in a hurry. "What?" one of them says. "Your dinner's more important?" The others laugh, and it's not a nice sound. I try to smile, awkwardly, as one of the girls waves someone across.

"Adam," he says as he comes over, a big, solid boy in a white tee-shirt and jeans. He puts out his hand to shake mine, like I'm his mother's friend or something. I touch his clammy hand briefly and find myself saying, "How do you do?" I'll be curtsying next.

"Riley was my best friend," he explains, his voice close to cracking. "I'm lost without him." The way he speaks, his words, the look of him tell me all I need to know. My instincts were correct. This is the teenage boy's first love. And I am moved by this, and I can't seem to find the words to reply.

He looks at me, sees I am emotional and, without warning, lurches forward and hugs me. It's not a polite touching, it's a warm embrace as though his life depends on it. I hug him back for a few seconds, and the two girls go "aah" and "ooh" before they turn to hand out more leaflets to other people now coming up to them.

As we part, I pat the boy on the shoulder, holding up the leaflet and mumbling that, "I'll put it up ... in my front window." He smiles and blows me a kiss. And my heart breaks for him.

I turn to go and see, watching me from a distance, next-door Emily pushing her mother in her wheelchair towards the Triangle. I wave. She just stares back. It unsettles me, that look. Like she's monitoring me, taking everything in, ready to report me to someone later.

Then I am away and walking home as fast as I can. I need to pack and be ready to leave. Do one or two other things. Honestly, I'd go tonight – now – if Matt hadn't booked flights for the morning. It can't come soon enough. I feel everything closing in on me ever so fast.

I'VE PACKED two suitcases and weighed them on the bathroom scales; both of them are just under twenty kilograms. Our whole life together totals thirty-seven kilograms.

It was hard to know what to take beyond passports and driving licences, clothes and bags and shoes, all of that – mementoes, too, of our marriage. Memories of our wedding and honeymoon. There's so much we'll be leaving behind. No room for Matt's tools; he'll have to buy some there.

I now sit by the living-room window, waiting for Matt to come home. *Be 45!* he texted twenty or so minutes ago. I feel suddenly melancholy; I will miss sitting here and this place. Our life really. I don't think you realise what you've got until it's gone.

It's busy on the road. I see, out and about for once, the man downstairs walking up the path. He's been shopping and is carrying a bulging carrier bag. I certainly won't miss him and his creepy watching of me. He stops and looks up, somehow knowing I am there. I think, for a moment, that he might smile and wave for once. But he does not. He maintains eye contact – like he's challenging me – and then he continues into the house.

I hear him clonking about, unpacking, coughing, dropping things. It strikes me again, so hard this time, how I can always hear his noise at any time of the day or night. He must hear us too. I go through it all. Our row with Lucy. Killing her. Our arguments after. Listening to the noises. The movements. The words we shouted.

I wonder why he hasn't gone to the police, revealing what he has heard. Perhaps it's not quite damning enough to be certain. Maybe he wants a quiet life. He might have secrets of his own, this odd man who flashes torches back and forward with the men over the road. Why would you do that? It's so weird. Even so, when we've gone, he'll remember all of it, and if asked by the police, it will come pouring out. The thought gnaws at me.

There is still no sign of the teenager's parents coming home, being returned by the police officers in their car.

So long now. Part of me hopes, prays, that they are being held by the police, being interviewed under caution, put in cells, interrogated. The police may have cause to suspect them.

If there are no bodies, the police may have to clutch at straws, looking at ideas and theories as to what might have happened. The parents, the father especially, will be a prime suspect. Even today, there must still be middle-aged fathers who hate the thought of their sons being gay.

Then I see next-door Emily walking up the road, from the far left, with three or four books under her arm. I guess she's been to the library, stocking up for herself and her mother. She too may have heard what happened in our house. Maybe not heard it quite as well as the man downstairs, and perhaps not taking it all in.

She has always wanted to be my best friend, but my

constant rebuttals have, I think, now turned her against me, souring our polite and neighbourly relationship. Certainly, the last few times I have seen her, she has either blanked me or stared right through me. I get the sense that she is now my enemy.

As she comes level with our gate, madness takes hold of me, and I bang on the window to get her attention. She turns and looks across at the man downstairs' window and then up at mine. I smile at her and raise my hand, more a farewell than a greeting. She looks back, thinks about it for a second or two, but then continues to her gate, her path, and then out of sight. She too will do me down if she gets the opportunity.

Matt arrives, parks and looks towards me. He does a thumbs-up with both hands and smiles widely as he walks to the house. I do the same back although I don't feel that cheerful. Not at all. Thing is, I am sick with worry.

Lucy. The woman from the care home. Lucy's father. Lucy's husband. The teenage boy. His parents. The needy father. The police officers who've seen me. The burnt-out van. The man downstairs. Next-door Emily. Prison. And me, with my precious baby, crushed and cowed in the middle of them.

As Matt comes in and hugs me tight and tells me about his day and what he's done – all is "perfect, just perfect" – my spirits lift briefly. My thoughts turn to leaving for the airport in the early hours of the morning. We'll be getting away in the nick of time.

CHAPTER TWENTY-EIGHT

FRIDAY, 4 OCTOBER, THE FINAL NIGHT

I'm sitting on the window ledge of the living room one last time, gazing out on the road below, waiting for Matt to return with fish and chips. I'm thinking about our baby, one hand curled around my tummy, the other holding my phone, skimming through Facebook with my thumb. Force of habit now.

I've just texted my line manager that I'm taking time out. I've told her I am pregnant. She is cutting me some slack, as she knows the journey we've been on to have a baby. She's sympathetic. I'm having what's left of my year's holiday allowance and, after that, we'll see how it goes. At some point, I'll text her and say I'm not coming back. But the money until then will be useful. I might need medical help during my pregnancy and will do for sure when our baby is born. I don't know what we'll do about that.

Whatever happens, I have to protect our baby. Nothing and nobody can prevent me from bringing our baby up. I cannot go to prison and lose our baby to adoptive parents. I couldn't bear it. I'm worrying endlessly at the thought.

And then – my worries turning to outright horror – I see

it. A copy and pasted front page of the local online newspaper on one of the Felixstowe Facebook group pages.

BODY FOUND IN FOREST is the headline, followed by a photograph of Rendlesham Forest and the basics of the story. *Remains uncovered by dog walker.*

Not Yet Identified the news goes, although there are references to the missing teenage boy. It may be him. Or Lucy. Whichever. My mind turns round and round. Thinking things through. It hits me so clearly. Matt will have buried them in the same place. I'm sure of it. Police dogs will no doubt soon discover the other close by.

Damn Matt and his utter stupidity. He told me they would never be found – could never be found, "no way" – and here we are, everything now unfolding.

I reckon all he did was take them into the forest and bury them in shallow graves close to the road. They've lain there since, waiting to be discovered.

I never asked exactly what he did, not wanting to know. Part of me thought he'd buried them deep in concrete at a barn on the renovation where he's been working. Or scattered parts far and wide. More recently, I'd imagined that he'd destroyed them with acid. Not just left them in overturned soil for a dog to dig up.

It can only be a matter of time before both bodies are uncovered, and then the assumption will be made that they are both victims of the same killer. It will all be over everywhere, including the national media. And the talk of everyone in Felixstowe.

The police will track back from the body in the forest. They know the night the teenager disappeared, and they will search CCTV between here and there for that time, looking for vehicles going there and back. They will see Matt's van driving to the forest and returning. The only vehicle doing so that night.

I guess, too, they have the report of Matt's burnt-out van – and it comes to me, suddenly, why would anyone want to burn it? Only if you wanted to destroy evidence. And they'll come for Matt, if not for me too. Behind the scenes, everything is closing in on us.

I want to text Matt, *Google! Front page of the paper!* Or better still call him, whispering urgently down the phone: "What the hell do we do?"

But it will leave evidence on both our phones. I have little knowledge of technology, but I don't doubt a police forensics geek will be able to extract something damning.

Matt, in his lumbering way, will simply say, "Not to worry, it'll be okay." But it won't, not now. We're done for. One day, perhaps even tonight if they are acting fast, the police will be at our door. I need to be ready.

In my head, I start to formulate a plan. In a perfect set of circumstances – where we are a hundred per cent sure to be safe – I'd want Matt, the baby and me to come through this and be a happy little family. But it's never going to unfold like that, is it? It can't. Not now.

So I have to think of the next-best alternative. I must make sure the baby is safe and brought up well. That is my one and only priority. And it must be by me. On my own if necessary. I can do it without Matt if I have to.

My thoughts from there shock me. There's only one way through. Matt has to take the rap for everything. The killing of Lucy and her burial in the forest. The murder of the teenager and his burial there as well. If – and only if – he does, one of us has a chance of walking free. Me, with my baby.

A sudden movement from the road below catches my eye. It is a police car pulling up outside of the house over the road. I sit and watch, transfixed, as a young female officer – that young female officer – steps out from the front passenger seat and opens the back door of the car.

The teenager's parents get out, slowly and painfully. This forty-something couple are now looking twenty years older. I guess they have been to identify their son's body. The officer who was driving the car joins his colleague on the pavement. Words are exchanged, and the police officers follow the couple up the path to their house.

As the man reaches the front door and puts his key into the lock, an extraordinary thing happens. He turns and looks back and sees me watching them. He gazes up, and for a moment, we seem to be looking into each other's eyes. A coincidence I'm sure. But then he says something – maybe, "Her, look ... she's always there, watching us" – and his wife and the two officers turn, and they all look at me sitting here watching them. It's the most unsettling thing ever.

I step back instinctively from the window ledge, moving away, feeling horribly like a voyeur. I don't know why the man turned or why he looked up at me, nor what he said to the others to make them look as well. It may be nothing important. But I feel it's more than that. I am, I know with dreadful certainty, now on the police radar.

WHEN MATT RETURNS HOME, I've worked myself close to a frenzy.

My mind has gone this way and that, running through

the possibilities over and again. But it boils down to one thing only.

The police will come at any moment. And then we're done for.

I confront him as he comes into the living room, looking for me, fish and chips in wraps of paper under his arm, telling me they were out of pickled onions. Like I care. I show my phone, the newspaper front page, the comments on Facebook, everything. I make him read them, with me watching as he gets increasingly agitated.

"How long before they find the other body?" I say, close to shouting. "And see your van on CCTV over there. Put two and two together and come for us? The weekend? Tomorrow? Tonight? Now?"

Matt moves to the window, looking out, not sure what to say. Then he sits, slumped, head in hands, on the sofa, the wrapped fish and chips rolling one after the other onto the carpet. I stay standing. I'm too angry to move and comfort him.

"You should have buried Lucy one hundred, two hundred miles away – and somewhere she'd never be found. In concrete or something. A bloody dog found her!" I am raging now.

"Did you bury the boy in the same place? Did you?" I shout, and he shakes his head briefly but then nods two, then three times to indicate, "Yes, yes, yes." Like a naughty schoolboy.

"Christ almighty!" I yell at him. "And the van? They'll see it on CCTV and match the number plate ... and they could be here any minute. You're so stupid, Matt. You've done for us. Me and the baby."

I stop suddenly, my voice so loud and echoing, as I hear a

noise downstairs, a thump-thump-thump as if the man is banging on the ceiling. Be quiet! Be quiet! Be quiet! Coincidence surely? He's just moving about.

But then I think maybe he's heard me shouting. Listened to the actual words. Taken in the unmistakeable sentences that spell out our guilt. As good as a confession.

"Yes," he'll say to the police when questioned, "I heard her screaming, 'Where did you bury the bodies!'" And I will be as damned as Matt now surely is.

"What are you going to do to save us, Matt, me and our baby?" I try hard to keep from shouting, my words still so tense and angry. "If I go to prison, our baby will be taken into care. I can't go to prison," I add emphatically.

"I don't want to go to prison either," he retorts, anger rising in his voice too. I had wanted – hoped – that he would say he'd go to the police before they arrive and confess he'd done everything and I knew nothing about any of it. That way, I'd have a good chance. But he's not going to. And I realise that it's too much to expect him to. He's not the one who attacked Lucy with a fire extinguisher.

Instead, he mumbles and stumbles through words I don't want to hear. Words that condemn us both. "We ... you and I ... we're ... a team ... we'll stand or fall together." He looks all sweaty now. I think he believes his words are noble and heroic. They're not. They're just plain stupid.

All he's really saying is that we'll go to prison, life sentences for both of us. Locked away until when? We're in our late forties or early fifties? By then our baby will be close to being a teenager, brought up in an adoptive home, never to be seen by us again. Never knowing us.

"You're going to prison, Matt. Whatever happens. The bodies, CCTV, your van ... it's only a matter of time. You're done for." I hear my voice as though it's someone else who's screaming so loud. "What you have to do is to stop me going there too, so I can bring up our baby. You ... you have to sort this."

"I can't," he replies in anguish, his voice stubborn and unrelenting. He puts his head in his hands again and repeats his words, condemning me to a life in prison, never to see my baby once it's been ripped from my arms at birth. "I can't confess. I just can't. I ... I could never admit to ... all of that. God ..."

I stand speechless, my plan – my only plan – in tatters. I don't know what to do now. I have to beg him. It's all that's left for me.

He shouts suddenly, emphatically, "Let's go, let's go now. I'll drive to Stansted. You book the next flight out to anywhere ... wherever, it doesn't matter ... Prague ... Budapest ... let's just go."

I nod quickly; it's our only chance. He dashes out along the landing, picks up the two suitcases, staggers back into the living room and puts them in front of me. "Passports?" he asks. "You've got the passports ... and your phone?"

I turn to the sideboard where our passports and an envelope full of euros sit beneath that ornate paper knife. I reach for them.

We see it before we hear it. A bright light circling and flashing up into our living room from the road below, followed by the briefest sound of a siren being switched on and off. It's the police. Already.

They've acted fast. Working on CCTV footage since the discovery, I'd guess yesterday. Matching Matt's van on CCTV to a report on the burned-out remnants of the van. The comments of the teenager's parents – "she's always watching from her window". Lucy being reported missing, her last known address here. Some smart police officer shouting, "No such thing as coincidences, go, go, go."

Matt is up, wiping his face with his hands and crossing to the window. He then turns back towards me, his face stunned, his mouth hanging open, speechless.

I STAND AND FACE HIM. Matt. My beautiful, stupid, thoughtless boy. Condemning us both to life imprisonment with his foolishness.

There are noises in the road below. Car doors opening. Shutting quietly. I imagine the police gathering, one officer gesturing at others where to stand, where to go. Ready to come for us.

And then, before Matt can speak, it comes to me. The only thing I can do. To save myself. Our baby. To give us a life together. I have no choice.

Instead of the passports and envelope, I pick up the paper knife from the sideboard.

Matt doesn't seem to notice. He's looking from me to the road below and back again. He has no idea what to do.

I take a step towards him, knowing I have to be strong and swift, to do this terrible deed before I have second thoughts.

I have to sacrifice Matt. It's him or me and the baby. I have no choice.

I'll tell the police he confessed to killing both Lucy and the boy.

That he was going to kill me right here and now. I had to defend myself.

One more step towards Matt. I grip the knife as tightly as I can in my shaking hand. I have to do this. I have to.

"Right, right," he says nonsensically, raising his hands, flat palms, towards me. "Um, um." He's still not seen the knife. He's thinking now, as fast as he can, reaching a decision.

I hear a knocking downstairs at the main door. It's a polite knock, but insistent. There will be more knocking, then banging and breaking in, in less than a minute.

Matt glances again, to and fro, out the window, then towards the stairs. He's beside himself now, frightened and distressed, and still not sure what to do.

I move forward, one final step, raising the knife. He does not see it; he's too distracted. There is a moment's pause when everything is in the balance. He goes to speak, to say, suddenly, unexpectedly, "I'm going to ..."

But I am already plunging the knife deep into his chest. Once, and then twice. I don't know why I do it again. To be sure, I suppose.

He looks at me then, properly, into my eyes, and tries to speak, to formulate the words, to finish his sentence, "... confess ... I love you, Soph."

To my horror, it is too late. He is already tumbling back, falling to the carpet, sprawling there dead. I have killed him.

I am sobbing, down on my knees, my head on Matt's chest, as the police come running up the stairs and into the living room.

EPILOGUE

It's been almost five years since Matt and Lucy and Riley died. Sometimes, it feels like it was yesterday.

Two by my hands. One by Matt's. Three terrible and unnecessary deaths. I think of Matt all the time.

I have to live with what happened for the rest of my life. My soul is in torment. The nightmares still come to me whenever I sleep.

I was arrested the night I killed Matt. I claimed it was self-defence and stuck hard to my story. That Matt had broken down and confessed he was having an affair with Lucy and had killed her in a fit of rage when she threatened to reveal all to me.

I said he then talked of Riley, who had seen Matt and Lucy together, and killed again so that his secret would not come out. I said Matt sometimes hit me. What else could I do?

I told the police he said I had to lie to protect him. Had threatened me. Even so, I said, I refused. He came at me, his hands raised to my throat. I stabbed him with the knife in self-defence, to save myself. "If I hadn't, he'd have murdered me too."

There was a trial. I was accused of murdering Matt. It was something of a cause célèbre. I seemed to be on the front page of the *Daily Mail* and others, the whole media, for days on end. Matt had already been judged to have killed twice, which was in my favour.

Even so, I was sure, as I listened to the prosecution and the defence, that I would be found guilty and sent to prison for life. The prosecution made much of my letter to the building society and returning the keys. The defence said I had been coerced to do so under the threat of death.

After so many hours of deliberating by the jury, I was acquitted and walked free. I was fortunate, I know that, not least because neither the man downstairs nor next-door Emily gave evidence. Turns out he was partially deaf, and she always had the television on loud for her mother.

That was not the end of it, though. Riley's father and Lucy's were in court every day, both of them staring at me throughout. They never took their eyes off me. There were shouts and threats from them as the verdict was announced.

The two fathers harassed me endlessly after the trial. They confronted me several times, out and about and at my gate, wanting answers to every little thing. Self-appointed detectives. They both believed I was involved in the deaths although neither of them offered any sort of proof.

After my complaints, the police spoke to both of them, and the face-to-face confrontations stopped. By that time, my spirit was broken. I stopped work. Ended up on benefits. I didn't go out much. Became something of a recluse.

Even so, there were other actions by, I assume, the two fathers – including dog mess through the letterbox on two occasions. The man downstairs dealt with both of those. The police came round and must have spoken to the two fathers again, as it all went quiet for a while.

I could not stay in Felixstowe. Whenever I went out, there were looks and muttered comments from passers-by. A man in a shop in town point-blank refused to serve me, simply saying, "Get out." He gestured to the door. I slunk out to the sound of raucous laughter from schoolchildren in the shop, humiliated. I've been jeered and spat at too.

My home was sold at below market value. I left most of the furniture there and headed off with my possessions in my old car, now with obscenities scratched in the side. My life had become a living hell.

Riley's father saw me loading the car as I was leaving. He still always seemed to be at home, looking out the window. I'd been told he was ill, had terminal cancer, two to three years to live. He sat there all day, seething with fury. He came out, running alongside the car, shouting that he would hunt me down wherever I went, and get even if it was the last thing he ever did. "Eye for an eye, Curtis."

I now live in a static caravan on a park inland from the North Norfolk coast. A lot of benefit claimants live here. I'm still on benefits. I expect I will be for a while yet. I'm hoping to get a part-time job from September. But it's a nice caravan, clean and tidy, and close enough to walk to the shops and the beach.

There are two bedrooms, one for me, and the other for Ava, my beautiful daughter. Our gorgeous daughter. Mine and Matt's. I love her so much. "You're all mine," I tell her every day. That and "I love you!" She's four now and going to the local school's nursery next month when summer ends. If it weren't for Ava, I don't know what I'd have done through the trial and all the abuse I suffered after that. I doubt I'd have come through it.

We've been here a while and are blissfully happy. We make and have breakfast together. Then go into town for a wander, to look round the charity shops, or go to the library, or do some litter-picking, which Ava adores. We have lunch on the decking of our caravan. After that, we walk all the way to the beach to look for fossils, have a paddle and eat a picnic. Then we come home, and Ava plays outside as I make our tea. That's what she's doing now.

I have high hopes for the future. Once Ava is at nursery and I'm working part-time, we'll have a little more money to spend on ourselves. It would be nice to get a runaround car again, as the last one gave up the ghost a year or so back. We can have days out in the countryside. We'd love our little trips.

We are both on our own here, really; no one knows us, although we did bump into the gay men in town the other week. I blanked them and hurried back to the park. Matt's family, such as it was, has never kept in touch. My mother and brother sent birthday and Christmas cards for a while, but not for the past year or two.

There is a youngish Jamaican man who works in one of the charity shops who likes me. I noticed his looks and smiles the first time we went in. We pop in most weeks, sometimes twice, and he now always gives Ava a lollipop. He suggested having a coffee "some time" when I last went in. I replied, "Maybe." He beamed with pleasure. When Ava is at nursery,

I'll say yes.

"Ava! Teatime! Cheesy beans!" I call. It's simply beans on toast with grated cheese on top. A glass of whole milk. A handful of jelly babies for after. Her favourite tea. She usually comes running quickly, her little feet clattering on the steps up to the caravan door.

"Hurry up!" I call, moving to the door and looking out. She always plays with her zoo toys and a bucket and spade to the side of the caravan. My little mud baby. She's not there.

And is nowhere to be seen. She never goes off. We keep ourselves to ourselves. I feel panic rising in my chest.

All is silent except for the noise of a car in the layby on the wooded road on the other side of the fence of the park. The slamming of a door, the revving of an engine, the roar of the car accelerating and racing away. As I run screaming towards the road, I reach for my phone in my pocket, pressing 999.

ABOUT THE AUTHOR

Did you enjoy *The Surrogate*? If you could spend a moment to write an honest review, no matter how short, we would be extremely grateful. They really do help readers discover new authors.

Iain Maitland is the author of five previous psych thrillers for Inkubator Books, *What Lies Inside* (2024), *The New Son* (2024), *The Soulmate* (2023), *The Perfect Husband* (2022) and *The Girl Downstairs* (2021).

He is also the author of two memoirs, *Dear Michael, Love Dad* (Hodder, 2016), a book of letters written to his eldest son, who experienced depression and anorexia, and (co-authored with Michael) *Out Of The Madhouse* (Jessica Kingsley, 2018). He has written a semi-autobiographical novel, *The Old Man, His Dog & Their Longest Journey* (2023) as well as other novels in different genres.

Iain is an Ambassador for Stem4, the teenage mental health charity. He talks regularly about mental health issues in schools and colleges and workplaces.

You can find Iain on his website:
www.iainmaitland.net

ACKNOWLEDGMENTS

It's been a thrill to have had six psych thrillers published by Inkubator Books over the past few years. I'd like to thank these key members of the Inkubator team ...

Thank you, Brian, for commissioning the books.

I have had an excellent editor, Alice, who has helped improve my original manuscripts.

Lizzie is in charge of covers, and you have delivered crackers time and again.

Thanks again to Brian for writing the blurbs.

Jodi has been my line editor on some of the books – and a fab job you've done too.

Pauline – thank you for your excellent proofreading all the way through.

And Claire – thank you for formatting and seeing the books through to publication.

Mentions too for Stephen and Garret – thank you very much.

It's been a blast, Inkubator Books – thank you for having me, and wishing you all the best for the future.

AUTHOR'S NOTES

Back in the day, before I wrote psych thrillers for Inkubator Books, I was traditionally published across a range of genres, including memoirs (*Dear Michael, Love Dad*), murder mysteries (*The Wickham Market Murder*), police procedurals (*The Scribbler*) and literary novels (*The Old Man, His Dog & Their Longest Journey*).

I always enjoyed promoting these books at author events, book signings, festivals and via the radio and press and, occasionally, on the television. It was especially nice to meet readers of my books and answer their questions.

I still receive questions about my Inkubator Books' psych thrillers even though they are a digital-first publisher. Emails and texts and so on come in on a steady basis. Let me answer some of those questions now, although, of course, I'd still love to hear from you if you'd like to drop me a line.

The most common question is 'where do your ideas come from?' Many of them are triggered by something that's happened within my family. I've been with my wife, Tracey, since schooldays in 1979. We have three lovely children who have three wonderful partners, and we have two beautiful grandchildren.

So, *The Surrogate*. One of my children had a great friend during childhood, and they drifted apart and then got back together a little later, and it kind of just fizzled out. Nothing like what's just happened in the book, I hasten to add. But there was a kernel of an idea there.

Family members have also experienced IVF, and although I don't really want to go into that in any detail, the premise of the book just fell into place. Two best friends in childhood. They part, get back together again, and one offers to have a child for the other. A set-up rich in potential mischief and mayhem!

I create a potent situation – Sophie cannot have a baby; Lucy offers to have one for her – and have the characters clear in my mind. That's all I have to begin with. I then start writing and let them take me wherever we are going to go.

I'm aware that readers generally like their main character to be a 'goodie', and in this thriller, Sophie is. But as the story unfolds, bad stuff happens, and she is forced to make instant and, at times, unbearable decisions in the heat of the moment.

I try to make my psychs as straightforward and as fast-moving as I can, with twists and turns coming out of the story as it unfolds. And everyone seems to love a big twist at the end – I hope you enjoyed this one.

I'm also sometimes asked if my characters are based on people I know, and to be honest, no, they all come out of my mind. I do have children in the age range of my main character – thirty-five-ish – so I sort of have them in my mind in terms of what someone of that age might say and do, but that's all.

Why do I set my books in Felixstowe in Suffolk in England? It's because it's where I live, and it's easier to write against a backdrop I know. I do move things about a bit though – for example, there is no caravan park in Felixstowe that's near an Asda and a petrol station. Generally though, it's much as I describe it.

I try to make everything as accurate as I can, but it isn't always – I had to jig around some dates at the line editing stage, and Saturday 31 August became Saturday 24 August. Ipswich Town were playing at home on the (original) 31st but were away on the 24th to Manchester City. So I've left that in rather than have Matt going to Manchester and back or, worse, make him a Norwich supporter. (My youngest son and I have ITFC season tickets … so I don't want Matt supporting them.)

I'm usually asked if I'm going to write a sequel. The answer to that is no; all my books are standalones. I've usually got one or two more ideas in my head by the time I get to the end of writing a book, and I want to explore those.

And finally, I'm almost always asked what I am going to do next. At the time of writing, late October 2024, I've just come out of hospital after fighting an infection for a couple of weeks. That's knocked me sideways a bit, and I've another month or so of treatment.

I'm currently working on a script of *Mr Todd's Reckoning*, a psych I wrote a few years ago, and finishing another psych thriller, *The Real Father*. They will keep me busy to Christmas and beyond. I hope they will see the light of day in 2025.

As for what I'm doing in 2025, I'm currently chatting to TV and publishing folk, and I'll surface again somewhere sometime later in the year. I hope I'll see you then.

See you again soon.

Best Wishes,

Iain Maitland
29 October 2024

ALSO BY IAIN MAITLAND

The Girl Downstairs
The Perfect Husband
The Soulmate
The New Son
What Lies Inside
The Surrogate

Made in United States
North Haven, CT
13 January 2026